"Anyone who knows anything about this lynching and don't come forth will be prosecuted with the lynchers. That will be a murder charge, too." . . .

"Maybe them Mannons can answer that," a boy in his late teens spoke up.

"What's your name?"

"Danny Egelstone." He removed his bowler hat in an instant. His freckled face shone in the midday sun.

"Why would they know?"

"He stole their horse—sir."

"Guess you boys would all testify in court to that . . . ?"

"We-we never saw that part—" Egelstone turned back to the others, and they all shook their heads.

"Wonder why he'd steal a horse anyway, he had one of his own?"

Hats shook again, and they all looked down at their boots and brogans acting uncomfortable.

Montana Revenge

DUSTY RICHARDS

BERKLEY BOOKS, NEW YORK

THE BERKLEY PUBLISHING GROUP
Published by the Penguin Group
Penguin Group (USA) Inc.
375 Hudson Street, New York, New York 10014, USA
Penguin Group (Canada), 90 Eglinton Avenue East, Suite 700, Toronto, Ontario M4P 2Y3, Canada
(a division of Pearson Penguin Canada Inc.)
Penguin Books Ltd., 80 Strand, London WC2R 0RL, England
Penguin Group Ireland, 25 St. Stephen's Green, Dublin 2, Ireland (a division of Penguin Books Ltd.)
Penguin Group (Australia), 250 Camberwell Road, Camberwell, Victoria 3124, Australia
(a division of Pearson Australia Group Pty. Ltd.)
Penguin Books India Pvt. Ltd., 11 Community Centre, Panchsheel Park, New Delhi—110 017, India
Penguin Group (NZ), 67 Apollo Drive, Rosedale, North Shore 0745, Auckland, New Zealand
(a division of Pearson New Zealand Ltd.)
Penguin Books (South Africa) (Pty.) Ltd., 24 Sturdee Avenue, Rosebank, Johannesburg 2196,
South Africa

Penguin Books Ltd., Registered Offices: 80 Strand, London WC2R 0RL, England

This is a work of fiction. Names, characters, places, and incidents either are the product of the author's imagination or are used fictitiously, and any resemblance to actual persons, living or dead, business establishments, events, or locales is entirely coincidental.

MONTANA REVENGE

A Berkley Book / published by arrangement with the author

PRINTING HISTORY
Berkley edition / September 2007

ISBN: 978-0-425-21758-0

BERKLEY®
Berkley Books are published by The Berkley Publishing Group,
a division of Penguin Group (USA) Inc.,
375 Hudson Street, New York, New York 10014.
BERKLEY is a registered trademark of Penguin Group (USA) Inc.
The "B" design is a trademark belonging to Penguin Group (USA) Inc.

PRINTED IN THE UNITED STATES OF AMERICA

10 9 8 7 6 5 4 3 2 1

PROLOGUE

A PATCH of light from the open schoolhouse window shone on the ground a few feet away from the pair. From inside the building, the sawing of Jake Iver's fiddle strings playing "Sally Good'n" sliced the breathless hot night air. Voices of the dancers and sounds of the activities going on inside carried out into the school yard crowded with parked rigs and hitched horses.

"Hush your mouth before someone hears us."

"I never—"

"Did you see that damn Texan Hanks in there dancing with my girl?"

"Hell, yes, let go of my shirt. You're going to tear it."

"I want him dead. He ain't taking her away from me—no way."

"What can you do about it?"

"Go get'cher brother. Before this night's over that sumbitch is going to be popping up daisies."

"How're you ever going to kill him and get away with it?"

"You leave the thinking to me."

"You'll have us all hanging."

"That's it. Hang the sumbitch." His steely eyes glared at the window.

"Damnit—you ain't thinking about what'll happen to us—"

"Hell with that. Go get your brother, we've got work to do."

Two hours later, the smell of sour vomit filled the air and the wind carried an aroma of the approaching storm. Thunder growled like a deep-throated bear galloping toward them. Lightning lines danced on the western horizon and illuminated the Texan's still body suspended by the rope around his neck.

"Quit puking!"

"Ah, damnit to hell." More dry heaves. Then tears ran down the boy's face in the darkness. "I never figured it would take him that long to die. Hell, oh, I don't ever—"

"Shut up. Now we need a note to pin on him. You sneak up to the schoolhouse. Dance's over. Get some paper and make a note says 'horse thief' on it."

"I can't spell that."

"What can you spell?"

"Hoss stealer."

"That ought to work. Now we can't let anyone see this pocket watch or his knives. I can get rid of 'em."

"How much money he have on him?"

"Close to ten bucks."

"Do we really need a note?"

"Hell, yes, we hung us a horse thief and the world needs to know it."

"Oh, God, I hope this works."

"It will. Get to cutting." The leader gave him a shove to start him off. "That rain's a'coming."

The boy mounted up and rode off.

The third one shook his head. "I didn't like you crippling his good horse."

"You're too young to understand. Just keep your damn mouth shut. Our lives depend on it."

"Pa ever hears about it, we all may be dead, anyway."

"Will you shut up."

Thunder rumbled across the rolling plains. Wind rustled through the box elders and cottonwoods. The second one finally returned with the note. With the paper pinned on their victim's shirt at last, the three rode off leading the extra horse.

ONE

THUNDER rumbled like a wagonload of loose potatoes over the house's roof. Herschel sat up in bed and listened above the rush of hard-hitting rain tearing at the house. Heckuva storm outside—but something else had wakened him. He turned an ear to listen.

"What is it?" His wife Marsha bolted up beside him and swept the lock of stray hair back from her forehead.

"Someone's downstairs at the front door shouting for me," he said, concerned, and threw the covers back.

"What time is it?" she asked.

He struck a match and checked his pocket watch. "Three in the morning." With a shake of his head, he blew the match out and continued to dress in the darkness while she lit a lamp. Who in the world wanted him at this time of night? No telling. This was one of the drawbacks of being the sheriff.

"Wonder who's down there," she said in a hushed voice. His wife of six months put on her robe. She was the light of his life, more than his new job, more than all his plans to bring equal justice to Montana.

"I have no idea," he said, finished dressing. "But something must be bad wrong."

The lightning flash filled the house's interior as he hurried down the steps to answer the persistent pounding on the front door. "I'm coming. I'm coming."

"Oh, Sheriff Baker—" the shorter man said when Herschel opened the front door for him. "You've got to do something. They've murdered poor Billy Hanks."

"Come in here, Cove. What's this about a murder?" Herschel used his shoulder to close the door behind the familiar rancher from north of Billings, and then went to light a lamp. Shaking the match out, he replaced the chimney and looked at the drenched man holding his sodden hat at his side. Puddles had begun to gather on Marsha's polished wood floor beneath the tail of Cove Tipton's canvas duster.

"Evening, ma'am," Tipton said to Marsha, who was descending the staircase in her robe. "Sorry to bother you so late."

"No problem, Cove," she said, and smiled at him.

"There's been a murder," Herschel said to her when she reached the bottom of the stairs.

She stopped and nodded calmly, but looked taken aback by the news. "Sorry to hear that. I'll make some coffee."

"Good idea, we'll need some. Give me your coat and hat," Herschel said to Tipton. "How was Hanks killed?"

"He was hung." Tipton looked around to be certain they were alone. "Oh, Lord, Herschel, it was the worst thing I ever rode up on. Him twisting on that rope in the wind and all—"

"I'm sure it was tough. Was he still warm?"

"What do you mean?" Tipton handed Herschel his duster and hat.

"I mean, was his body still warm when you got there?" He hooked the coat and hat on the wall pegs. Though it knifed his conscience, there was nothing he could do about the water on Marsha's floor.

"I don't remember," said Tipton.

"That's fine. Any idea why someone would want to hang Billy?" He herded the balding man into the lighted kitchen.

"No—I can't think of a soul. He was just a fun-loving cowboy."

Herschel pulled out a chair at the table for Tipton and nodded to Marsha, who had finished stoking her range and was dipping water out of the reservoir to fill her granite pot.

"Water's still hot. Shouldn't take much to get it boiling," she said.

"Good, I'll watch it," Herschel said. "Better go see about the girls. They may be upset."

She agreed with a nod and left them.

"Did I do that—" Tipton started to get up, but Herschel waved him down.

"They'll be fine. You need to start back at the beginning."

Tipton swept his thin, gray-streaked hair back with his hands and looked at the table as if he didn't know where to begin. "There was a dance last night up at the Sharky Schoolhouse. Afterward, I drove the widow, Missus Wynne, home in her buggy, and then I was riding my horse back to my place when I saw his body swinging there on a tree when the lightning struck close by."

"Any trouble up there at the dance tonight?"

"Oh, that big Swede Yarman got a little tipsy and loud.

We sent him home early. It was a pretty peaceful dance, all in all."

"Is Hanks's body still up there?"

"Oh, no. I cut him down and he's out there over my horse." Tipton gave an involuntary shudder.

The pot on the range had begun to boil. Marsha wasn't back, so Herschel rose and added ground coffee to the boiling water. "His horse wasn't around?"

"Never seen it—who'd do such a thing—" Thunder cut Tipton's words off, and the house shook hard enough that the china dishes rattled on the shelves.

"Cove, I have no idea, but I guess I'm going to have to find out." Herschel took his seat across from the man. Visions of the happy-go-lucky Texas cowboy Billy Hanks went through his thoughts. Handsome. Wavy, dark brown hair. Devil-may-care attitude—Billy rode some tough broncs at the city park contests. Polite, but always with an eye for the ladies. Worked for the Bar 9. Never in any trouble—oh, a scuffle or two—but that was just young-fella stuff. He'd come up from the Lone Star State with a herd of cattle and, like Herschel had earlier, had obviously liked Montana and stayed. "Coffee will be done here in a few minutes. Then we better go wake up the coroner."

Looking prim and proper, Marsha returned wearing a blue checkered dress and inspected his handiwork in the pot as she put on an apron. "Girls are fine. Getting dressed. I see you've fixed it—" A new blast of rain slashed the house. The windows became instant bright lights and the rain's loud voice rolled off down the valley. "Oh, I'll be glad when all this storming is gone."

"Sure good for the grass," Tipton put in.

"If a rancher ain't wanting rain, it'd be a strange day, wouldn't it?" Herschel sat back and squeezed his chin.

Who would want to kill that boy? Much less hang him? Oh, well, he'd have to figure it out—somehow.

"I could use less fury when it rains." Marsha busied herself putting skillets on the stove and getting out a sack of flour. "You two men will eat breakfast before you run off, won't you?"

Herschel agreed with a nod. "Maybe the rain will let up by then and it won't be so stormy."

"Oh, I found this, too, pinned on him." The rancher drew out a piece of paper. The damp sheet was from a tablet that children used in school with lines for cursive writing. Using his hand, Tipton flattened it out on the table. HOSS STEELER was hand-printed on it in big letters with a pencil. The S's were backward.

"They weren't very smart. Couldn't write or spell very good." Tipton used his index finger to point it out.

Herschel nodded. Or they wanted the reader to think that. At this point, he wasn't certain of anything. "When did it start raining up there?"

"Oh, I don't know. I only saw him 'cause of the lightning, but it hadn't rained there then. Why?"

"Guess I'll have to ask a million questions to ever solve this. This paper is dry. Or almost."

"Yeah. Got a little wet in my pocket. Sorry."

"No problem. I am trying to piece this all together." He stopped and smiled at his oldest stepdaughter, Kate, age ten, who'd entered the kitchen. "How are you this morning, Kate? You know Mr. Tipton?"

She nodded quickly and made a small smile for the man. "We've met—Mother said that Billy Hanks was murdered last night?"

"Yes, he was."

"My, he was sure a nice cowboy." She wrinkled her nose. "I have to go milk now, you will excuse me?"

"Yes, and I'll be back later to pitch the hay," Herschel said.

"Oh, I can do it." She turned and spoke softly to her mother, who was busy making biscuits. Then she lit the small lantern and took the tin bucket from the sink. With a swish of her blondish braids, she was gone out onto the back porch to put on her rain gear.

"You've sure got some nice young girls in your marriage to Marsha."

Herschel agreed. From a bachelor rancher's life to the stepfather of three young girls, plus sheriff of Yellowstone County—things had changed fast in his life over the past six months.

"Got him a handful of headaches," Marsha said, popping the pan of floury biscuits into the oven. The aroma of bacon cooking filled the kitchen while she swept around the men filling their cups.

"It's a good handful," Herschel said, stretching his arms over his head and sharing a wink with his wife.

"I've been to Herschel's cabin down on the ranch before the fire and he never had nothing like this." With a wave of his hand, Tipton indicated the kitchen and the house.

"Shh," Herschel said, holding his finger to his mouth. "Folks will think I'm on the take."

"Naw, they know you better than that. But this sheriff business, I can see, is going to be a tough job for you." Tipton nodded and chewed on his lip. "You want to keep this paper?"

"Yes, that's evidence."

"I just figured you'd better read it."

"I need all the evidence I can get—you think Hanks was stealing horses?"

"Why would he? Had that good sorrel he rode. He never

acted sneaky to me. I'd bet Paul up at the Bar 9'll say that's a lie, too." Tipton jabbed his index finger at the note.

Herschel accepted the man's words with a nod. Damn lynchings anyhow. Slow-acting law and short sentences had added up to lots of vigilante activity in the Montana Territory. He'd hoped to stop them in his jurisdiction and here was the first one, not sixty days into the job. Was this lynching really over horse stealing, or a convenient murder? Wouldn't be the first lynching done as a cover-up. The thunder growled farther away, and Herschel felt better about the weather and Kate being alone out at the barn.

"You liking living up here in town, Marsha?" Tipton asked her.

"Oh, yes and no. That ranch down there was my home for several years. Now this place must become that." Busy turning bacon, she smiled back at the rancher.

He turned to Herschel. "You liking law work better than ranching?"

"I guess. I chose it."

"You certainly did and lots of us small fellas are glad. Who's taking care of the ranch?"

"I sold mine to buy this place, and we have a family down there taking care of things at Marsha's outfit. Matson's their name, come well recommended."

"You're lucky, good help's hard to find."

Herschel agreed. "Did Hanks have words or get into any scuffles up there tonight with anyone that you know about?"

"No, not that I seen. He danced a lot and with lots a females. You know Hanks. He was a real hand at that dancing and he could swing them ladies." Tipton smiled for the first time, like he was recalling the evening's entertainment all over again.

"Scrambled eggs fine?" Marsha asked him.

"Heavens, Marsha, I'm a bachelor and any kind's fine with me, so long as I ain't cooking 'em." Then he laughed.

Herschel rose and turned when he heard Kate coming in the back porch door. She smiled and pushed her way into the kitchen, her right arm holding the tin pail half full of milk, the lamp in the other hand. Herschel stepped over and put the bucket on the dry sink for her.

"Go okay?" he asked her when they exchanged smiles.

"Fine—hateful thing. She switches her tail at me all the time." Kate tossed her braids and went to wash her hands.

"Cows can be cantankerous," he said with a grin, and went to sit back down. Marsha began putting their breakfast on the table.

"Can you think of one person hated that boy?" he asked Tipton, and took his seat.

"Naw, I had all the way in here to think about that. I can't point at no one." The rancher busied himself filling his plate.

"Bet you're tired, Cove, being up all night and everything?" Marsha asked him, refilling his cup.

"Why, ma'am, I ain't had time to think about it."

"We'll have to take the body to the coroner. Then I need to ride up there and look the place over if you can make that ride back?" Herschel said to Tipton.

Busy forking food in his mouth, Tipton looked up. "I'll be fine 'cept I'll miss church with Lucille."

Herschel winked privately at his wife. This business with the widow woman and Tipton must be getting serious. Tipton was in his early forties, never married, but it sounded like the younger widow might have him on the string.

"I bet she'll understand," Marsha reassured the rancher.

"Oh, she's a real understanding woman." Tipton took two more biscuits, popped them in half on his food-stained plate, and lathered fresh butter on them. "Guess she'll learn all about this when everyone else does."

And Herschel knew outright that this hanging would be sure to upset lots of folks. Small outfits would start blaming the big ones for this crime, and he wasn't ruling that out either. There was still bad blood, even after Herschel's upset win over the old regime of crooked politicians serving the big outfits' interests.

He blew the steam off his coffee. No one said this job was going to be easy, but hanging Billy Hanks was like a knife stuck in his guts. There was no way that he could be everywhere and prevent every bad thing from happening. He only wished it hadn't happened so soon on his watch.

TWO

E VEN before sunup on Sunday morning, a body draped over a horse drew the curious. Herschel had gone up to knock on the coroner's door. After some time, a sleepy-eyed lady wrapped in a robe and nightcap came to the door, and with a dry voice inquired as to the nature of his business.

"I'm the sheriff, Herschel Baker, and I have a body out here for Mr. Peabody to examine."

"Oh—"

"Is he up? I know this is dreadful early, but I need his opinion."

She blinked her eyes and leaned to see past him in the darkness. "He's dead, isn't he?"

"Yes, ma'am, but—"

"Well, then, you have the answer. I am sure it can wait until Monday morning, and Mr. Peabody will be in his office then."

"I need him to examine the body—tonight."

"Well." She lowered her voice and looked peevish. "He can't."

"Why not?"

"'Cause he's not here."

"Very good. Where is he?" Herschel asked in a lowered voice.

She gave him a hard look before she spoke. "Where he is at every Saturday night."

"I have no idea."

"I can tell you. He's down at the Big Horn sleeping with some dove."

"Yes, ma'am, sorry to bother you."

"Yes," she said with finality, and closed the door in his face.

"He ain't here?" Tipton asked under his breath when Herschel reached the gate.

"No, you take the body to Nelson's Funeral Parlor. I'll go round up Peabody and meet you there. Don't do any more to the body than unload him."

"What's going on, Sheriff?" one of the four onlookers that appeared out of nowhere asked.

"A man got killed last night. Take him down there," he said to move Tipton along. "You can all hear the story later."

"Who is he?"

"That can wait, too," Herschel said, and hurried Tipton off in the predawn light. He still had to get Peabody from the whorehouse—what next? He'd need to have a hearing with a justice of the peace. "Lots to do," he muttered to himself, making long strides over mud puddles and around the flooded spots, all the time wishing he'd brought his own horse along to town. Being sheriff sure wasn't a glamorous job. He needed to send word to have his deputy, Barley Benton, meet them where the body was found.

Benton was a real tracker and any help was better than none on the scene.

He checked the sky, which was beginning to lighten up. The rain looked like it was over for the time being. He entered the new two-story courthouse and bounded up the stairs. The night jailer, Wally Simms, came from the jail office door to meet him.

"What's up?"

"There's been a lynching up at Sharky. I need some help. I need Art Spencer woke up so he can be in charge while I'm gone to see about all this. I want Barley Benton to meet me at the murder site."

"Best we send that Fellars boy up there to get word to Benton. And I guess Spencer's sleeping at the boarding-house, isn't he?" Herschel agreed and led the way back to his office. He lit a lamp on his desk.

"Who got lynched?" Wally asked.

"Billy Hanks. Cove Tipton found him last night before the rain."

"My Lord, what did they hang him for?"

"I don't know. Who's in the jail?"

"Them two cowboys robbed the Cross Creek Store and a couple of town drunks."

"They'll be fine till you get back. You go send that Fellars boy after Benton and tell him to meet me at the Sharky Schoolhouse. I'll go wake up Art. Give him the news. Guess I can find Peabody, too."

Wally cocked a thick eyebrow at him. "Where's he at?"

"Sleeping with some dove at the Big Horn."

Wally laughed aloud. "Lordy, I'm learning a lot tonight."

"So am I, Wally. So am I."

Ten minutes later, Herschel had Art Spencer awake in his boardinghouse room and was explaining the problem.

The shorter barrel-chested man combed his hair back with his fingers, sitting on the edge of the bed and trying to wake up.

"Sounds like a mess to me. Anything you need done at your place?"

"No, but if you can, go fetch Peabody out of the Big Horn." Herschel watched his man shake his head and then grin as Herschel completed explaining his plans. "I'll go home, get Cob, and meet you at the funeral parlor. I've sent word with a boy for Barley to meet Cove and me up there at the Sharky later this morning."

"You reckon the big outfits are behind this hanging?" Art was up, busy buttoning his shirt and getting dressed.

"No. They'd spell better than whoever wrote the note that was pinned on the body. It was crudely written."

"Who do you reckon did it, then?"

"Maybe someone wanted him out of the way?"

"Who in the hell would that be?"

"Art, if I knew that I'd be a fortune-teller."

The man yawned and nodded. "I'll get Peabody out of the whorehouse. Meet'cha at the funeral parlor in twenty minutes."

"Good. Be thinking about this. There's a rhyme and a reason to everything. We'll find out who did this."

The rain's passage left a northerly wind to usher in some cooler weather. The wind hit Herschel's face like a slap to waken him when he exited the boardinghouse. He reached his house and hurried into the kitchen. Marsha was feeding the girls breakfast, and their faces all turned to greet him, filled with youthful questions their mother had no doubt already answered.

"Morning, you all going to church?" he asked, and kissed Marsha on the cheek.

"Yes," came the chorus.

"Well, I have some sheriff business to attend to and won't be able to go with you this time."

"I really liked Billy Hanks," seven-year-old Nina said.

"I guess he had lots of friends." He tossed the blond curls of four-year-old Sarah and winked at her. "How's your doll this morning?"

"She fine. Herschel, you see a pony today, we sure need one."

"Sarah!" Marsha frowned in shock at her youngest. "Don't you be pestering him about no pony."

With effort, the youngest scooted off the chair and beat a path to him. She held her arms high, and he swooped her up. "If they've got any ponies up at Sharky today, I'll try to buy one."

"Yay!" Nina shouted.

"Girls," Marsha said with a hard look. "Herschel has bought us this nice, warm, big house. We have a good place for the cow, our chickens, and the pigs. Let's not ask for everything."

"Aw, ponies ain't everything." Herschel put down Sarah with a wink.

"These girls, I swear."

"Pretty nice crew. I'm going up and meet Barley at the schoolhouse and maybe we can find something."

"A pony," Nina said, and went on eating her pancakes.

Herschel shook his head and hugged his wife, laughing as he did so. "Might not be back tonight. Can't tell, but I'll try."

"It's important for you to be careful," Marsha said, fussing with his vest.

"I will."

He saddled his big roan gelding, Cob, in the barn alleyway, loaded his bedroll on behind the cantle, and tied it down. The sweet smell of alfalfa filled his nose, and the cow in her stanchion mooed to some far-off one. He led Cob outside and cheeked him by the headstall close to his knee. The grain-fed rascal might buck. Wouldn't be the first or the last time either. In the saddle, he let go of the cheek strap and checked him with the reins. For the first hundred feet, the roan walked on eggs. But after that, he settled into a long swinging walk and Herschel headed him for the funeral parlor, hoping all parties would be there. And grateful his frisky horse hadn't bucked.

At the funeral home, Tipton jumped to his feet and came to meet Herschel when the overhead bell rang.

"Anyone else here?" Herschel looked around the empty room.

"Only me and Tom Nelson. You never found Peabody?"

"I sent Art Spencer after him, and that Fellars boy to get Barley Benton to meet us at Sharky's."

"Good. Tom has him laid out. I was napping in the chair."

"I bet you could use some sleep."

Tipton stretched his arms. "I'll be okay. What's Peabody got to do?"

"A coroner has to fill out a report on any unusual death, and then I need to have a J.P. hold a hearing."

"Guess there's more to being a sheriff than I ever figured—here they come."

Lots more than Herschel had ever figured. It wasn't just catching criminals or preventing crimes; it was lots of paperwork, too.

"He have any money or valuables on him?" Herschel asked.

"None. That's funny. He didn't even have a jackknife on him. Reckon they took it?"

"No idea." Herschel shook his head. The lynchers must have taken some items from him—was that their real motive? Robbery? Too much remained unanswered at this point.

A scowl was etched on Peabody's face when he came in the door and put his bowler hat on the hall tree. Art Spencer came in behind him.

"Where is he?" Peabody asked.

"Back room," Tipton said.

Herschel and Tipton followed the man in his rumpled green suit into the back room. Tom Nelson looked up from his desk and said, "Good morning."

His greeting only drew a grumpy growl from Peabody, who took off his coat, hung it up, and then went to the prone corpse. He picked up the short piece of rope trailing off the table and scowled.

"Boston hemp. Kills them every time." Peabody turned to Tipton. "You cut him down?"

"Yes."

"His feet were how many feet off the ground?" Peabody asked Cove.

The rancher held out his hand about chest high.

"Death by strangulation. He still alive when you reached him?"

"No."

"Then at the hands of parties unknown. That's my report."

"Good, fill it out and we'll have a J.P. investigation next week," Herschel said.

"Waste of time."

"The law requires it."

"I know that, I'm the coroner."

"Sorry to bother you," Herschel said, and turned back to Art. "You watch things here. We'll go meet Barley."

Art nodded. "I can handle it if it don't get any worse."

When the bell rang as Peabody left by the front door,

the three men looked at each other and then laughed at Peabody's behavior.

Nelson came over and shrugged. "Guess I'll fix Hanks up. Funeral will be at two tomorrow, if that's all right?"

"I can't see doing anything else about it," Herschel said. "Try to send word to the Bar 9 outfit, he worked for them."

"I will."

"Good. Cove and I are headed back up there. Rain and all, I doubt we can even find the tracks, but we may."

"Good luck," Art said after him.

"Yeah, thanks for finding Peabody."

"Oh, anytime." Art shook his head and smiled. "I'll go by and check on the jail and keep in touch."

"Good," said Herschel. The ex-teamster was a great head deputy. Herschel always felt covered with the man in place during his absence.

Two hours later, Herschel and Tipton crossed the last rise and could see the grove of cottonwoods and the Sharky bell steeple. Wagon tracks sliced the wind-whipped short grass and wound up to the front door of the whitewashed schoolhouse. Herschel dismounted and wrapped his reins on the hitch rail.

"Guess Barley ain't made it," Cove said, looking around.

Herschel agreed and headed up the steps for a look around the classroom. "He'll be coming." The front door on the right opened with a twist of the knob, and he stepped inside. A faint aroma of perfume, food, and body odors was still contained in the large closed-up room. Sunshine poured in the south windows, and a red-covered tablet was on the table along the wall. He picked it up, lifted the cover, and turned it to the light. There on the paper was the indention off the previous page. HOSS STEELER.

"Find anything?" Cove asked, coming inside.

"They wrote the note on this tablet."

"Pretty damn brave. I figured several folks were camped all night up here after the dance."

"Give me some names."

"Ralston, Scopes. Fred Danberry's bunch."

"Guess I better ask them some questions." He drummed his fingertips on the table. When he raised his gaze, he looked through the distorted glass panes and watched a buckskin horse and rider coming out of the creek crossing. Barley Benton had arrived.

"They had lots of nerve," Cove said. "Coming back here and stealing the paper for the note."

"Or was it organized?" Herschel rubbed his mouth with his calloused hand and considered his latest theory. Had they held vigilante court in the building after the dance?

"I swear I never heard a word of it at the dance," said Cove.

"I ain't accusing you." Herschel turned and nodded to Barley entering the door. The man was in his fifties. He wore a buckskin shirt, and an eagle feather trailed from his hatband. The white-flecked beard stubble looked a few days old, and the steel-blue eyes shone like deep pools of sky.

"Boy said you had trouble up here last night."

"We sure did. Someone lynched Billy Hanks after the dance."

Barley frowned, then pushed his hat back on his shoulders by the leather string at his throat. "What in the hell for?"

"Left a note pinned to him that he was a horse thief." Herschel handed Barley the folded paper to look at.

"And they wrote it on this tablet," Cove added.

Barley held the paper at a distance to read it. "They

must have went to my school. Can't write or spell worth a damn." A chuckle rose in his throat and he smiled, handing the paper back. "What else have we got to go on? You know who wrote this?"

Herschel shook his head. "Cove'll show us where he found him last night before the rain struck."

"I take it you ain't buying the horse-rustling business?"

"All I know is a cowboy was hung last night. Horse thief or not, we've got laws in this territory and taking the law in your own hands is over."

"Let's go see where they hung him," Barley said, and nodded to Cove.

"I'll show you. Been a heckuva long night for me." Cove went out the door shaking his head.

"Bet it has been," Barley agreed, clapping the rancher on the shoulder as they walked to their horses.

Herschel closed the door behind them and looked over the sparkling, clear countryside. Rain would sure boost the grass. Lots of folks had had a good time in the school the night before. Someone had sure ruined it all, and it was his job to solve the crime. He hurried on to his horse.

The hanging tree stood a mile east of the school on the creek road. To the left and up the hill, Herschel could see how, with the lightning brightening the sky so much, Tipton had seen the corpse. The heavy rain had obscured the tracks around the site. Barley came back afoot, leading his horse and shaking his head. "Not much left here."

"I figured that. Only hoped we'd get lucky." Herschel had searched around the site for a hopeful sign or clue.

"That his horse?" Barley asked, pointing to a sorrel across the creek who'd raised his head to study them.

"Sure is," Cove said. "Where's his saddle and bridle?"

"I have no idea." Herschel shook his head in grim disgust. The puzzle grew greater by the hour. "We better go round him up."

"He won't be hard to catch. He's running on three legs," Barley said, feeding out some rope to make a loop.

The gelding held his right front hoof up, and obviously something was wrong with it. A dead cowboy, a crippled horse, a scribbled note, and a clearing sky—it all weighed heavy on Herschel's conscience. They forded the rushing creek, hemmed up the cow pony, and dismounted to examine him.

Its hoof in his lap, Barley used his hunting knife to pry a stone out of the horse's frog. He handed the sparkling object to Herschel. "See what it is?"

"An arrowhead. Unusual, ain't it?" With a frown, he studied the sharp-edged rock that his deputy had handed him.

"I guess you can step on anything."

Herschel turned the small chiseled stone over in his palm. "It's a good one, too. The kind people like to collect."

"Well, old sorely here collected it all right." Barley clapped the horse on the shoulder. "He should be all right. Little gimpy, but he can walk enough to follow us."

"If he was mine, I'd pour some turpentine in that cut and burn it so he don't take lockjaw," Cove said, looking concerned.

"Good idea. We find some, we'll do that. Let's go look up at the tree again." Herschel pocketed the arrowhead in his vest, stepped in the stirrup, and swung in the saddle.

"Indians around here use that kind?" He twisted around for Barley's answer.

His deputy frowned and scowled at the notion. "I never seen one that exact color before."

"What the hell does that mean?" Cove asked, booting his horse in between them.

"Means it might not be from around here." Herschel knew he'd have to answer the next question, too.

How did it get up there and get in that horse's foot? Good questions, no answers. He lifted his gaze to the tree limb and watched the wind swing the tail of the rope. The night before, Billy Hanks had left lots of things unsaid.

THREE

Never seen a thing, Sheriff." Bert Ralston stood on the front stoop of his log cabin. He was bareheaded. The wind tossed his thin hair, and his gray-black chin beard stuck out like a billy goat's. He held on to his red galluses and rocked on his brogan heels.

Herschel leaned over the saddle horn and stretched his back muscles. "You stay all night at the schoolhouse last night?"

"We camped up there."

"Who all was there?"

"In our camp?"

It struck Herschel this man didn't like being asked anything by the law. No matter, he'd get answers. "Who was there with you?"

"My boys, Tucker, Farrel, Jimmy, and girls, Effie and Wanda. My wife stayed here."

"You see or hear anyone in the schoolhouse after the dance?"

"No."

"Are the boys around?"

"Naw, they went off to trade for a dog. Left as soon as we got back. What you need from them?"

"Billy Hanks was hung last night less than a mile from that schoolhouse. Someone knows something about what happened. You have those boys stop by my office and see me the next time they're in Billings. I want to talk to them about it."

Ralston shook his head. "I can tell you now, they don't know a damn thing about no hanging."

"Ralston, I never said they did. But they might have heard something or seen something that night I need to know."

"I'll do it."

"Thanks." Herschel turned and nodded to Barley and Tipton. "We can make the Scopes place before dark if we ride hard."

As they trotted their horses to cover ground, Tipton rode up close to him. "He wasn't very friendly, was he?"

"Bert's like most folks from back in the hills. Suspicious of any kind of law."

"Where's he from?" Tipton asked.

"Kentucky or Tennessee. I'm not sure."

"Bunch of them kin to him, ain't they?"

"Holisters and Treys are, I think, or at least I heard that somewhere." He twisted to look for Barley, who was on his left. "Kin, ain't they?"

"Some kind of kin."

They reached the Scopes place and dropped off the ridge toward the smoke trailing out of a rusty stovepipe. The low-walled cabin was roofed with dirt and the new grass was green on top of it.

Herschel rode around the unpainted wagon and dismounted, hissing off the barking dogs that acted threatening.

An attractive young woman came to the doorway, drying her hands on a towel. Clare Scopes was perhaps sixteen. With a budding figure and a straight back, the dark-eyed girl was no doubt the center of attention of the young men at most dances.

"Hello. Your father home?"

"No, is something wrong?" she asked, looking at him and the other two on horseback.

"Yes, there is. Clare, Billy Hanks was murdered last night."

Her face paled and she put her hand to the door facing to support herself. She blinked her long lashes in disbelief and shook her head. "Oh, no."

Herschel bounded to her side at the sight of her distress. "We better go inside and you sit down. I'm sorry, I didn't know—"

"Come in." She turned, went to the gray table, and sat down. Chewing on her lower lip, she clasped both hands. Then, shaking her head, she drew out a kerchief from her dress pocket and began to sob.

"I had no idea." Herschel felt helpless.

"Oh—" She indicated for him to take a seat. "Billy was such a nice—" Across the table from him, her eyes glistened in silver wetness as she raised her chin. "Billy wasn't the kind a girl married—though he asked me—" Caught up in her sadness again, she chewed on her lower lip and shook her head in disbelief. "Oh, Sheriff, he could really polka."

"Yes, he sure could. Why couldn't you have married him?"

"Oh, he was like a wild mustang. He'd never settled down. Had no place. Could you imagine a bedroll for a house?" She swept the reddish-tinged hair back from her face. "Marriage to me means having a home, kids, and settling down." Her dark eyes met his gaze. "Billy Hanks wasn't cut out to be that kind."

"I understand. Can you think why anyone would want to hang him?"

"Hang him—" Downcast and looking at her folded hands in her lap, she shook her head. "I have no earthly idea."

"He never said anything last night about troubles he had or anything I can go on?"

"No." With the corner of the handkerchief, she dabbed her eyes. "I'm no help."

"Oh, you have been lots of help. I hate to leave you all upset. When will Ed be back? Soon?"

"Before dark. He just went to find a heifer he thought was close to calving."

"Clare, if you think of anything or your dad does, get word to me. I want these killers brought in."

"I will—oh, why Billy?"

"It problems me, too. No talk at the dance, no fights?"

"I didn't hear a word. In fact, I thought at the time it was too peaceful. We all could see that storm coming in."

"Tell Ed I said hi, and don't forget to tell him I need anything he can add."

When the men were on their way again, Barley asked, "She know anything?"

"Said Billy wasn't the marrying kind."

"One thing for sure, that girl's sensible enough." Barley grinned. "She's sure a looker."

"He wanted to marry her?" Tipton asked, booting his horse up with them.

"She said he asked her."

"Last night?"

"Didn't say—guess I'll have to talk to everyone that was there." Herschel rehashed the whole thing in his mind. It was like a box canyon for him, nowhere to go and no way to get out. But someone knew something. He'd keep asking till he found that individual.

"That'll make a list as long as your arm," Barley said. "What's next?"

"I've got to set up an inquest. We all better ride for home. Thanks."

"Want me to poke around some more tomorrow?" Barley asked.

"Yes, see Fred Danberry and then start making a list. After the funeral tomorrow, Cove, you better come by the courthouse. I'll have the inquest at four." He reached over and shook Barley's hand, then Cove's. "Thanks."

The men nodded and separated. Barley rode off east and Cove went north. Herschel checked the setting sun. Be two hours getting home and seeing his wife and girls. Didn't find a pony either. Maybe Nina and Sarah would forgive him. He put his boot heels to Cob.

FOUR

"STAGE's been robbed!" The out-of-breath youth collapsed against the door facing of Herschel's office.

From his swivel chair, Herschel blinked in disbelief at the boy. What else would happen? Better get down there and see what he could do.

"What's going on?" Deputy Phil Stevens asked from the doorway. Phil took care of the office and had been gone when the boy burst in.

With the gun belt around his waist, Herschel hitched the buckle. He looked up. "They've robbed the stage."

"What do I need to do?" Phil asked.

"You may need to ramrod the hearing on Hanks's death. Right now I better get down to the stage and see what happened."

"They shot up Hoffman," the boy said, some recovered.

"He was the shotgun guard," Phil said.

Herschel nodded. "I'll let you know what I think I better do. Young man, run down to the livery and get my roan horse, Cob. Afton will help you saddle him."

"I sure will, Sheriff."

"Wait." Herschel stopped him. "Donnie Fellars, isn't it?" At the boy's nod, he continued. "That roan will sure enough buck, so if you ride him back, walk him."

A crowd was gathered at the stagecoach half a block up Main Street. Herschel made his way to the front of the curious and nodded to the agent, Jim Brooks. "How's Hoffman?"

"He may live. They got the bank shipment."

Herschel nodded and looked around for the driver. "Where's Argle?"

"He's getting a drink. Needed one after all he'd been through. Said he'd be right back."

"How much money did they get?"

"Fifteen hundred dollars."

"Lordy, they did get the right one this time." Herschel tried to see over the crowd to look for the driver, who he hoped was returning. "He say how many holdup men?"

"Three."

Herschel nodded and then faced the crowd, holding his arms up. "I'm sure we can catch the ones did this. Let's all of you go about your business. The law can handle it."

"You need anyone, Sheriff, a bunch of us sure would be happy to help," a rancher he knew from over on Deer Creek said.

"Thanks, Slim. I'll sure call on some of you if I do."

Looking hard-eyed enough to fight a bull, and hatless with his too-long black hair in his face, Argle Bailey stalked across the street toward him. Bailey nodded to Herschel, opening and closing his hairy fists at his sides.

"Them devils done made me mad. No reason to shoot Hoffman."

"They were masked?"

Argle nodded. "Flour sacks and wore dusters."

"See their horses?"

"No."

"Any wear spurs?"

Argle shook his head and then swept the errant long hair back. It was hopeless in the afternoon wind. "They even wore cloth gloves. 'Cept one swore a lot."

"What did he say?"

"Sumabitch. Used it all the time."

"He the leader?"

"No, a short fella spoke in a tough voice ran the show."

"How tall was he?"

The driver raised his face and looked up at Herschel. "My size."

"Must have planned it well."

"Must have. Still, they never needed to shoot Hoffman."

Herschel agreed with a nod. "Was the money in sacks?"

"Yeah, they emptied the strongbox in the road."

"Any passengers?"

"Couple of drummers."

"I want both of them to give a statement to my deputy Phil. Can you find them, Brooks?"

"I will."

"Where did they hold you up?"

"Foot of the mountain. They were in the road and had us covered like they'd popped out of the ground."

"I better go see if I can find any tracks. They sound like tough ones."

"You ain't taking a posse?" Argle blinked in disbelief.

"Places you need them, others you don't."

"They're killers, Baker. Cold-blooded ones."

Herschel acknowledged the warning with a nod. "I need help I'll send word."

The Fellars youth came leading Cob up the street. He jumped off, and Herschel paid him a dime, which he smiled at in his palm. "You need me, you just call, Sheriff."

"I'll do that. Argle, if they ain't fled the country, I aim to find them." He nodded to him and Brooks, then swung into the saddle. He motioned to the boy. "Donnie, you run up and tell my deputy to send word to my wife I may be late for supper."

"Yes, sir." And the youth was gone up the boardwalk in a flurry of dirty bare feet. His flight parted women and men as he dodged through them. The eager efforts brought a smile to Herschel's lips. That boy'd do well when he grew up.

"Be careful," Brooks shouted after Herschel when he reined the horse around to leave.

Herschel waved he'd heard the man's warning and set Cob into a long lope. Highwaymen like this bunch sounded well organized. It would pay to be careful—but he needed to find them while the trail was fresh.

An hour later, he was at the robbery site, marked by the empty strongbox with its shot-up lock at the side of the road. He searched around the area of the crime. His gaze went to the hilltop roached in short pines. Had they gone that way to their horses? Nothing but rolling prairie for a long ways to the north, hardly a place to hide horses. Still, climbing the steep hillside would have been a task while carrying the loot. He dismounted, and soon found the obvious boot tracks. Uphill was the way they'd gone.

He stepped in the stirrup and started to ride up there. Cob cat-hopped over the steepest part, and when they reached the top, he let the roan catch its breath. Not twenty yards over the rim, he found the piles of horse apples where their ponies had stood. From the tracks, four horses had headed south. Herschel felt certain the fourth was a packhorse—carrying camp stuff, bedding, and probably the loot in the panniers.

The bandits were headed in the direction of the Wolf Mountains and Wyoming. Several undesirables lived down in that country—some small outfits in that region fed and boarded passersby overnight and never asked any questions. Lots of horse thieves threaded their way through that region. Many of the residents were suspected of being wanted someplace else themselves. From there, robbers could weave their way east into the sparsely settled lands of northwest Nebraska and then head south for the Indian Nation or Texas. It was the trail for the wanted—not a highway, but a more general route. Some called it the Owl Hoot Trail—lawmen called it an outlaw railroad.

With four hours of daylight left, he pushed Cob southeastward. The Wyoming line did not bother him. They could argue that legality of their arrest from one of his jail cells as long as they wanted. And he still stood a good chance he might catch them this side of the border, especially if they were confident there would be little or no pursuit. Their horse tracks were clear, he only needed to check them once in a while. The stout roan under him could run all day. It was grain-fed and rock-hard. He let the roan run and, at once, flushed up some grouse from the sagebrush. Their loud burst into flight caused the big horse to shy, and he reined it back—never losing a stride.

With the sun firing in the west, he dropped off the ridge and eyed the pole corrals and low dirt-roofed outfit. The sunset cast long shadows of him and the hard-breathing Cob. The outlaws' tracks led down there. He checked the gun on his hip. Been nice to have brought a long gun—but he'd never thought about it. This being sheriff business would teach a man a lot about going prepared if he lived long enough.

The horse between his knees was still breathing hard and snorting out his nose from the long run. Repeatedly bobbing his head, Cob danced some coming downhill, as if he knew more than his rider did about what this place might hold for them. His pace took on more of a high step, and only made Herschel that much more aware and uneasy.

The question any lawman faced in a situation like this was would they run, fight, or surrender. He'd considered all their options and since he had no backup, he decided to charge in and throw the devil to the wind. Lots of such criminals were simple enough out-of-work cowboys and in the face of authority surrendered. However, there could be some real hard cases down there. The next few minutes would sure tell.

When he was a hundred yards from the main building, someone came outside and used a hand to shield the last of the sun and look in his direction. The man could see who was coming off the hill, but maybe because it was one rider and not a posse, it might not throw as much suspicion.

"Sumabitch!" the man swore, and ducked inside.

That sounded like one of the robbers Argle had mentioned. The .44 in his fist, Herschel charged the roan for the cabin.

Three men spilled out of the doorway in a panic-filled retreat. The one in chaps stopped and began shooting at him. Mushroom smoke out of the muzzle obscured the man, and Cob shied when the hornetlike bullet sent up dust beside them. By then the shooter was headed for the cover of a shed after the other two in full retreat. Herschel drew up the horse enough to aim, then squeezed off a shot. The shooter went down, dragging his leg and crawling for his goal.

"Stop!" Herschel shouted, and reined up the roan at the foot of the hill. He piled out of the saddle and hit the ground running. In his heart, he knew the other two were already beyond the corrals fleeing on their horses. Damn the luck. He headed for the wounded one, a small man in his forties with gray beard stubble on his pained face, when a voice behind him commanded him to drop his gun.

Ready to face down the challenger, he spun on his boot heels, six-gun at his hip ready to fire. He found himself staring at a hard-looking woman, thirty or so, in the doorway, dressed in a wash-faded, long-sleeve, black dress buttoned to the throat and holding a double-barrel Greener on him.

"Put the gun away!" he ordered. "I'm the law."

Her eyes hard as rock coal and her mouth drawn in a thin line, she never moved at his words, only stuck the shotgun out farther.

"Put the damn thing down," said Herschel. "Now!"

"It's your chance, Felton," she said, looking past Herschel at the wounded man on the ground.

"Let it go—I'd never get on my horse." Lying on his side, he waved her efforts away and shook his head in defeat.

"If you can run, you better now," she said.

"That sumabitch is the damn law. Don't make it worse for you, Bertha."

"I'll sure send him to hell."

"Naw, he won't bother you. He come for me and them."

Herschel holstered his pistol and waited until she let the muzzle down. Then, after a stern look at him, she dropped her square chin and snorted out the end of her sharp nose. "Worthless damn law, took my man, now Felton."

"Lady, I never took anyone, except that stage robber. You better go see how bad he's hurt.

"Where's the loot?" Herschel asked, standing over him.

"On that dun hoss they led off. Sumabitch, this hurt."

He was holding his bloody pants leg and wincing in pain as he rocked on his butt.

"Who were they?" Herschel asked, looking off in the direction they'd ridden.

"Smith and Jones."

"Mister, you want to live, you better get a tongue in your head."

"I don't figure my life's worth much anyway if that shotgun guard dies."

"You cooperate, I might do you some good."

Kneeling on the ground, the woman ripped open his pants hem and looked in anger at his wound. "Tell him. Hell, they won't never know."

"They come by here couple of weeks ago." Felton closed his eyes as she bound his leg up in some bandages ripped from her petticoats. "Said they needed some help—sumabitch, that hurts, too." He motioned to her bandaging.

"Got to stop the bleeding," she said with a scowl.

"Go on." Herschel waited, seething inside over the fact he only had one of the three robbers and the moneybags were gone. Then he spotted a loose dun horse coming around the shed, trailing a lead rope. It wore a diamond hitch, and Herschel nodded in approval. In their hasty flight, those two hadn't gotten the loot after all.

"Sumabitch!" Felton swore at the sight of it.

"I told you they'd never get away with it," she said privately to Felton.

"Would have if it wasn't for him," Felton said.

Herschel nodded. One outlaw and the money taken back would be enough. "Who were those other two?"

"Casey Ford and Jim Riggs," she said, helping Felton to his feet.

"He got a horse to ride?" Herschel asked her.

"Why, he can't—"

"He better or he's going belly-down back to Billings."

"My Gawd, mister, you're damn sure tough." The look of disapproval on her face was as cold as any blizzard.

"Tough ain't got nothing to do with it, lady, I've got a job to do. Go get him that horse."

She wrinkled her sharp nose at him, swept back the wind-loosened, fine black hair that had escaped her severe bun, then gathered her dress to go after the horse. Be a long ride back—but the distance made no mind; he had one of the three outlaws and the money.

Long past three in the morning, he rode the weary roan horse up the dark street. His man was in a jail cell, the moneybags were locked in the office safe. He dropped heavily to the ground in front of his own barn, found his sea legs, stretched his stiff back, and rolled the aisle door aside in a long creaking noise. He promised himself he'd grease it, and in the darkness fumbled with the still-wet latigos. At last the girths were free, and he lifted the heavy saddle and pads off the roan. A strong smell of sour horse sweat filled the air. He set the saddle on its horn and turned in time to be tackled around the waist.

"You're safe!" Marsha cried.

"Safe and sound," he said, throwing his arms around her and kissing the top of her head. A rush of euphoria filled him. He was back with her and it was no dream. To savor the moment, he rocked her in his arms.

"Oh, I've worried all night about you." She hugged him harder and buried her face in his chest.

"Now, you can't do that. I'd say a sheriff is going to spend lots of his time on this job out looking for bad guys."

"If anything ever happened to you—"

"Marsha, ain't nothing going to happen to me."

"Did you get them?"

"One, and the money."

His arm in her grasp, she headed for the house under the stars. "Good, I have some food in the oven. You must be hungry."

"I am starved." He smiled down at his wife. Marsha and the girls were the stars in his life. Shame he'd missed getting Ford and Riggs, too. Then another spear stabbed him—the lynching of the carefree Texas cowboy Billy Hanks.

FIVE

A RT Spencer walked into the office and picked up the paperweight—a piece of polished petrified wood. With a pained expression on his face, he looked troubled when Herschel glanced up from his report for the county treasurer on the past month's county jail food and other expenses.

"What's up?"

"Guess you better come downstairs and see for yourself. Rath Mannon and his boys are down there. They brought you something you need to see about."

His mind still on the figures, he pushed himself away from the desk and strapped on his six-gun. Then, with his Boss of the Plains Stetson hat on, he slipped into his suit coat. Been cool outside. What did Mannon want? Tough old man. Folks spoke about Mannon's overuse of the running iron, but nothing was ever proved against him.

"What's on his mind?" Herschel asked his chief deputy going down the stairs to the lobby.

"He's got more story to go with the Hanks lynching."

"Figure they did it?" He looked over at Art.

Art shook his head. "He says no."

Wind caught Herschel when he stepped out the front door. In the street, he could see the family of boys all mounted and an extra horse. Out in front, with a week's black whiskers on his hard-chiseled face, Rath Mannon sat a big gray horse, grasping the saddle horn in both hands. His dark Injun eyes could have bored a hole in steel plates.

"Rath." Herschel nodded to the three Mannon sons, ranging from their twenties to a kid in his teens. "What can I do for you, boys?"

"We had a horse stole at the dance Saturday night. I first figured he'd broke loose. Boys'll tell you the same thing. So Harry, he's the youngest, rode home double. I was mad as hell at all of them, me a-thinking they was so stirred up about the dance they hadn't hitched him up better. Good horses don't grow on trees, you know."

Herschel nodded. "I'm listening."

"Well, we heard about that Hanks—the Texan being hung. . . ." Mannon acted like he wanted the go-ahead to continue.

"Yes."

"Well, me and the boys never hung him."

"Never accused you of it. What happened next?"

"Yesterday, the bay we call Sam showed up. The one we thought got loose." Mannon turned in his saddle and indicated the empty kack on the bay horse. "That's his rig."

Herschel nodded and walked over to look at the outfit. "He came home, huh?"

"Most horse'll come home, sooner or later. We never bothered nothing on him. Earl recognized the saddle. It was made in Lampasas, Texas. It's Billy's, all right."

"I'll need the saddle and his things for evidence."

"Sure, sure, but we brung that pony and rig here like it was, 'cause we never hung that boy. I don't want no talk either about the Mannons doing that. If Hanks had needed a horse, we'd loaned him one. He knew that."

"You and your boys left the dance together when it was over?"

"Earl stayed and rode home with Miss Kelly, Barbara Ann, then he came to the house. Me and the other boys, we left when it was over—we had work to do Sunday."

"This horse was gone then?"

"Yeah, I already said how mad I was about him getting loose. Must have been about eleven when we discovered him gone—I didn't check my watch."

"Didn't see anyone or anything?"

"I said, we don't know a damn thing about the lynching." The impatience rose in his voice.

"When I accuse you, I'll let you know," Herschel said. "Earl and Hanks had a scrap, as I recall, out at the City Park last fall."

Earl booted his roan forward. Not near as Indian-looking as his pa, he wore leather cuffs and looked the part of a fancy-dressed drover. "Me and him had a disagreement is all."

"Nothing a black eye and a bloody nose wouldn't heal?" Herschel's words drew some laughs.

"It was over after that. I hated to hear he was dead." Earl met Herschel's gaze. "Us Mannons didn't lynch him."

"None of you heard a word about lynching him while you were up there at the dance or anytime before that?" Herschel looked at them for any sign.

The row of riders under their wide-brimmed hats all shook their heads. Cold-eyed as fish, almost like they'd been practiced at it.

"Anyone see this horse coming back to your place?"

Herschel looked at them, and when they didn't answer, he continued. "What I mean is, where was he for two days?"

"He just showed up," Rath said.

Herschel went to undoing the girths. Art, who'd been listening all the time, removed the bridle and put the halter back on the horse. Why did Herschel suspect they knew more than they were saying? He looked down the street trying to tie all he'd learned from them together; then he finished ungirthing the rig and lifted it off the horse. Now wasn't the time to press them, it could wait until he found out more.

Saddle and pads in his hands, Herschel nodded to the riders. "I want to thank you for bringing this in. It may not prove anything, but if any of you learn of any new leads, let me know."

"You're convinced we done the right thing, bringing him here for you to see?" Rath asked, reined his horse up close.

"Rath, it was the right thing. I don't know who lynched him, but I aim to find out."

"Well, the Mannons never did it."

"Thanks."

Rath jerked his horse around and booted him up close to Herschel. "I ain't convinced you believe us, Baker?"

Unmoved by the threat, Herschel looked him in the eye. "I ain't convinced I know who killed that boy."

For a full five seconds, Rath held his contemptuous gaze at Herschel; then, at last, he turned the horse around. "Let's go, boys. We've done our piece here."

The riders and the spare horse galloped away.

"Tell me something," Art said from behind him. "Why in hell was Billy's rig on their horse?"

Herschel watched them disappear in the street traffic. "One of two things. Either someone aimed to point the finger at them as the lynchers, or they did it and now they're covering it up."

"They never said where that pony came from. Hell, they're all cowboys enough to backtrack a shod horse."

"I thought about that, too. Let's get this upstairs and look through his things."

"I forgot to tell you, Paul Allen at the Bar 9 is sending you Hanks's war bag. Told me so at the funeral."

"Good, grab a newspaper." Herschel's arms full of the saddle, he went sideways in the courthouse front door.

When he was upstairs at last in his office, he put the saddle down on the floor and stretched his tight back muscles. "What's the headlines say?"

"Sheriff refuses citizens' offer of assistance—" Art frowned and shook his head as he read on. "This fella at the *Herald* must not like you. Instead of bragging on the recovery of the money, he's saying you should have taken a posse and got all of them."

"I guess that's his privilege." Herschel knelt down and unbuckled the saddlebags. His hand closed on the six-gun and holster wrapped up in a belt with ammo loops. He drew it out to examine the weapon. The rubber grips with a rearing horse were typical of most .44/40-caliber Colts.

"'Our inexperienced lawman'—why, this son of a bitch needs this article shoved down his throat," Art said.

"Maybe he's right. I haven't been sheriff all that long." He took out a handful of old letters from the saddlebags and stood. At the desk, he smiled at an angry Art and set the Colt down beside him. "Opinions are free."

"Not when they smear a hardworking man's reputation." His deputy was slapping the newspaper with the back of his fingers and scowling.

"Get a chair. You can't change what's in type and we need to read Hanks's letters."

"I can damn sure make him retract it."

Herschel stopped, seated himself, and grinned big at the red-faced man. "We're the law now. No strong-armed business. I'll drop by and meet this man if I find the time. Phil, come in here. We need to read some correspondence."

"Don't read the damn paper, it'll only make you mad," Art said to the younger member of the team.

"These are Hanks's letters," Herschel told Phil. "Mannon and his boys brought us his saddle a while ago, seems it got on one of his horses. Start reading with us and see if there are any clues as to who hung him."

"I was out getting the mail," Phil said, scooting up a captain's chair to the big desk. "I miss much?"

"Just another piece of the shattered plate I'm trying to put together for the answers to who hung him.

"Who's the new reporter down at the *Herald*?" Herschel asked, beginning to read the flowery handwriting on a page of stationery.

"Ennis Stokes," Phil said.

"Guess I'll meet him." He turned back to read the letter in his hand.

Dear Billy,

It has been some time since any of us down here have heard from you. I hope this letter finds you fit and fine. Shane Coburn, who returned last year after spending a winter up on the Big Horn, told us it was worse than anything we ever see in Texas day in and out, cold and snowy. I really can't understand why a young man like you with such a bright future would consider such a frigid place to live. Why, I shiver at the thought of it.

Your Uncle Harry died this past spring. Weak heart they say. Two weeks ago Madge Dayton's son George was killed in a buckboard wreck with some broncs that a twelve-year-old never should have been driving. Nonetheless, Madge is very depressed. All the ladies at the Stone Creek Baptist Church are trying to comfort her.

Your sister Twaine is marrying Joey Ruckers in the fall. I know you hate Germans, but Joey is a nice boy and has his own farm down by Kerrville. Your father is not doing well, but he insists that you are busy and not to bother you. I doubt you would make it in time to see him alive if you came at once.

Your mother
Moore Ann

"He has a sister named Jo Anna who lives in Mason, Texas." Art turned over the envelope. "Her last name's Lincker."

"May be why his mother said he hated Germans. His sisters all married them," Herschel said and laughed, picking up another letter from Hanks's mother.

He was halfway through it when he stopped—*I guess you have not found a proper young lady yet to accept and wear your grandmother's golden wedding band.* Herschel closed his eyes. He leaned back in the chair and wondered where the ring was. Might be in the war bag. No telling. Hanks might have hocked it somewhere, with all the intentions in the world to go back for it.

Be just like a mother to give her sugar-foot son his grandmother's wedding ring hoping he would use it on some girl and settle down. Mothers had their own ways and schemes. Why, they all must have sat up at night thinking how they might work on a wayward progeny. His late mom included. His own sister about died of shock when he wrote to her that he was marrying Marsha, and three pretty young girls came in the deal. All he could think about was that Hanks had tried to please his mom—he'd proposed to Clare Scopes. But she considered him too wild to ever break to marriage traces and settle down. Maybe if she'd accepted his offer, he'd still be alive. Damn.

"Finding anything?"

"Just news about Texas," Phil said, not looking up from his reading.

"He must have written some. They answer him and then complain he don't write enough," Art said.

Herschel handed him the letter he'd read about the ring. "Maybe we can find this and return it to his family."

After a minute or so, Art agreed. "I recall, too, he had a pocket watch. He gave it to me to hold one time when he was about to ride a big bronc down at the City Park. I'd know it on sight. It had a silver case and a big D engraved on the cover. Stood for his grandfather's family on his mother's side."

"He give you his jackknife to hold, too?"

"No. I never seen it, but Bar 9 boys, I bet, can identify it."

"Phil," Herschel said, "start a list of his things we haven't found. I want every little store and saloon in south central Montana to have a copy of the items when we get them all and to be on the lookout for them."

"Wonder what that ring looks like?" Art asked.

"No telling, but leave that off. I don't want the killers plumb spooked off." Seeing the question in Phil's look, he went on. "It was his grandmother's ring, his mother mentioned it. She thought he might use it and settle down."

"Why, I'd bet he could of had any girl in the territory that he wanted," Phil said, and shook his head. "He could sure dance."

"Hmm," Art snuffed. "Dancing is like roping, you got to practice a lot to ever get good at it."

"I ain't got anyone to practice with."

"Why, Phil, I bet Kate could show you how in a minute," Herschel said, thinking how his eldest could teach his deputy to dance.

"But she's just a girl."

"Better take his offer. That's some little girl," Art said, amused, and picked up another letter.

"All I want to know is how to dance." Phil looked at both of them.

"Hell, we know your intentions are honest." Herschel stood and stretched. "Ask her, she may be flattered enough to show you how."

"Sure. Sure."

"I can see you now, cutting a rug in two," Art said and never looked up. "We're going to know it all, I guess, when we get through reading all of this."

"It ain't spelled out a thing about why he was hung or who hated him. Has it?"

"No."

"I'm going to ride up and see Barley. He may have learned something. Phil, did you get the descriptions to the printer for the Ford and Riggs posters?"

"I did that when I got the mail."

"Good. You get time, look over the expense list for last month. I'll ride up and see what Barley's found out."

"Can I go stick that reporter's head in a thunder mug?" Art made a grim face at him.

Herschel laughed and shook his head. "No. Ignore him. He's chosen a different route to go than ours. And controversy sells papers. And if he sells enough, his ad sales will go up."

"What if I tell people to not buy ads in it?"

"That sounds like the last bunch's strong-arm tactics."

"I figure if the big outfits hadn't lost so damn many cattle last winter—why, I'd bet he's on their payroll."

"I doubt they've got much to pay. Cowboys all over are out of work. That pair we got in there now held up that grocery for food to get back to Texas."

"I don't have to like his insinuations about you and the job you're doing as sheriff."

Herschel clapped Art on the shoulder, then went to the wall. He unchained a .44/40 Winchester from the rack of six and put the chain and lock back on the rest.

"Taking a long one?"

"I needed it yesterday."

Art nodded. "Don't take any chances."

Herschel got a box of cartridges out from the drawer and began filling the receiver. "I'll try not to."

"Anything else we need out of these letters?" Phil asked, gathering them in a pile.

"Yeah, save them," Herschel said. "What we really need to know is who killed Billy Hanks."

SIX

A T mid-afternoon, Herschel reined Cob up in sight of the Deer Creek Store. The big roan dropped his head and snorted in the road dust. Several rigs and horses were parked around the log building and pens Mike Mellon-camp used for his store and trading business. There was something going on and he'd bet it was a fistfight, the way a circle of onlookers had formed around the action. Or they were having a cockfight.

When he rode up, he could hear them taking sides and cheering the fighters on. Big Mike, in a red-checkered flannel shirt, was holding up one post on the high porch and gazing off at the altercation.

"Howdy, Herschel," he bellowed.

Twisting in the saddle, Herschel looked back at the two shirtless fighters dodging in and out to give each other glancing blows. When he turned back, two boys in their teens came around the corner of the store, saw him, and looked shocked at the discovery. They fled the porch and went around the building like he'd sicced a big dog after them.

"Them two out there been at it long?" he asked, dismounting and loosening the girth.

"Naw." Mike took a toothpick out of his mouth for a pointer. "The skinny one's Berry Kirk. The taller one is Wayne Farr."

"What's it all about?"

"Hell, who needs a reason to fight at that age? Got into it about nothing, I suppose."

"They fight often?"

"Oh, that Kirk boy, he stays on the prod a lot. They won't hurt each other. Ain't got any sticks or singletrees to use on one another."

Herschel wiped his mouth with his calloused hand and considered his next move. Should he consider fist fighting as disturbing the peace, or just two big boys settling nothing, as Mike called it? Be unpopular with the crowd to stop it. He took off his hat and beat his leg.

"Let 'em fight awhile," Mike said, no doubt seeing his concern. "Take some of the piss out of 'em. Come on in, I've got fresh hot coffee."

"Who were them two boys on the porch when I rode up?" Herschel asked, going inside after the broad-shouldered storekeeper.

"Guess that was the Cross brothers—Sidney and Roman."

"Strange, they spooked like wild geese upon seeing me."

"Hell, the sheriff of Yellowstone County don't come out here often enough. I'd run, too." Mike poured him a tin cup from the granite pot on the stove.

"Not unless you had something to hide." He thanked him with a nod and took the steaming cup.

"I sure don't know anything that they're into. Their old man is a damn gray-back and he's still fighting the war after all these years. Why in the hell did such a reb ever come to Montana for, I'll never know."

Herschel went to the front window and watched Kirk pile into the bigger Farr in a windmill of fists. Kirk sent his opponent to the ground and then moved in to kick at him.

In a swift second, Herschel was out the door. "Berry Kirk! Berry Kirk!" He didn't get the boy's attention. "Kirk, this is the sheriff talking. Get up here. Right now!"

Kirk was rawboned. His ribs stuck out of his snow-white narrow chest with some black hair in the center. He glared with a hard look in the direction of the store. The obvious disdain was written on Kirk's face. For a moment, Herschel considered setting down his coffee and going down there to get him. But he bided his time, and finally Kirk said, "I'm coming."

Putting on his pullover shirt, he tucked the tail in. He was followed closely by his bunch of five fans. Boys his own age or younger.

"What do you need?" Kirk asked. Someone handed him his vest and then his hat as he dressed at the foot of the steps.

"Were you at the dance last Saturday night at Sharky?"

Kirk shrugged and swept his dusty black hair back to put on his hat. "Yeah, sure, lots of us were—" He got vocal backing out of the handful of others in the crowd. Satisfied with their support, Kirk nodded. "Why're you asking me?"

"Someone or some party hung Billy Hanks after the dance."

"Why ask me?" He chuckled. "I never done it."

"You must be glad he's dead."

Kirk blinked at him and drew up defensively. "I said I never done it."

Herschel looked off at the pines on the ridge to the east. "I never said you did. But someone knows who did it. Do you?"

"Hell, no."

"Guess you have an alibi for that evening?"

"I went home early. I've got friends will tell you I did."

Herschel could see the heads nod in the crowd. "You and Hanks have a fight up there?"

"No. I never had no fight with that Texan."

"Not ever?"

"Not ever."

"I kinda take it you like to fight. And Billy Hanks did, too. If you're lying to me about never having a fight with him, I won't take it kindly."

His arms folded over his vest, Kirk spoke. "We never had no fight at the dance last Saturday night."

His shoulder to the post, Herschel took a sip of the hot coffee, but he held Kirk in place with his hard gaze. "What did you and Billy fight over?"

"I can't remember."

"You're mighty young to be having memory problems. You carry a grudge against him?"

"No."

"Any of the rest of you see or hear of any vigilante talk up there?"

The hats, from bowlers to Stetsons, all shook no.

Herschel ran his tongue over his molars, then said, "Anyone who knows anything about this lynching and don't come forth will be prosecuted with the lynchers. That will be a murder charge, too." He took another sip of coffee looking into the young faces. "So anyone knows even a peep better get it off their chest right now."

"Maybe them Mannons can answer that," a boy in his late teens spoke up.

"What's your name?"

"Danny Egelstone." He removed his bowler in an instant. His freckled face shone in the midday sun.

"Why would they know?"

"He stole their horse—sir."

"He did?" Herschel asked, looking hard at the youth of sixteen or seventeen.

"Sure did. That old man was mad as a hornet, too. Cussing and fussing around the womenfolk as well."

"About someone stealing it, huh?"

"Yes—sir." Egelstone was supported by more head nods in the group.

"You see him or his boys do anything about it?"

"No—sir."

"Anyone see that loose horse on Sunday?"

"Naw, it never was loose. They got that damn horse back when they hung him."

"Guess you boys would all testify in court to that; Hanks stole Mannon's horse and they hung him?"

"We-we never saw that part—" Egelstone turned back to the others, and they all shook their heads.

"Wonder why he'd steal a horse anyway, he had one of his own?"

Hats shook again, and they all looked down at their boots and brogans acting uncomfortable. "I want each one of you to sign a list inside the store, so I can call on each of you when we have a grand jury hearing."

"Why? We never did anything," one of them complained as they filed in the store.

"That may be right so, but someone did and someone knows who hung him." He finished the coffee and looked off toward the defeated fighter. Farr was climbing stiffly on his horse.

"Hold up, I need to talk to you, too."

"I don't know nothing."

"You know, I'm getting about tired of hearing that. A hundred folks at a dance and no one knows how Billy Hanks got hung." He stepped down and walked over to look at the fight's loser. There would be one black eye for certain. And his other cheek would be purple by morning.

"What was the fight over?" Herschel squatted down on his haunches.

"Aw, nothing."

"Don't tell me nothing. You two were fisting it out about something not five minutes ago."

"Nothing."

"Damn it, Wayne. I'm not buying your answer."

"All right." Farr glanced up at the store. "I told him to stay away from my sister."

"He courting her?"

The freckle-faced youth of sixteen or so shook his head. "He's too old for her."

"How old is she?"

"Fourteen."

"She like him?"

He shrugged. "I guess if I was fourteen, I'd think he was something. You know what I mean?"

"What's your folks think?" Herschel wished for a stick to whittle on when he shifted his weight to the other leg.

"Aw, I guess they don't care. I just don't like him, don't trust him, and this ain't our last fight." His green eyes cut an angry look at the store.

Herschel could see Kirk and his followers were coming outside. Big shots laughing and chests thrown out like banty roosters—swaggering conquerors would be the term. A bunch like that led by a tough troublemaker could get into lots of things—even a lynching.

"Sheriff?" Kirk shouted at him from the porch.

Herschel nodded, half-turned to him.

"You better make damn sure and see he signs that list in there, too." Kirk was pulling on a pair of thin black gloves, using his fingers to fit it and preparing to mount a bulldog dun stud horse. "I got to be there, he does, too."

"I'll do that." *Thanks for telling me how to do my job.* He gave them a touch of his hat and the Kirk bunch rode out.

"I never hung Billy Hanks." Farr's green eyes looked hard at him. "And I swear to God, I don't know who done it. But they must've been ready."

"Why's that?"

"Hanks didn't leave till the whole thing was over. I was taking sis home in the buckboard and I saw him ride out on that good pony of his. He left laughing and a-waving at everyone, especially the women. 'Course I went north and he went south—well, down the creek, and I figure he went south after that at the crossing."

"Didn't leave with any female?"

"Naw, him and that good horse was all I saw in the night. But lots of folks were leaving then, too. It was coming, that rain. You could see the lightning and I figured we'd stayed too long as it was and would get wet. But it was slow getting there."

"No idea who hung him?"

"No, sir. But if I hear something I'll send word."

"Good. You know my deputy Barley Benton?"

"Sure, I bought a Crow horse off him last year."

"You tell him and he can tell me. Save you a trip."

"Hanks was a nice fella. A little wild, but he sure turned heads. Still, I think he was a gentleman—" Farr pursed his lips together and shook his head.

"I guess you're telling me more so than Berry Kirk."

"Guess I am."

"Thanks. Better go put your name on the list in the store. I wouldn't want Kirk saying I treated you better than him." Herschel rose to his feet and nodded at the youth as he led his horse past him for the hitch rack.

"Me, either."

Big Mike knew nothing more than rumors about the death. So Herschel rode over to the Bentons'. Barley's Crow wife, Heart, straightened up from her gardening and wiped her copper face on her sleeve. With a big smile, she gathered her many skirts and started for the gate, looking pleased to see him. Heart was a full-blood and some thirty years younger than her husband. Before Herschel found Marsha, he used to be envious of his friend finding such a lovely young Indian girl for his bride. Wife number three for Barley, the other two had died. One from cholera in Omaha and the other in childbirth in Kansas.

She hushed the barking stock dogs, and they came slinking over to sniff Herschel and the horse when he dismounted and loosened the girth.

"I will make some coffee for the sheriff," she said when he finished, and clutched his arm possessively guiding him to the low-roofed cabin.

"Where is he?"

"Went to find Danberry and ask him about the lynching. That was a bad deal. Wasn't it?"

"Danberry wasn't home?"

"No, it was strange. Barley said his wife didn't know where he went. But he thinks he went on a big drunk."

"I don't know him. Just heard his name."

She looked at the open log rafters and shook her thick braids with the coffeepot in her hands. "Oh, he's a drinker at times. Fell out of the wagon coming home from Billings one day last summer. His horses went home without him and all the food and feed was fine. Meanwhile, he had wandered off, and the neighbors finally found him the next day panning for gold."

"Panning for gold?"

"Oh, yeah, he must have had some whiskey on him 'cause he was still drunk."

"Whew. Barley tracking him down?"

"Sure, his wife was worried." She sat down across from Herschel.

"Got a good garden started?" he asked.

"Fine one with all the rain. How's your life with girls and a wife?"

He nodded, thinking about them. "Very nice, except I need a pony."

"Barley can find you one." She smiled big.

"I was afraid of that." He turned at the dogs barking again.

"I bet that's him coming now. Stay seated, I'll tell him you're in here. He knows Cob."

Barley came in, hat in hand, and hugged her. "Just the man I need. We better ride up and talk to Danberry." He shook his graying head.

"What is it?"

"You need to hear his story about Saturday night."

Herschel stood and finished the hot coffee in the thick mug. "Thank you, looks like I better run," he said to Heart.

She smiled. "Come any time. You at least talk, he never does."

Outside, he girthed up Cob and listened to Barley's conversation with his wife.

"He needs a pony," Heart said to her man when he was mounted.

"We can find him a good one or three good ones, I bet," his deputy said, reining his horse in closer.

"I ain't sure I don't need three, but one for now would be great," Herschel said.

"We get back, I'll show you one I traded for."

Herschel agreed, swung in his own saddle, and they hurried off. Close to Barley's stirrup and the roan matching his bay's gait, he spoke to him. "What's this all about?"

"I want Danberry to tell you."

"About the hanging?"

"Yeah, let's lope."

An hour later, they found Fred Danberry bailing out buckets of sour-smelling wet grain from weathered gray barrels to his squealing hogs. He wore only his red underwear and pants. The sty's powerful aroma struck Herschel's nose, and he nodded to the red-eyed man who still looked hungover. Danberry shook his head in defeat at the sight of Herschel.

"Howdy, Fred," Herschel said, and the man wiped his hand on the seat of his pants before he shook with him. "Barley says you've got something to tell me."

"Aw, I ain't too proud of it." He shook his head and looked off to the hills in the north. "Guess I was drunker than I imagined when I was leaving that dance Saturday night."

"You see something that can help us?"

"Boy, I was drunk, Hersch, but I know I seen three riders and them leading off an extra horse down on the creek road after the dance."

"Where were they going?"

"I studied on that." He scratched his mussed-up hair. "Damn. I've been thinking how I knew one of them horses."

"One that they rode or led."

Danberry turned his calloused palms up in exasperation. "I just can't say, but when I come to I saw that boy swinging by his neck, not thirty feet from me.

"I got sick as can be 'cause I knowed them three had done that. Well, I heard a horse coming, so I crawled back in the willows. The rider cut him down and took him with him."

"You see who did that?"

"No. But the body was gone when I came to again, and so was the rider."

"Was it raining then?"

Danberry blinked his eyes and, downcast, shook his head. "Started after that—damn cold rain sobered me up some when it finally got there. Then that blasted lightning—it was a helluva bad night is all I can say."

"But you first saw three men ride off leading a spare horse, then when you came around again you saw Hanks hanging there?"

"That's what I saw."

Herschel leaned forward and looked hard at the man. "How did you see them in the dark?"

"That lightning—she lit up everything for a long time before it rain."

"You hear them talk?"

"Naw, I was down by the creek and they was on the hill."

"Cove Tipton cut him down."

"Oh, I didn't know that."

"But you saw him ride up there?"

"I saw somebody."

"Fred, you keep thinking, you recall that horse or a shape of their hats, I need to know."

"Never thought about a hat. I'm sure they had them on."

Herschel clapped him on the shoulder. "I appreciate what you told Barley and me. I want those killers. You think of anything else, you remember you get me or Barley word."

Danberry half-smiled at them and agreed. "I'll do her." He went back to slopping his hogs, who let out earsplitting screams fighting over space.

When they rode out of Fred's hearing, Barley asked. "What do you think?"

"I think he may have seen them ride off."

"We may never know why or how they did it, but we do have a lead."

Herschel was studying the late afternoon sky. No clouds, a simple blue emptiness that spread from horizon to horizon. He finally nodded. "A drunk saw part of something. It's a lead all right, but heavens, what a lead."

"Suppose it was the Mannons? I've heard lots of talk lately they ain't telling it all."

"I figured that when they said the horse came in. Why didn't they backtrack it?"

Barley twisted in the saddle and glanced back. "I don't know either. And the Ralston boys been brought up, too."

Herschel agreed. "What about Berry Kirk? He was into a fight down at Mike's place today. And he has followers. Bunch of boys with him."

"I know him. He's trouble all the time. Got a temper and gets into fights a lot. Who was he into it with this time?"

"Wayne Farr, and it was supposedly over Farr's younger sister. Seems like Kirk's been flirting with her and Farr don't like it."

Barley shook his head in disapproval. "One day, Kirk will get so mad and in his rage he'll gun someone down. You going to use Danberry's testimony at the grand jury?"

Herschel shook his head. "They won't put much stock in a drunk. I ain't ready for a grand jury yet. Besides, all he said he saw were three riders and a spare horse. No names, no identification, nothing. He didn't even recognize Cove as the one cut Hanks down either."

"But he said he saw someone ride up there."

Herschel rubbed his left palm on his pants leg and nodded slowly in deep concentration. "That's why I want to believe he actually saw three riders. I know about Cove finding Hanks."

Close to sundown, Herschel came riding up the street leading Chico, a spotted Welsh pony wearing a youth saddle and a bright red Navajo blanket. Jailhouse expenses, court cases coming up against Hamilton and Raines over the grocery robbery, and another story in the *Herald*'s latest edition complaining that the Hanks lynching had not been solved and what was the sheriff doing about it. At the moment—he grinned to himself—*not one damn thing.* He had bigger fish to fry. A pony that Barley had traded for in his horse deals, well mannered, who liked people, was a present for the three girls to ride.

"You found him!" Nina shouted as she burst out of the house, ran across the porch, and took the steps two at a time.

Dismounted, Herschel sent a grin at his wife, drying her hands in the doorway. He captured the excited seven-year-old around the waist, swung her up into the saddle, and nodded to her—you're there.

"What's his name?" she asked in an awed whisper.

"Chico, and it's a her."

Her blue eyes drew in tight lines and she looked sternly at him. "She's ours?"

"She's all of yours." He took the bridle from the horn and slipped the bit in her mouth, then handed the reins to Nina. "Go easy until you're sure you can ride her."

Stiff as an ironing board, she nodded and pulled the

mare around. Chico obeyed a step at a time, and then Nina gave it some rein. The chunky-built pony began to walk away, and a great "whew" escaped Nina's lips. By this time, Herschel held Sarah in his left arm, Marsha clung on the right one, and Kate, shoes set apart, hands on her hips, was making a silent caustic appraisal of how her sister was handling the pony.

"You are spoiling us to death," Marsha said, looking up at him.

"It was time somebody did." Then he laughed.

SEVEN

A PENCIL stuck behind his ear and a small pad of paper in his left hand, the tiger reporter of the *Herald* stood with one shoe on the captain's chair ready to collect another story. Ennis Stokes wore a cheap green-checkered suit, a collarless, once-white shirt he'd slept in, no socks, and his dusty shoe propped on the chair was coming apart at the sole. Maybe twenty-five years old, he had a mustache crop on his upper lip and his blue eyes surveyed the desk of the Yellowstone County sheriff.

"What's new on the hanging?"

Herschel leaned back in the swivel chair and folded his arms over his chest. "I don't know, I haven't read the latest edition of the *Herald*, my chief source of information."

Stokes raised his eyebrows from the pad in his left hand and paused. "Now, reporting is my business. You're the law. You're supposed to know about everything." He waved the pencil around in a large circle.

"I ain't biting on that bait. The investigation of the

lynching of Billy Hanks is ongoing. At such a time that we get sufficient evidence, we will have a grand jury hearing and at that hearing we will name the accused killer or killers."

"What are you doing about it?"

"Interrogating everyone that was there."

"You mean, of course, those that attended the dance?"

"And others that might lend any information on the murder."

"Do you expect any more lynchings?"

"No. Do you know about any more that are planned?"

Stokes frowned at him, then smiled knowingly. "I ain't heard of any. What evidence do you have in the lynching?"

"A shank of Boston hemp rope from a lariat that about ninety percent of the stockmen in Montana use."

"So stockmen hung him?"

"Or they borrowed it from one."

"You gave out a list of things to stores and saloons this week." Stokes fished through his paper looking for the information. "Yes, a pocketknife and a watch with D monogrammed on the silver case and a red horsehair fob on it."

"You seen any of those items?"

Stokes shook his head. "Don't you figure that they will destroy them now you have a description out on them?"

"I'm counting they can't read."

"Did they rob him, then?"

"He was missing those personal items. You can judge the rest."

"What about the stage robbers Casey Ford and Jim Riggs?"

"We think they've gone to Nebraska and we've sent out wanted posters."

"Many people in Billings think you aren't doing enough

to combat crime in the county. What is your answer to that?"

"This meeting is over. Thanks for dropping by. Have a nice day, Ennis."

"But I need to know—"

"You heard the sheriff," Art Spencer said, coming in the office. "The meeting is over." He used his thumb to indicate the open door.

"You know—the press can defeat you in the next election," Stokes protested as Art herded him out and shut the door.

His back to the door, Art shook his head. "You got more patience than I'd ever have with that sumbitch."

Herschel laughed and shook his head amused. "You have to admit he's sure persistent."

"That ain't the word I'd use."

"Well, we can look for some good spirited reporting in the next edition."

"Anyway, I got word a while ago that one of them stage robbers may be back."

"Which one?"

"Casey Ford. Bartender friend of mine up in Miles City sent me word by Argle that Ford may be gathering a new gang."

"Any ideas where or how many?"

"I figure he needs to find work or do another robbery pretty soon. You got back all the loot on the last one, save the little money they took off those drummers on the stage."

"Maybe I should drop down and pay Bertha a visit. She would probably know if they were around that country."

"But would she tell you anything?"

"I doubt it. She's mad and mean enough she might shoot me this time." Herschel chuckled. "I really thought for a second I was dead that day looking down those two barrels of her Greener."

"Luck's what I say. But this Ford must be pretty smart; bet you can't catch him with a fast horse next time."

"Sounds like we better get ready for more trouble. One of us needs to ride that stage when it has money on it—" Herschel slammed the desk with his fist. "That's it. Ford has an inside track somewhere and we need to know who it is."

"You're saying?"

"I'm saying someone is feeding him information when that money is on it. That stage runs every day with only mail sometimes, and the very day it has cash, Ford and his gang heist it."

"Maybe just luck."

"Too damn convenient. One of us better ride up to Miles City and talk to Sheriff Tommy Clarendon about setting a trap."

"Clarendon ain't your biggest fan. He rides with them big ranchers up there."

"I know, but when it comes to crooks, the big outfits hate them."

"It's worth a try."

"We better get to going on it. If Ford's going to try something, then I'd like him to meet four armed lawmen."

"You want me to go up there and set it up?"

"You better, I'd be too obvious. I figure Ford could see me a mile off and run."

Art agreed. "We put out the word that the money is on the stage, and then we replace the passengers after it leaves Miles City and take him when he tries to rob it."

"Let the banker do it like he usually does. I want to think the spy is in the organization, or whoever is passing out the word is in the middle. Could even be a deputy, I don't know Clarendon's men."

"Where do we fit in?"

"Carson Station, we get on and ride it into Billings."

"What if they hold it up in Big Horn County?"

"Clarendon can run them down."

Art laughed and then looked at Herschel hard. "This job doesn't ever get to you, does it?"

Herschel rose and nodded, hitched up his pants, and walked to the window that looked down on the street. "Art, I made up my mind when I got elected to slow down, be methodical, work things out. But it gets to me. Them two getting away might have been because of my bullheadedness."

"How's that?"

"I hate posses. They aren't hardened riders. They aren't lawmen."

He stared out the distorted glass window at the bull wagon plodding down the street. Several yokes of roan steers crawling like an ant army up the street. Even the loud swearing voices of the drivers carried to him in a faint way. "I hate we ain't found Billy Hanks's killers and that eats at me every waking hour. No, this job gets to me. I just have a good rein on my anger right now."

Art looked hard at him and nodded. "You damn sure do. Lots better than I have."

"Go up to Miles City and learn all you can. Set the trap and I'll be ready to help you spring it."

Art agreed. "I think we may get him that way."

"You handle Clarendon the best you can."

Art chuckled, going out the door. "I'll try your way."

While Art was gone to Miles City, Herschel planned to ride up and see Faye Ryan, the widow woman who never missed a dance and never missed seeing a thing either. "Phil, handle things. I'll be gone a couple of hours."

"Ah, Sheriff, did you ask, ah, your—daughter Kate about lessons?"

Herschel took his hat off the rack and smiled at the young man. "She said she'd be pleased to."

"Thanks—"

"Anytime," Herschel said, and went out the door. He took Cob out of the stall and went around in a circle before he could get his toe in the stirrup. At last in the seat, he spoke sharply to the gelding, who danced sideways for fifty feet up the empty street, drawing surprised looks from some ladies on the boardwalk. Cob's foolishness somewhat resolved, Herschel sent him off in a long trot for Widow Ryan's farm.

The weather was warm and strong gusts came out of the south. His Stetson never threatened to leave his head, but after years of wearing one, Herschel had learned how to tilt his head a certain way to buff the eternal wind. Like how he reset the six-gun on his hip out of habit, time and again until he didn't think about it.

He rode off the rise, and could see the green cotton-wood leaves around her white house and picket fence. She raised up in her garden and used a hand to shield the sun's glare to see him. Then, with a nod, she headed for the end of the row, and he knew she was smiling.

"Well, hope you aren't out here to arrest me, High Sheriff," she said from the gate, busy pulling off cotton gloves.

He dismounted and wrapped the reins on the worn-smooth hitch rail. His gaze met her bright blue eyes and he shook his head. "Naw, Faye, I need information today. You stole anything lately or done anything immoral?"

"Is it a sheriff's job to enforce morality now?"

"No, but it would make good gossip if I knew something on you."

The willowy woman in her forties laughed out loud, took his arm, and led him to the porch. "Now wouldn't it. How's that wife and those pretty girls?"

"Best thing ever happened to an old cowboy."

"I agree, and they're lucky to get such a fine man. Sit in the rocker and I'll bring us out some tea and then we can talk sheriff business." She paused in the open doorway. "You did come out to talk business, didn't you?"

He nodded, grim-faced. "Yes, ma'am. Billy Hanks."

"Yes," she said, and chewed on her lower lip. "It crossed my mind when I saw you and that fine roan coming. He's coming to ask me about Billy."

Herschel rubbed his palms on the top of his pants legs. "Get the tea. I've got some time."

"Oh, yes—I almost forgot my business." She hurried off, and he studied the short grass beyond the yard fence that was whipped and tossed by the growing wind. In the past few days, some small violets had begun to bloom in patches, and tiny yellow blossoms had also burst open to feed the bees hungry from winter. Mother Earth was healing over the bones and carcasses of the thousands of storm-lost cattle piled up in ravines. Losses that would bring an end to many big outfits, and some small ones, too.

"I hope you like cream puffs," she said, putting a dish of them in his hand as she moved the delicate china cup and saucer to the nail keg beside him.

"Trying to bribe me?"

She laughed, and the wind swept her long skirt around her high-button shoes in a hard rush. "I may blow away before I get this all ready. Sugar?"

He nodded and winked at her.

She used the small silver spoon to add sugar. "Cowboys

never use sugar in their coffee, but drink my tea and they all need sugar."

"'Cause it's handy," Herschel said, and sat back in the rocker to try the pastry oozing with stiff cream filling. The first bite flooded his mouth with saliva. He closed his eyes to savor the flavor. "Wonderful."

With her blondish hair swept back from her face, she sat opposite him in the other rocker. "Have you arrested anyone for his murder yet?"

"No, but I hoped you could give me a lead. Did he get into it with anyone up there?"

She looked at the teacup in her hand and shook her head. "I've thought hard about it—since I heard the bad news. Something was strange about that night. We all knew it was going to storm, but the storm sat out there and growled like an old toothless dog for hours."

"Hanks never got into any kind of altercation that you saw—with anyone?"

"No." She shook her head warily.

"I need to ask kind of a tough question."

She nodded for him to continue.

"Hanks wasn't having an affair with someone's wife, was he?"

"My, my—" She squeezed her chin and then shook her head. "No, but he was so good-looking and charming he could have. But I'd say no. Why?"

"I think this horse-rustling business was a frame-up. I don't buy it. I think he made someone mad over him flirting with their wife or girlfriend and they put him out of the way."

"Jealousy, you mean?"

"Yes."

"You have a long list of suspects, then?"

He nodded and went on. "Did he dance much with Barbara Ann Kelly?"

"You mean Earl Mannon's girl?"

"Yes."

"Oh, Herschel, I can't say. I'm not certain. No, not particularly. He danced with me and he sure did polka with Clare Scopes. Those two cleared the floor every time. He really knew how to do that dance."

"Must have learned how from his German in-laws down in Texas."

"I would bet so. Have you talked to Clare?"

"Yes, she was taken aback by the news. He had proposed to her."

"Oh, no."

"Actually, she declined his offer."

"Oh, really?"

"She was very forthright about the matter, said he wouldn't settle down, and it would be like taming a wild range horse, probably ruin him. She wanted a husband who would make her a place to live."

"Smart girl, not many her age are that smart. They all think they can tame them and they never do." She wrinkled her nose at the notion.

"You can't think of a soul that wanted him dead that was at the dance?"

She rose and took his cup. "One more cup of tea and I will twist my brain some more."

"Twist it hard. I have a reporter at the *Herald* that is on my backside for not solving who did this."

"Well, doesn't he know the wicked crew that you replaced?" she called out from inside.

"Folks' memories are short."

"Short indeed. Here." She handed him the cup, then administered two teaspoons of sugar to it. "More cream puffs?"

"No. They are wonderful."

Taking a seat, she went on. "You think the Mannons are suspects?"

"They brought me his saddle on a horse of theirs. They say he was taken from the school yard and eventually wandered home."

She thought for a moment. "I heard all the shouting and cussing he had at the boys in the school yard over some horse getting away."

"He admitted it." Herschel dug in his pocket and handed her the arrowhead from his vest pocket. "Found that in the frog of Hanks's horse."

"I never saw one like that before from around here. Strange-color flint." With her fingers, she turned it over in her palm.

"Barley says he's never seen one like that, either. Don't mean anything, I guess. But what are the chances a horse sticks that in his frog?"

"Hmm," she said, holding the point up to the sunlight. "This isn't flint, it's more like glass. No, it would be hard to do unless someone drove it into his hoof on purpose."

"Why cripple a good horse?"

"Oh, my, Herschel, so they would make it look like he needed another horse and stole one." She looked shocked at her own words.

He turned, deep in thought, and gazed at the pines on the ridge and nodded slowly. "Half the folks there would have loaned him a horse if he needed one. I really believe the boy was murdered for revenge or it was over a woman."

"That leaves lots of speculation."

"Didn't you teach at the school when you first came here?"

"Yes, but no one thought it proper for a married woman to teach. So I only did it one semester, and they found Mary Ann Childs to teach."

"I recall her. She married a drover and went back to Texas in the spring." He chuckled. "The note they pinned on him, I have it here. Look at it hard and tell me who wrote it."

"How can I do that?" A peeved expression swept over her face.

"I'm teasing. Read it." He handed the paper over.

"Oh, my, the backward S's."

"Seen them before?"

"Yes, several students make them like that and think they're right. In fact, I think they see them like that and reproduce them the same way in their writing."

"So I need to find someone that writes like that."

"This was the note pinned on him?"

"Yes."

"It very well could be a grown-up."

"His spelling isn't the best either."

"No." She chuckled and handed him back the paper. "'Steeler' would get you a failing grade in spelling."

"Whoever wrote this went back, snuck in the schoolhouse after the dance, and wrote it on a tablet they found in there. I have the imprint on a second page."

Her eyelids narrowed and she cocked a suspicious eyebrow at him. "What else do you have?"

"Four feet of hemp rope. Cove Tipton found him and cut him down."

"I wish I could help you more. I just have no idea who would do such a cruel thing."

"Thanks for the tea, those dandy cream puffs, and the conversation. I better get back to Billings and see what else fell down today. And all your ideas."

"Heavens, I have done little."

"Yes, you have. That arrowhead is made of obsidian and I hadn't thought of it until now."

"Volcanic glass, yes, that's what it is."

"Now all I have to find is who packed it up here." He stepped off the porch. Then he turned back and saluted her.

"Tell Marsha and the girls I said hi," she said.

"I will, and I am certain they would have sent the same to you had they known I was coming up here. The girls are busy today riding a new pony called Chico, and if they haven't mauled each other over who rides next, I'll be surprised."

Her warm smile and wave sent him homeward bound.

EIGHT

"A<small>RT</small> sent you a note from Miles City," Phil said when Herschel walked into the office.

"So soon?"

"I didn't read it."

Herschel began to read it.

> *Money will be on the Thursday stage. I want you to meet the stage about nine* AM *at Carson Station just across the county line. Argle will stop and pick us up there.*

"What do you need to do?" Phil asked.

"Meet him day after tomorrow. Maybe catch us some stage robbers." He held his finger to his mouth and shared a nod with his deputy. "Secret."

"Oh, I know. Will you be home tonight?"

"I reckon. Why?"

"Kate said you had to make the music so we could, ah—dance."

"Oh, sure, we can do that after seven."

"Good," Phil said, looking relieved.

"Well, no trouble today, then?"

"Me and Dave Allen, the town marshal, brought in a drunk kid that was making a ruckus and stuck him in the jail."

"Who's that?"

"Egger-stone?"

"Danny Egelstone?"

"You know him?"

"I met him out at Melloncamp's store. Is he passed out?"

"He was a while ago."

"Go get him and bring him in my office."

Phil frowned. "He was really drunk."

"I know. I have a test for him."

"Well, all right, Sheriff, but—"

"Get him, then we'll see."

He took a seat behind his desk, drew out a pad and pencil. In a short while, Phil was back with Egelstone, who still looked drunk.

"What'cha yah want—" Egelstone put both hands on the desk, and the only thing that saved him from being jerked away was Herschel's hand signal for Phil to let him be. Herschel shoved a piece of paper across the desk. "Print 'horse rustler' on this."

Egelstone blinked. "This a trick?"

"Print it or else."

The kid held up his hand. "I ain't got nuffin to hide." He took the pencil and began to print in shaky letters. The S's were all right and despite the tremble in his hand, the words were spelled right. Egelstone raised his smarmy gaze. "What next?"

"Put your name on it."

"I did that at the store. I never rustled no horses."

"Never said you did."

He finished writing his name and looked at Herschel. "What now?"

"Phil's going to take you back to your bedroom. Sweet dreams."

"Aw, hell, I thought I was getting out of *cheer*."

Herschel shook his head in disgust as his deputy took the kid away. Not the same printing for sure, and he'd never flinched spelling "rustler." That was one down, and he still had an army more to test. Good idea, but working alone would take some time. Maybe if he looked at the list of names that bunch had left at Mike's store, there might be a clue on it.

He'd get the list on his way to Carson Station. His mind was more on the stage robbers than the lynching. He wondered how many men Casey Ford had recruited for his next heist, and if he'd be able to find the one who was feeding the outlaw the information. He went back to his expense figures for the jail. Holding criminals over for trial had doubled his budget. Of course, the little four-eyed fellow from the treasurer's office said his costs were considerably under those of his predecessor, who, he mentioned, might have been padding them. Herschel went to the open window and studied the traffic in the street below. It would soon be roundup time. Breaking a few fresh horses for a string sounded so much better than doing book work in his spacious office, but he'd chosen this new career and better get to liking it. When he'd finished with Casey Ford, he needed to go down to Marsha's place and see how the new help was doing. There would not only be a roundup, but haying as well.

After looking over the figures, he gave Phil the ledger and told him he was going to check on some things. He planned to drop by the mayor's office and see if he had found a chief of police to hire. Billings was growing fast in anticipation of the railroad arriving in a year or so, to the detriment of other communities that had wanted it for themselves. The die was cast and right-of-way staked despite tons of political wrangling—Billings would be the railroad town. He noticed three familiar riders coming down Main. The hat no doubt belonged to Rath Mannon, his eldest son, Earl, was on his left, and the youngest, Harry, in his teens, rode on his right.

Herschel stepped outside and waited for them.

"Morning," he said, seeing the sharp distrust fill the older man's gaze.

"Morning yourself," Rath said.

"I am starting a list of everyone involved in the Hanks case. If you three would swing by and sign in at my office, I'd sure appreciate it."

"What's the meaning?" Rath shook his head to cut off his boys from speaking.

"I am making a list of everyone involved in the case. Now, if stopping by my office and signing in is too much work, I'll go get some paper and you can sign it right here."

"I told you—"

"Rath, if I ever accuse you of his murder, I'll damn sure look you in the eye and tell you so."

"I don't like you acting like we done it."

"Trust me, when I have the proof, I'll be after whoever done it. There won't be no pussyfooting around, either."

"We're going to Wheeler's." Rath nodded toward the store. "We can sign your list there."

"Fine."

Herschel stepped back and let them pass. Wheeler's sign hung a half block down the street. He didn't miss Rath's wolflike look at him as the man booted his horse past. Harry's freckled face looked innocent and a little uncomfortable. Earl's stern nod toward him was like his father's. A tough bunch who lived under harsh circumstances, matched against the large ranches they caught lots of ire from the big outfits, guilty or innocent of using a running iron. The stigma remained, little outfits were all rustlers in the eyes of those big ones. That attitude made men like Rath defensive, too.

Herschel arrived at Wheeler's and followed them inside the spice-and-harness oil–smelling store. He walked to the counter and borrowed a pad from the clerk. With a pencil from his coat pocket, he handed pad and pencil to Rath, who'd been talking in low tones to his boys. No doubt giving his orders how to handle the situation.

"I can't see any reason to—"

Herschel waved Rath's complaint aside. The rancher put the left elbow of his brown suit coat on the counter and concentrated on putting down his signature.

"There."

"Print 'horse rustler' on the next page."

"Listen—"

"I don't give a damn what you think. Print it."

For a long moment Rath looked ready to rebel. Then he growled under his breath and turned to the next page. "Spell it, Harry."

"H-o-r-s-e-r-u-s-t-l . . . e-r."

Rath nodded with a grin when he finished. "Good thing one of them boys went to school anyway."

"Didn't hurt him none," Herschel said as Earl came up to write next.

Finally, Harry signed his page. The task completed, Herschel gathered the sheets and thanked the Mannons.

"You got any more leads on who done it?" Rath asked.

"Not yet, but I'm looking. You all know any more?"

"We do, we'll tell you," Rath said, raising his hackles again.

"Oh, I had a man by the office looking for some good arrowheads to buy. You all collect them?"

Rath shook his head, and the other two followed his lead. "Couple of million out there. What does he pay?"

"Certain good ones, a dollar."

"Hell, boys, we've been walking on millions of dollars." Rath laughed and waved at his entourage to follow him out.

Herschel put the papers inside his coat pocket. He liked the arrowhead idea. It was a long shot, but he couldn't see how one got in a horse's frog without being driven into it. That made no sense, except it forced a man with a crippled horse to beg, borrow, or steal. Or else it was done to make the crime look real. In that case, the one who planned the lynching might be much smarter than Herschel had been giving him credit for.

Once in the café, he spread the sheets out. No backward S's. Rath's printing looked very shaky, but didn't resemble anything on the note that Cove had found.

"You hungry?" Maude Corey asked with a big smile, standing above him in an apron.

"No, is Buster busy? Oh, I need some of your good coffee."

"Coffee's coming. He's always glad to escape work back there. I'll tell him you're here."

Buster shuffled into view from the kitchen door, spotted Herschel, and came over in his carpet slippers. He removed a toothpick from his white-whisker-bristled mouth and smiled. "How's the sheriff doing?"

"Depends who you listen to."

The ex-cowboy scratched his dark spot-blotched cheek and nodded. "You've been making headlines."

"Oh, yes. Have a seat."

"I will." Buster sat down and fetched the makings out from under the soiled apron. With his gnarled fingers, he began to roll a smoke. "Folks were pleased you got the money back. That Yankee boy at the paper is crazy."

"I'll get Ford, too. What have you heard about the lynching?"

Buster put the twisted, licked-shut cigarette in his sun-whitened lips and struck a match. Small puffs of smoke began to issue out the side of his mouth, and he drew it away between his forefinger and thumb. "Not much. Mannons are mentioned."

Herschel nodded. "What about Bert Ralston's bunch?"

"I wouldn't put nothing past them. Been several things they've been involved in that were shady."

"But there isn't any word out that I've missed."

Buster shook his head. "Not a thing, but I'll go to listening."

"I don't think Hanks stole any horse."

"Why did they lynch him, then?"

"I had that answer, I'd have the killer."

"I'll keep it in mind."

"Good." Herschel lifted the thick cup to his lips and blew on the steam. "You ever see an arrowhead like this?" From his vest, he fetched the stone point and set it on the table.

Buster took it and fingered the edge examining it, then shook his head. "No, never seen anything like that. Looks like it's made of glass. Where did it come from?"

"The frog of Hanks's horse when we found him."

"Hmm, I've seen some small rocks and sticks jabbed in frogs, but never got an arrowhead out of one. Guess they can step on anything."

"Or they can be drove in on purpose."

Buster nodded slowly as Herschel drank some more coffee. "I sure liked that boy. He was me a hundred years ago, I reckon. Devil-may-care, rode bucking horses like he just knowed they couldn't throw him. He was a sight on one."

"Yes, and he didn't need to die. I have to see the mayor next. You learn anything, let me know."

"I sure will, and thanks for thinking of me. I get plumb lonesome back there wrangling dishes and peeling spuds." Buster laughed, then puffed on his smoke.

"I'll be back."

Buster waved off the dime Herschel put on the tabletop. "Coffee's on me."

"Thanks." Herschel left with a wave for Maude.

Mayor George McKay wasn't in. His secretary, a young man named Winston at McKay's law office, said he'd taken the stage to Miles City earlier for law business and to talk to the railroad officials who were supposed to be coming up there.

Back on the street, Herschel recognized a big red-faced man on the seat of a wagon, Nels Hansen from down on Horse Creek by Herschel's old place. Nels reined up at the sight of him.

"What brings you to town?" Herschel stepped off the boardwalk to speak to his ex-neighbor.

"Order some mower parts. Get some things the wife needs and to shake your hand." He bailed off the seat and stuck out a large ham of a hand.

"How's things up on Horse Creek?"

"Smells like dead cattle like the rest of Montana. We had a few workdays, and finally got all the carcasses out of the stream, but they sure ain't going away very fast. Damn wolves and magpies are so fat they can't move to get out of the way. I shot a gyp last week, and she never ran she was so fat."

"Be all summer getting rid of them."

"We will be. We heard you got the stage robber single-handed."

"And the reporter at the *Herald* didn't like it."

"Aw, them newspapers live on that crap. Folks are proud you're up here in charge. That dumb newspaper ain't turning no one against you."

"Good. Come next election, we may have a battle on our hands."

"Bring them on."

"Guess you heard about a cowboy being lynched. His name was Billy Hanks."

Nels nodded grimly. "We talked about it up at the store. Didn't get any details, though."

"Parties unknown hung him last Saturday at the Sharky Schoolhouse after the dance."

Nels nodded. "Vigilantes?"

"No, I suspect foul play."

The big man looked deep in thought and folded his thick arms over his chest. "How can we help?"

"Listen. Someone knows who did it. They'll talk eventually."

"Got any leads?"

Herschel shook his head. "Only notions."

"You must think he was murdered."

Herschel nodded. "I do." But proving it looked like a hard mountain to climb.

NINE

WITH the harmonica in Herschel's mouth as he sat on the high-back wooden chair, he began tapping his foot for the timing. In the center of the kitchen floor stood his young deputy Phil and a very straight-backed Kate holding Phil's left hand up. The notes for "Oh, My Darling" began to float from the mouthpiece, and Kate took her stiff student across the room with her. At first her one-two count sounded unsteady, but her voice gained courage, and she soon had the still-stiff Phil moving across the room.

Under the scrutiny of her two sisters, who'd been warned by their mother against making comments, his deputy's first dance lesson had begun. Soon, the notion of watching their older sister and him circle the room must have lost its charm, for they began to dance like a couple, ignoring Phil and Kate.

Herschel played until he gave out, and Marsha served

dried-apple pie along with lemonade to the dancers and the musician as well.

"You're doing very well, Phil," she said, handing him his pie and drink.

"I'm sure it is Kate who's doing it," he said, taken aback by her words.

Herschel shared a private wink with his eldest, and took a forkful of the warm treat. He could tell she was very proud of the invitation to teach the young man. It struck him that he might be matchmaking and that was not a good idea, but he felt Kate was very grown up for her age and hardly some giggly girl.

So the lesson went on after the intermission, and Phil left about nine. Nina had the last word when the girls started upstairs for bed. "I'm sure glad you're teaching him. He's too stiff for me to ever try to do anything with him."

Herschel hugged his wife and chuckled. "We have Nina's opinion now. I need to get up early and ride over to Carson Station and meet Art."

"How early?"

"Like four in the morning."

"We better set the alarm. Business?"

"I wouldn't get up that early for anything else."

"Sounds real early."

"I need to meet Art and the stage at the county line."

"Fine," she said, and turned up her face to be kissed.

How lucky he was.

The bell on the windup alarm jarred him awake. Short night, he decided on one side of the bed as his wife, on the other side, put on a robe and lighted the lamp.

"I'll go down, make coffee and breakfast."

"Fine, I'll saddle Cob and hitch him out front."

She paused in the doorway as he put on his socks. "Be very careful today. We need you."

"I will," he said, and drew on his boots.

"Counting on that," she said, and was gone.

The barn smelled of manure and sweet hay. Cob snorted at the lamplight when Herschel opened the stall door talking softly to the big roan. When the saddle was in place, he blew out the lamp and under the cool starlight led Cob around to the hitch rack. Cob's reins were wrapped on the bar, and Herschel stretched his arms over his head and went in the front door.

The smell of Marsha's cooking filled the house.

"Cool out there?" she asked from her position at the stove.

"No heat wave, but it'll warm up in a little while."

"You be back this evening?" she asked as he hugged her shoulder and laid his cheek on top of her head.

"I'll try."

"Try hard. I sleep better that way."

"Well, don't stay up. I may have some problems."

"You're expecting stage robbers?" Coffeepot in hand, she narrowed her eyes as she questioned him.

He picked up the coffee she poured him. "Art's been up there working on it. He must think they'll try a robbery today."

"Maybe we should go back to ranching after this term is over."

"As I recall, I got beat up and burned out doing that."

"Yes, things are not that bad here—yet."

He put the mug down and threw his arms around her. Rocking her back and forth, he drew a deep breath. "You have to stop worrying. I'm going to be sheriff until they turn me out."

"All right, Sheriff Baker, but your eggs may burn if you don't release me."

They both laughed.

He took Cob the long way around rather than by the main road to Miles City. In case the robbers were on or near it lying in wait, he wanted to avoid them. No need to spook them. He wanted to catch them in the act. Well past Tow Creek, he took Parrot's ferry across the Yellowstone River, and was at the Carson stage station by nine o'clock.

Art came out to meet him when he rode up.

"Right on time. Anything go wrong while I was gone?"

"No, quiet in town." Herschel dropped out of the saddle, put his hands on his hips, and stretched his tight back.

"We can put our horses in with the stage stock. Argle's trying to keep any passengers from taking the stage today."

"May piss off the mayor," Herschel said, undoing the latigos on his cinch.

"Why's that?"

"He was supposed to be coming back today."

"Another day might not kill him." Art laughed out loud.

"You feel this is good bait? This shipment today?"

"Oh, yes. We have over a thousand in currency in the strongbox."

"Anyone you suspect of telling them?" Herschel jerked off his saddle and set it on the ground.

A gray-whiskered man waved at them from the porch. "Come on in when you get him put up. Wife's got hot coffee."

"Thanks, Carson, we're coming," Herschel assured him, and led the roan off toward the pens. He put Cob inside the corral, slipped off the bridle, and patted him on the neck with a promise to be back for him. The roan moved off, ears back, toward the other horses to eat at the rack.

"Getting back to who's telling them," Art said as he closed the gate. "I'm still looking."

"Maybe we can learn more today. I can see the dust."

In a short while, the stage appeared, and Herschel took up the saddle to load. No time for coffee. Argle reined the double team up and shouted to him. "Good to have you two aboard."

Carson's men switched the teams with precision.

The shotgun guard took Herschel's saddle up top and with his rifle in hand, Herschel climbed in the coach. He nodded to Art, who already sat on the back bench holding a double-barrel Greener in his arms.

"You must have got up early," Art said with a grin.

"Too early. Guess those buzzards are up the road?"

"I sure think they'll try for this strongbox."

The stage left in a rocking jolt, Argle's loud voice in command and the fresh horses off in a hard lope. A few miles farther, the horses began to slow up, and Art stuck his head out in time to hear Argle say, "We've got company up ahead."

"Masked men on horseback," Art said at the side window, then settled back in the seat.

"How many?" Herschel asked.

"I saw three, maybe more."

"You use that scattergun on that side and I'll get out on the other side, while they're distracted," Herschel told his deputy.

"Be careful, they've shot one guard," Art said.

Herschel agreed with a nod. Things were about to break loose and he turned his ear to listen for the robbers' words.

"Throw down them guns," someone ordered.

"Easy on the trigger," Argle said to the highwaymen from on top. "We're doing it."

"Where's the strongbox?"

Herschel nodded to his partner as he heard the approach of a horse coming in closer.

"Get your hands up, we're the law!" Art shouted, and the blast of the shotgun was echoed by a horse's scream.

Herschel bailed out the door on his side and drew aim at the masked rider fighting with his spooked horse. Six-gun in the outlaw's hand, he could see this one wasn't surrendering. The rifle in Herschel's hands spoke, and the masked man pitched face-first out of the saddle.

In a run, Herschel was soon beside the second team and looked up at Argle and the guard—both appeared to be unscathed. Off in the west, two of the holdup men were burning the breeze down the road. He jammed the stock in his shoulder and took aim, but neither of the next two rounds stopped them.

"Get me a horse out of these teams," he shouted, and set down the rifle.

The guard tossed down Herschel's saddle and bailed off the seat. In seconds, they had the yoke off the front team and were piling his saddle on a dancing lead horse.

"Reckon he's been rode lately?" the guard asked with a grin as he fit the bridle on.

Herschel gave him a smile, shook his head, and followed the circling horse to tighten his latigos. The big black was lathering at the bit, and moved nervously in a wide circle as Herschel tried to finish cinching up the girth. Argle joined them and nodded toward the outlaw that Herschel had shot. "He's dead."

"We've got two of them, but Ford and the other one got away," the deputy said, joining them. "What do I need to do?"

"Go get our horses and send the bodies in. I'm going after them," Herschel said, taking the rifle from the guard.

"I can ride along."

Herschel shook his head. "I need you to load their bodies in the stage and get our horses and catch up with me. We may need them. It could be a lengthy chase."

Art agreed with a concerned look on his face. "Be careful."

Herschel nodded and with both Argle and the guard hanging onto the upset stage horse's bridle, he bounded in the stirrup. "Got him," he said, and drew on the reins.

Ole Black took off in long bucking strides. He might have been drive-broken, but he sure was not saddle-broke. He ended his first fit in some bone-jarring crow-hops as all four feet struck the road surface at the same time. Herschel slapped him on the butt with the rifle stock, and he shot out in a wild gallop.

No telling how fast he was. Herschel decided a Texas cow pony would not outrun him, if he could only control him when he found where the robbers left the road. In a few minutes, he could see the robbers in the distance, taking to the sagebrush and headed for a ridge. Whipping their ponies, the two were soon cat-hopping up the steep side of the hill. He set Black in their direction, and the big horse went to leaping over patches of sage. He began to wonder about his choice of mounts, but he was closing in on the pair of outlaws.

At the base of the hill, he saw them going over the top. If Ford was one of them, he already knew Herschel wouldn't back off, so he wondered if they'd keep going or try to ambush him. No time for caution. He sent Black up the steep hillside, and was prepared to jump off if he ever floundered.

Black's breath roared out his throat, but he never slackened. His efforts came in large lunges that about tore Herschel out of the saddle, but he rode him, sometimes forced to grab leather. The top was in sight. How far ahead were they?

Then a rifle shot cracked the air. A bullet slapped his mount in the chest, and Herschel felt the horse shudder between his knees clamped to the leather. Black screamed, hard hit, and threw himself sideways. No time to think about it. Herschel shook his boots out of the stirrups and dove to the side, hoping not to be rolled on by the big animal falling over backward. His rifle went one way, he went the other. His back hit hard in the brittle sagebrush; then he went rolling and pitching off the mountain through the blunt sage. When he stopped, his mouth was full of dirt. Out of breath, he tried to clear his head, and simply rolled off the last clump that he'd ended his fall on and lay flat on the steep hillside.

Screams of the injured horse filled his ears, but he lay still, not daring to move, knowing he still could be in the rifle's range. His body felt in one sore piece, but he knew the sage had cut his face for the liquid running down his cheek was blood.

"Come on—you got him—" The voice on the wind sounded confident. Sprawled in the bristled bunchgrass, softly spitting the grit from his mouth, he silently vowed he'd get them.

TEN

❧

"WILDCAT get'cha?" Art asked, blinking at the sight of him.

Standing in the stage road, Herschel shifted his saddle to the other shoulder and shook his head. "Worse, sagebrush, when I took wings off that hill back there."

He went by Art and tossed his kack on Cob. "It gave them a lead, anyway."

"What happened?" Art was off his horse and helping on the other side to reset the girths for the roan.

"They shot Black out from under me. Oh, say, a hundred feet from the top." He drew up the latigo on the front D ring.

"You're lucky to be alive."

"They are, too."

"You still going after them?"

Herschel nodded. "Only more so."

"Could I offer my assistance?"

"Thanks, but you better go and help Phil," he said. "Give me your rifle. Broke the stock on mine in the fall."

Art jerked it out of the scabbard and handed it to him. "You need a doc to look at your face."

His foot in the stirrup, he swung his leg over the roan. "I can do that later. You tell Marsha I may be late."

"How late?"

"Don't know, but if they think I'm dead, they may ease off some."

"I'd sure go along—"

"Thanks, anyway. I need you in Billings. Phil's good, but he's just a kid. Be sure to clear those two bodies with the coroner. I'll see you in a while."

Art shook his head in disgust. "You sure can be hard-headed."

"My mother said that." He checked Cob with the rein. "See yah."

He booted Cob for the ridgeline bristled with pines. This time he promised himself to find an easier way to the top. A wave to Art and he rode off.

The sun was bleeding in the west when he found a small outfit nestled in the brakes. No sign that the pair was there, but he loosened the Colt in his holster in case. Lucky he'd found the .45. He'd lost it in the fall off the mountain, but climbing back up, he'd spotted it on the ground. Wonder he hadn't lost more than that.

A woman came out on the porch and squinted against the glare. She hushed the barking dogs and studied his descent off the hillside. No sign of the robbers.

"You looking for your partners?" she drawled.

"They go on?"

"Yeah," she drew out. "Watered their hosses and shook a leg."

"How long ago?"

She wrinkled her nose. "Couple of hours ago."

She was younger than he first imagined when he rode up to the hitch rack, and he wondered who else was there. "Your man home?"

"Pa?"

"Yes."

"Naw, he's gone to look for work. I'm Ida, Ida Crowley."

"Herschel. I'd like to buy some supper."

She looked pained at him. "I ain't selling no supper. I ain't got much, but you're welcome to what I have."

He removed his hat. "Be pleased to, ma'am."

"Oh, heaven sakes, I ain't that, either. Wash up and come in." She turned to go inside, and he noticed that she was barefooted. Maybe sixteen. And all alone out here. Wonder someone didn't take advantage of her with her pa off looking for work. He tied Cob to the rack and loosened the girths.

"You know those men rode through here?" he asked her, drying his hands from the porch.

Her eyes narrowed. "Oh, you don't know them?"

"One was Casey Ford." He waited for her response.

"Yeah, Casey and Chub," she said.

"You know they were stage robbers?"

She slapped her forehead with her palm. "No wonder that they were in such a hurry."

"They been here before?"

"Oh, Pa knew them."

"What's Chub look like?"

"Bowlegged, must be past forty, hmm—" She cupped her chin and closed her eyes. "A dried-up little cowboy who needs false teeth."

"They stayed up here?"

"Some." She became tight-mouthed, and dipped him

out a bowl of beans from a pot on the stove. "Ain't much meat in 'em."

"They smell good," he said when she delivered them to him.

She nodded and closed one brown eye to look at him. "You're the law, ain't'cha?"

"Yes, I'm sheriff of Yellowstone County. That bad?"

She shook her head, sat down, then put one foot on the chair and hugged her knee, which was covered with the calico dress. "I hoped he wouldn't get in no trouble."

"Who's that?" He looked up from spooning his beans.

"Casey, Casey Ford."

"Guess you were sweet on him."

"Guess he never looked at me. But a girl can dream."

"Ida, you can find a better man than him. He's an out-law. Killed a man robbing the stage a week ago."

"Best man that ever came by here." She made a face and shook her head in defeat, then hugged her knee. "Till you showed up."

"I have a wife."

"Too late again." She threw her hand with the spoon in the air. "Just my luck."

He shook his head. "You'll find one. You don't know where they were headed, do you?" When he raised his gaze for the answer, she was chewing on a knuckle.

"The Swaggards," she finally managed to say.

"Who are they?"

"They're across the line in Wyoming on Dutch Crick."

"Big hideout?"

"Oh, I ain't sure. Old man makes whiskey."

"Ever been there?"

"Once—I ain't going back—" She shivered under the dress. "His boys were nasty to me."

"I won't ask you to, but how do I find it?"

"There's a pretty good trail south of here. Them two struck it. Pa never liked that kind to come up here, so he usually wiped out any tracks."

"He liked Ford?"

"Naw, he put up with him. Chub was always out of work, and Pa let him hang around and work for his meals. Chub brung Ford by a week or so ago."

"Must have been after the robbery and killing."

"Chub said Ford was down on his luck. Lots of cowboys out of work up here. Want more beans?" She stood and looked in his empty bowl.

"I don't want to eat up all your food."

"No worry." She snatched the bowl and went for more on the stove. "Ain't often I get a nice-talking sheriff to share my food with."

"He left the loot from the last robbery behind was why he was broke."

"Never mentioned that." She put the bowl before him and slid the saltcellar over. "They can use some more."

"If you can't make it, come to Billings. You can find work there."

"I ain't working in one of them houses." She looked affronted.

"I didn't mean that. Folks need help. My friends have a café, and some lady may need a cook and housekeeper, or you could become a nanny."

"That mean being a goat?"

"No, it means take care of children." Amused at her question, he busied himself eating. "There's work and a place in Billings, if it gets too rough out here."

"Good. Pa went to Miles City looking for work. I hope he finds some."

"So do I," he said, bothered by the fact he'd never looked at the two dead robbers—didn't even ask Art about their possible identity. Better keep that business to himself. "How many men are down at this Swaggard's place?"

"Him, her, and two boys. They ain't nice. . . ."

Herschel nodded, no need to make her upset. "Do they guard the place?"

"Yeah, they've always got guns standing around."

"Good, I'm going to ride that way tonight."

"Don't get lost."

"Been that before." He chuckled and pushed the bowl toward her. "Thanks. I can pay for my food."

"No, but I may be up there to see you if Pa don't find no work."

"Come on."

"Go easy on Chub. He ain't no bad guy. He ain't too smart, and I figure he was just going along with them." She looked pained at the end of her plea.

"I'll remember that, Ida."

"Thank you." She hugged her arms to her budding chest and acted uneasy.

He went out, pulled up the cinch, and undid the reins. She leaned against the door facing and nodded in approval as twilight spread over the hills. "Good to meet you, Sheriff."

Mounted, he checked the roan. "Yes, ma'am." And he rode away.

He could hear the rooster crowing before he topped the ridge, reined up the weary roan, and looked down on the buildings and pens. All night long, he'd dismounted, lit matches to check the robbers' tracks, and they'd led to this place. Close to the cabin, he spotted two hip-shot horses asleep on their feet in the gray of predawn. If it wasn't the Swaggards' place, he felt certain it was where the two stage robbers had ridden. The bay horses looked familiar enough to be theirs.

A ball-mouth hound began to bark. A woman came to the door loading a shotgun. Long black hair fell in her face when she raised the muzzle up and blasted away. Lucky she couldn't see. The blast made lots of dust in the hillside below Herschel, and the roan shied. Herschel spun him around and sent him for the ridge.

"Don't come back, either!" she shouted after him.

Beyond her shotgun's range on the ridge, he stepped out of the saddle and jerked out Art's rifle. Be hard to shoot a woman, but he had no time for her foolishness. Three or more hounds were baying around in front of the low-roofed cabin and no one was in sight.

He knelt down and took aim at the door. "This is the sheriff talking. Hands up and come outside."

No answer.

He took aim at the shiny new washtub hanging on the side of the cabin. The first round made a loud report, and the drum of the bullet penetrating the bottom could be heard where he was standing above the cabin. "Can you hear me?"

She came out unarmed this time, waving her hands and fighting the stringy hair back from her face in the wind. "Don't shoot no more. That's brand-new."

"Who else is down there?" Herschel shouted at her.

"Me and my boys."

"Tell them to come out hands high." Rifle ready, he started down the steep slope on his boot heels. "Where's Ford and Chub?"

"Who?" She used her hand to keep the hair back and shade her eyes from the slanting sun.

"The men who rode those horses in."

"Didn't know them."

"You always lie like that?" he asked, feeling on edge as he looked around for the boys' appearance.

"They was my man's friends." She shook her head. "They needed fresh horses."

Herschel nodded he'd heard her. "Them boys don't get out here in an instant, I'm going in there shooting."

"Pal and Eddie, get out here!" she shouted, and her screechy voice echoed off the buildings.

Two boys in their teens, half-asleep and in their faded red underwear, stumbled out the door and blinked in disbelief at the long gun in his hands.

"Who the hell're you?" the younger-looking one asked. His blond hair stood up like a rooster's comb.

"Sheriff he said," the woman explained. "I told him them two took fresh horses and rode on."

"They damn sure did. One took my best pony."

"Steal it?" Herschel asked.

"Naw, but close. He only give Pa ten bucks apiece for them."

"Where is your man?"

She turned up her palms. "He never tells me nothing."

"You boys know where he's at?"

"Pa don't never sleep under a roof, mister. He may have his old buff gun pointed at your back right now." The younger one gave a stupid grin at his silent brother.

"Aiding and abetting known outlaws is a serious offense. It can draw you some time up in Deer Lodge Pen."

"How were we to know them was outlaws? They said they was out-of-work drovers and needed fresh horses," the elder said, scratching himself. No wonder Ida hated them. They reminded Herschel of lazy curs rather than humans.

"You better remember what I'm telling you. Helping these owlhoots is going to fly back in your faces."

In the rising sunlight, he wondered where Old Man Swaggard was at. Herschel didn't have a warrant for him, but there must be one out there somewhere. Honest folks slept in beds every chance they got. If he ever got back to his office, he would check through the warrants for one.

No need to argue or flap his jaws at these three miserable hunks of humanity. He shook his head and started up the hill.

"Who's going to fix my new washtub you shot all up?" she demanded from behind his back.

Halfway up the hill, he paused and looked back at them. "Next time, don't try to gun me down." Besides, he'd only put one hole in it.

She stomped her foot. "It was brand-new."

"Such are the ways of war," he said, and went on, not expecting anything out of them but their bad mouths.

At midday, he found a small crossroads store, bought two cans of airtights, one tomatoes and one peaches, and some corn for the horse. Outside on the porch, he punched a hole in the tomato can and drank the liquid out of the V-shaped hole. The sharp-tasting juice cut the dust out of his throat and quenched his thirst. Hitched at the nearby rack, Cob chomped on the whole corn.

"Traveling through?" the storekeeper asked, coming out the front door and using his jackknife to sliver off a slice from a tobacco plug.

"Looking for two stage robbers," Herschel said, looking at the man.

"You the law?"

Herschel nodded and speared another tomato out of the can.

"I ain't seen any strangers passing through."

"Funny thing about that," Herschel said when he finished chewing on the juicy fruit. "Their horses' hoofprints are at the hitch rack where they stood tied."

The man didn't say anything for a long moment, then he turned to go inside. "Pays not to see things, if you like living."

"Maybe," Herschel said after him. He opened the peach can with his knife and made up his mind. On fresh horses, those two had a good lead on him, and all he was doing was finding their tracks and horse apples. He'd better toss in his hat on this chase and head back to Billings.

ELEVEN

Hardly able to keep his eyes open, Herschel reached
Billings long past midnight and checked on the jail.
Wally shook his head at the sight of him. "Man, you had
any sleep the past few days? You look terrible."

"Very little. Feel the same way. I'm headed home to
sleep for a week."

"Good. Things are fine here. Go get some sleep."

"Who were the two dead stage holdup men?"

"One was Newton Crowley. A nester over in that country."

Even half-asleep, Herschel winced and leaned his
shoulder against the door facing. *Looking for work all
right*. Had they sent word to the girl? Damn. "Who else?"

"Randy Smith—out-of-work cowboy."

"Has word been sent to Crowley's daughter?"

Wally shook his head that he didn't know. "Better ask
the day fellas."

"I will if I ever wake up."

"Sweet dreams," Wally said after him.

At last inside his barn, he took the saddle off, then led Cob outside and turned the stiff horse out in the lot to roll. There was feed and water there, too. He closed the gate and gazed at the two-story house in the starlight. Sure looked good.

He put his boot on the bottom step with effort and the back door flew open. "Thank God. You're back."

A smile cracked his sore sunburned lips. Wonderful to have a wife like Marsha. She tackled him around the waist and both about went down.

"My gosh, Hersch, I've been so worried about you."

Then he realized how filthy he must be, three days of whiskers, scratched face, lots of dust and sweat. Who cared? Obviously not his wife. He stood on the back porch and rocked her back and forth in his arms and closed his weak eyelids.

"When did you eat last?"

"I don't recall." A huge yawn gaped his mouth wide open, and he threw his hand up to cover it.

"Why, you're all scratched up." She frowned at her discovery in the starlight.

"I'm fine. Wrestled a sagebrush or two was all."

"I suppose you didn't have any sleep, either?" She guided him inside the kitchen and lighted a lamp. "You want some food?"

"I can eat later." He dropped in a chair and tried to clear his numb mind.

"Can you make it upstairs?"

"I made it this far. But I'm too filthy to lie in the bed."

"No, you're not. I can wash sheets." She dipped some water out of the reservoir into a wash pan and brought it to him. "I'll get some soap and a towel for you to wash your face and hands. But don't worry about anything else—"

She stopped and sucked in her breath. Then, with a knuckle to her mouth, she shook her head, about to cry. "I was so worried about you."

"I'm home now."

"Yes," she said, and rushed over and hugged his head to her flat stomach. "And I'm thanking the Good Lord he sent you back to me, too."

"I'll be fine after some sleep."

"Wash your hands and face, that will make you feel better and I'll tuck you in."

"Sure."

She swept her robe under her legs and took a seat opposite him. "I know you can't think right now, but do you want a boy or girl?"

Struck by her words, he felt something he'd never felt before. He was going to become a father. Didn't seem right. Have his own child. He loved the girls like his own, but—he reached over and squeezed her hand.

"So it has five toes on each foot, I don't care."

"I'll try to provide you with that."

That was the last thing he recalled until he woke up in their bed. How long had he slept? Must be sundown, he decided, and threw his legs over the side. Combing his hair back with his fingers, he considered all he could remember. They had a baby coming. He needed to put out a new warrant on Chub and Ford. Get word to Ida about her father. And find Billy Hanks's murderers.

"Ah, you're awake," Marsha said from the doorway. "Come down. I have ham, green beans, and potatoes cooked."

"Fine. How are the girls?"

"All excited and ready to talk your head off."

He nodded, putting on his shirt. "I'm ready to listen."

"Oh, Art needs to talk to you when you can see him."

"He here?"

"No, he's at the office, but he said when you got up for you to eat and everything first. He could wait."

Herschel scoured his whisker-edged mouth with his calloused hand and nodded. "Wonder what he's got."

"He never said."

He pulled on his pants. "I better go assure those girls I'm here."

She shook her head like she didn't envy what lay ahead for him. "After you eat, I'll have the hot water ready for you to take a bath. And fresh clothes for you to wear."

"Why? These can stand in the corner by themselves."

They both laughed.

After his reunion with his girls, who were full of questions about his adventures, and the tasty meal, hot bath, and a shave, he headed for his office in the twilight. Stiff, he decided to walk the four blocks and loosen up.

Art sat behind Phil's desk when Herschel entered, and threw his boots off the desktop. "Hello, stranger."

"How're things?"

"Pretty quiet."

"Marsha said you needed to talk to me."

Art had an angry set to his eyes as he threw the paper at him. "I may jerk that reporter through his own necktie."

Herschel smiled at him. "Maybe he wants to be sheriff."

"That's foul play. He says the sheriff took the opportunity in the midst of the crime to go on a hunting trip. So far, no word on the game he's killed. But it may be snipes."

"Art, I'm more worried about Casey Ford getting away than what this reporter writes about me." He went to the window and looked at the busy street traffic below. "I also want Billy Hanks's killers brought to justice."

"He's trying to turn the whole county against you."

Herschel tried to appraise the anger written on Art's

face. "We know—" He thumped his own chest with his fingertips. "We're doing the best job we know how to do. Now I need you to ride up tomorrow and tell a young lady her father is dead."

"Who's that?"

"Ida Crowley. She's up there on a homestead all alone. Nice young lady. Hate that her father was shot, but that couldn't be helped."

"Draw me a map, maybe I can ride out some of my anger."

"Sorry I'm sending you on my job."

"No, no, that damn reporter—"

"Ease off, Art. He wants to get under our skin."

"I'll try."

With pencil and paper, Herschel drew him a map to Ida's homestead. "She may have the word by now. I suggested she come find work with a family here in Billings."

Art nodded and after examining the map, folded and put it in his pocket. "I'll go see about her."

"Anything else?"

"Mayor's heard some rumors. The Bar 9 cowboys are so upset about Hanks's hanging that there may be trouble at this Sunday's bronc fanning."

"You and I better be there at the City Park Sunday," he said to Art. "I'd give a lot to have a shred of evidence on that matter. Sometimes when tempers flare, so do mouths. You reckon anyone knows more than we do about it?"

Art narrowed his blue eyes and nodded with a grim set to his jaw. "The killers do. But I ain't heard a word about who did it."

"We will." Herschel gazed at the open office door where Phil stood—waiting. "Yes?"

"Cove Tipton is here to see you."

"Send him in." He strode to the door and shook the rancher's hand. "Cove, you know Art?"

The two shook hands and Art excused himself. "I'll ride up there and tell her."

Herschel nodded and showed Cove the chair in front of his desk. "Have a seat. What do you know?"

"I came by to tell you there's lots of talk about them Mannons and that horse under Billy's saddle."

Herschel nodded, taking a seat behind his desk. "They said he came home."

"There's folks think they did it all to cover the hanging."

"Cove, thinking and proving are two different things."

"I want to say there's some bad feeling about it up my way."

Herschel stiffened. "No one can take the law in their own hands. Montana has laws, judges, and juries. No more vigilante stuff. You even hear of any talk about it, you burn the saddle leather and get me."

Cove nodded that he would. "You have any real leads?"

"No, but I will." Herschel leaned back and the chair's springs squeaked in protest. He tented his fingers and tapped his nose.

"Them Ralston boys told Sam Evans that Billy Hanks got what he deserved."

"When was that?"

"Oh, in the last few days. I think they all were jealous about how he could dance and spin them gals around. It was a sight."

Herschel nodded. "I'll go talk to Sam in the morning. Anything else?"

"No. I wanted you to know what I found out."

"Cove, keep your ears open. Someone is going to slip up."

"That's why I came by."

He rose and shook the man's hand, realizing that what looked like blood on the wall was the sun's sinking glare on the plaster.

An out-of-breath youth stuck his freckled face around the door facing. "Sheriff, come quick. They've got a big fight going on at the Yellowstone."

"I better go see about it," he said to Cove, then told the fresh-faced kid in the doorway, "Tell them I'm on my way."

"Need any help?" Cove asked.

"No, Phil and I can handle it."

"I'm breaking out the Greeners," Phil said. "I was checking on the jail."

"Everything all right over there?" Herschel put on his suit coat.

"Yeah, Wally's here now."

Herschel took the shotgun his deputy handed him and inserted the two brass shells in the chambers.

Cove nodded in approval. "Hope there ain't no bad trouble."

"I hope there isn't, either. Go ahead, Phil," Herschel said, and nodded to the rancher as he left. "We have to run. Thanks for everything."

"Dave Allen working?" Herschel asked Phil about the town marshal as they were going down the stairs.

"Supposed to be."

The Yellowstone sat a block west on the next corner. When they were halfway there, two shots rang out. Herschel winced at the sound, and then grimly nodded in pained disgust at his deputy, running beside him.

"Now they're shooting each other," Phil said, sounding upset.

"You get behind me," Herschel ordered as they hurried. "Don't shoot unless you have to."

"Yes, sir."

It was the first time under fire for his man. If he had any time to think about it, the twenty-two-year-old would have lots of misgivings about this whole thing. As curious folks came running from all directions, Herschel became concerned about public safety.

"Tell them all to clear the streets," he told his man. He stopped and held the shotgun barrel-up. Acrid gun smoke boiled over the swinging doors of the saloon and two coughing cowboys came staggering out, bent over.

He caught the close one by the collar and jerked him upright. "What's going on in there?"

"Helluva fight and then Kirk drew his gun."

"Berry Kirk?"

When the man nodded, Herschel let go of him and took the double-barrel in both hands. His eyes narrowed against the smarting of the spent gun smoke as he faced the green batwing doors. "This is the sheriff. Hands high and don't try anything unless you want to die."

He pushed open the doors and knew he'd be silhouetted against the last light of sundown and make a perfect target. The decision would be with those inside. The percussion of a shot always doused the lights in a room, so the saloon's interior was in darkness save for the light coming over the half curtains in the windows.

"Everyone file by the bar and outside," he ordered, stepping aside from the doorway and using the shotgun for a pointer.

"Is anyone who's shot still alive?" he asked, trying to see in the hazy room.

"Yes, one fella," someone said.

He pointed the gun barrel at the man who'd said it. "You go get Doc." Then he spoke to Phil. "Line them up outside."

"Yes, sir."

"Who shot him?" Herschel asked.

No answer.

"Who shot him?"

"I did and it was self-defense." Berry Kirk stepped out of the line of men. "The sumbitch had a knife."

"Plenty of time for that. Give me your gun."

Kirk stepped over, his hands raised, and Herschel took his pistol.

"Go on with the others, but stay around."

"I told you—"

"Get out of here with the rest and do what I say." Herschel frowned after the surly youth.

"Do I got to go, too, Mr. Sheriff?" one of the doves asked, swiveling her hips and ample midsection as she filed past the bar.

"I said everyone."

"Well, darling, if you want me—I'm coming." Her words drew some laughs from the drunker men.

He caught the glare of Berry Kirk as he went through the doors hands held high.

"Mike," he said to the bartender, who was relighting lamps. "Doc's coming. He'll need more light."

"I'll let down the chandelier and light it first."

"Good." Herschel went over and knelt beside the un-conscious young man. His wounds looked serious, both in the chest. At last, he recognized the ashen-faced victim. Tucker Ralston, Bert's oldest son.

"Bad?" Doc asked, setting down his black bag and put-ting on his stethoscope as he joined him.

"Looks bad to me. I'll be outside if you need some-thing."

On the boardwalk, Herschel looked over the downcast

men lined up in a row on the main street outside the Yellowstone.

"Phil, collect all their guns and knives." He glanced at Berry Kirk standing in line with the rest. For a brief moment, the two locked gazes, then Kirk looked away. That boy was trouble with a capital T.

"He had it coming," Kirk said. "He had a damn bear-sticker out."

"A judge will decide that." Herschel raised his voice. "Now you're all going to march down to the justice's office and pay a fine for disturbing the peace."

"But I never—" someone protested.

"Mike told me everyone in the place was fighting. You can tell Judge Watson your story."

"I have their weapons," Phil said, standing over the stack of revolvers and knives on the boardwalk.

"Get a couple gunnysacks. Weapons can be reclaimed at my office for one dollar apiece. Did you all hear me?"

"What about mine?" Kirk asked.

"Right now it's evidence." He indicated he should move on with the others. Dave Allen had shown up, and was taking over the march of the dozen or so prisoners to the judge's office.

"Darling, what about me?" the dove asked, walking up with her hands on her hips.

"What's your name?" He cradled the shotgun in his arms and considered her.

"Sweet Rose."

"You see the shooting?"

"No, I had my back turned."

"I'd say you were watching it all to keep from getting hit."

A grin on her painted lips, she nodded. "Naw, I was pulling a fella up off the floor."

"Handy. When you get any memory back, send me word." He dismissed her.

"Well, darling, I sure will." She sashayed back inside the Yellowstone.

He looked at the dimming sky for help before he spoke to Phil about the stacks of guns and knives. "Get someone with a cart to haul them up to the office. Then go help Dave. I'm going to see what Doc knows about the victim's condition."

"I'll get it done."

"We also need a statement from everyone about the shooting—"

The somber face of Doc Hunter in the doorway cut him off. "Tucker's dead, Herschel."

"What's next? Thanks, Doc," Herschel closed his eyes to shut out reality, and then swiveled on his heel. "Phil, send someone to get the coroner. I'll need to look over the death scene."

"What else?"

"Tell all those rannies to stay at the judge's. I've got questions to ask them."

"I can get a wheelbarrow, Sheriff."

"There's my man," Herschel said, seeing his errand boy, Donnie, arrive on the scene. "Borrow a wheelbarrow, Donnie. Then take these guns to my office. They're probably loaded, so be careful."

"Yes, sir." And he was off running for the wheelbarrow.

Herschel went back inside the Yellowstone. "Mike, what happened in here?"

TWELVE

A LL I know is they had some kind of argument going on when I spotted the trouble." Mike, the Irish bartender, put down the glass he'd finished polishing.

"Who was arguing?" Herschel asked, looking at the stein of draft beer that Mike had set up for him. Foam from the head spilled down the side of the glass as he waited for the Irishman's answer.

"Kirk and that Ralston boy."

"What about?"

"I wasn't sure. I was drawing a beer when I first heard them and had my back to 'em. It was mostly cuss words. Then the whole place boiled into a fight. A couple of Bar 9 boys were in here. I guess the others were backing Ralston."

"Billy Hanks mentioned?"

Mike nodded with a sad look in his blue eyes. "That's all them cowboys talk about in here."

Herschel took a deep draught of the beer and set it

down. He'd already looked under the blanket at the corpse—no need to look at him again. With the back of his hand, he wiped his mouth. The hunting knife had been near Ralston's hand on the floor. Herschel wrapped it in a kerchief and put it in the side pocket of his suit coat. With Kirk's revolver in his waistband, he had both weapons from the scene. Nothing else he could do there. "I better get to Judge Watson's place and help Phil."

"Sorry I ain't any more help, Herschel," Mike said.

Deep in his own thoughts, Herschel absently nodded and thanked him. Was this all over Hanks's death? He pushed out the Yellowstone's swinging doors into the night, and his boot soles treaded the boardwalk for the block-long walk to Judge Watson's office. Four storefronts away, he could see in the light coming from inside that several cowboys and the other saloon customers were seated on the porch floor, with their backs to the wall, hugging their knees, waiting for their turns before Judge Watson.

He nodded to them and went to the open door.

"Wait your turn," a sharp voice commanded. The clerk named Dewey never looked up at him until the crowd's laughter forced him to raise his head. "Oh, Sheriff Baker, sorry."

"Where's Berry Kirk?" Herschel could not see him anywhere.

"Fined two bucks for disturbing the peace and released," Dewey said, and looked hard at Herschel for an answer.

"Should've held him." He said his thoughts out loud as Phil came back from the proceedings in the room.

"What's wrong?" the fresh-faced deputy asked.

"I guess we need to get a warrant and go after Kirk," Herschel said in a soft voice.

Phil shook his head. "Oh, I should have known he'd light a shuck."

"And I didn't expect him to get through here that fast. No problem." With a wave of his hand, Herschel dismissed it.

As the judge finished sentencing the next cowboy, Herschel spoke up. "Everyone here is a witness and will be called when the hearing is held on Tucker Ralston's death."

"You all hear the sheriff?" Phil asked from beside the front door.

A grumble from those waiting outside indicated they had heard him.

Dave Allen came in. "Sorry, I was eating supper."

"We all have to eat. Besides, no way anyone could have stopped this deal. They were in it right at the start, I think."

"What's happening here, Sheriff?"

Herschel turned, and a familiar-looking green-checkered suit was trying to get by him. The *Herald*'s star reporter, Ennis Stokes, had arrived on the scene.

"I heard the shots. What happened?" Stokes asked.

"Someone was shot."

Stokes grasped the pencil from behind his ear and began to scribble down notes. "Who was killed?"

"A body to be identified by the coroner."

"Who shot him?"

"Parties yet unknown." He wasn't giving Stokes one ounce of help or information. Besides, he'd twist it to suit himself when he wrote the story—good thing Art wasn't there.

"You aren't much help. Any of you fellas see any-thing?" No reply. Stokes stuck his head out the door for those still seated on the porch. "Any of you see anything?"

"Yeah," one smart aleck said. "We all seen the white

elephant come through." His words drew more laughter from those waiting.

Dewey called for the next plaintiff. With Kirk already gone, Herschel wondered what he should do next. There would probably be a coroner's hearing held over the matter and then a decision it was self-defense on Berry Kirk's part. Still, he had to treat it like a crime. Bert Ralston might not think it was self-defense, either. The whole thing was liable to stir up a hornet's nest. That was the part he dreaded the most and he saw no way to avoid the eventual collision.

"What in the hell is going on?" Stokes finally demanded.

Herschel caught him by the arm and guided him toward the front door, talking through his teeth. "A party was shot in an altercation in the Yellowstone Saloon amidst a large brawl."

"Why are all these men here?" Stokes asked the clerk in passing.

"Disturbing the peace," Dewey said, his voice ringing with impatience. "Now we're holding court, so shut up."

"I'll be at the office when you get through here," Herschel said to his deputy in a subdued tone, and turned the reporter loose.

Phil nodded.

A block away, Herschel turned off Main Street and rounded the corner. A shot rang out and tiny splinters flew off the clapboard siding on the apothecary where the bullet struck close to his face. He ducked for cover in the darker shadows. In a crouch, his fist closed on his gun butt, he searched the inky night. Close—where was the shooter? Must have been a rifle. He tried to see back across Main. The shot had to come from the side of Younkin's Harness and Saddle Repair Shop—he'd never seen the muzzle blast behind his back.

His measured breath came as fast and loud as his heart's palpitations. That bullet had been intended to kill him. The shooter no doubt was long gone. Was it over the lynching or something else? No way to know.

"Herschel? Herschel? Who's shooting?" Phil was coming on the run, his heels clacking on the wooden boardwalk.

"I'm fine." He stepped out to hail Phil down. "He must have been over there." He motioned across the street.

"What happened? I heard the shot."

"Someone tried to drygulch me a minute ago."

"Who?"

"Damned if I know, but they'd been a better shot, you'd've had a new boss."

"Oh, hell. Where did he go?"

"I figure back into the alley and rode out."

"What else is going to happen tonight?"

"Damned if I know." Herschel struck a match and squatted to look at the ground between the two buildings.

"See anything?" Phil asked.

Not finding a thing, except scuff marks, Herschel blew the match out, dropped it, rose, and stepped on it. "No. You can go back to the judge's. He's gone."

"Will you be all right?"

With a laugh, he clapped his deputy on the shoulder to reassure him. "I'm fine. And in the morning we'll try to figure out who shot at me."

"Strange night." Phil shook his head and headed back for Watson's law office.

"Yes," Herschel agreed. A real strange night.

When he started for the jail, he recognized the familiar hat coming down the shadowy street.

"What's happening?" Art asked, catching him and looking around. "Gunshots all over town. Wally said you were putting down a brawl at the Yellowstone."

"Judge Watson is fining about a dozen cowboys and hands for disturbing the peace. Tucker Ralston is dead and someone took a shot at me right here."

"Glad they missed. Why didn't you send word?"

"I figured Phil and I could handle it."

"Where did this shooter go?"

"Best I can guess, he ran out to his horse behind Younkin's and left town."

"Holy cow, you're lucky."

"I've been thinking the same damn thing. Let's go to the office. Need to sort out a few things. During the big brawl at the Yellowstone, Berry Kirk shot Ralston in self-defense, he says."

"What were they fighting over?"

"Mike thinks it was over Billy Hanks's hanging."

Art shook his head and opened the front door to the courthouse for him. "Guess that's a burr under his friends' saddles."

"A big sand burr." Somehow, he had to solve that case, too.

THIRTEEN

Billings's mayor, George McKay, was a big man and stood over six feet tall. He had a full brown mustache, and was an imposing man in his forties. His complexion was rosy red, and his breath roared in and out of his large nose like a circus lion's.

"We have much more trouble in this town and the Northern Pacific is going to bypass us. Look at the headlines!" He tossed the latest edition of the *Billings Herald* on Herschel's desk.

"Mr. Mayor, you may have come to the wrong office this morning to complain. Some hands got into a big brawl last night in the Yellowstone. Phil and I stopped it, but unfortunately, not before someone was shot. Now as to the hysterics of Mr. Stokes's headlines that point to Billings as the next Tombstone, they're ridiculous."

"The railroad could still change its mind. Bad publicity has made them go around lots of places." McKay was shaking his head in firm disapproval.

"Tombstone Style Law Enforcement. . . ." Herschel looked at the headline, drew in a deep breath, then pushed himself out of the chair. He went to the window and looked down at the traffic. "Stokes is the man you need to talk to. The *Herald* management needs to know what they are doing to upset our chances of getting a railroad. Blowing up a barroom brawl into what happened with the Earps, Clantons, and Lawrys down there is like saying that outhouse fire the other night rivaled the Chicago one."

McKay frowned and looked hard at him. "We can't afford to upset the railroad officials."

Herschel nodded and turned back. "You need to hire a chief of police and several policemen. Dave Allen can't be everywhere. He tries hard."

"I would, but I don't have the funds to pay them. You know what they want for pay?"

Herschel shook his head.

"Fifty a month, twenty-five percent of the fines, and a house to live in is what the last one asked me for." McKay continued pacing the office.

"What can you afford?"

He stopped, looked back, and scowled. "Thirty, maybe."

"Land's sake, what do you pay Dave Allen?"

"Oh, he gets twenty percent of the fines. But I can't pay fifty and give the new man part of the fines." McKay shut his eyes and shook his head. "No way."

"My deputies get forty-five and expenses."

"I can't afford that much. But we've got to stop this bad publicity," McKay said, getting back to his original complaint.

"You better speak to Ennis Stokes. He's the one making the sensational news out of little or nothing. Well, we did have a man shot, but I am satisfied no charges will be filed over it. Figure there's enough witnesses to say it was self-defense. Both men were armed."

"What if Stokes won't quit?"

"I guess you'll have to kill him and tell God he died."

"Oh, my, Baker, your solution sounds terrible."

"Then you think of a better one."

Shaking his finger in Herschel's direction, McKay gave him a sour look. "Just remember, Herschel Baker, if the rails don't come to Billings, it could be your fault."

"I'll remember. I have things to see about."

"Well, I'll go speak to Jim Townsend at the *Herald*, maybe he'll listen."

Phil appeared in the doorway with a frown as if needing him.

"What is it?" Herschel asked.

"Them Ralstons are downstairs and want to talk to you."

"Oh, dear God, more trouble in our city," McKay said, looked at the square tin ceiling tiles, and then swept out the doorway.

Herschel shook his head after the mayor's dramatic retreat. Then he spoke to his deputy. "You go down and tell Bert and his tribe I'll talk to them in my office."

"What if they won't come upstairs?"

"Act like we expect them to."

"Yes, sir."

Herschel cleared his desk and considered what they'd want from him. No doubt they were there over the death of the eldest son, Tucker. He looked up when the hard-eyed patriarch of the family came storming in the office door like a sore-toed bear. Behind him came two whiskerless boys in their late teens, dressed in ragged clothing, and a fat girl about eighteen or nineteen years old wearing a scarf tied under her chin and a too-tight dress.

"Hello, Bert. Have a chair."

"I'll stand. What are you doing about Tucker's murder?"

"That's a case for my office." He looked up hard at the defiant-faced man with his arms folded over a wash-frazzled shirt, wearing stained pants that needed washing.

"By Gawd, I'll handle it myself."

"Ease off. I'm holding an inquest. Let justice work."

"I'll let justice work all right." His dark eyes narrowed and his whisker-bristled mouth disappeared in a straight line. "I ain't letting that sumbitch Kirk—"

Herschel rose and glared across the desk. "Listen to me, this eye-for-an-eye business is over in this county. I'll fill Deer Lodge Penitentiary with all of you if you even lift a finger."

"Like hell you will!"

"Bert, don't try me." They were face-to-face and only the desk separated them. "I've been up there, took a prisoner up there. You don't want to rot up in that prison for murder."

The two boys, Farrel and Jimmy, frowned at each other. The pie-faced girl looked upset and ready to pull her father back.

"I'm going to find that smart-mouthed bastard and kill him."

Herschel straightened and narrowed his gaze at the man. "No. Take that boy's body home and pray for him and your own soul."

"Pa, he ain't going to help us." About to cry, the girl pulled on his sleeve.

"Hush up, Wanda." He jerked her hand off his arm and whirled back. "Baker, you better ship that boy's killer up there to that prison, so's I can't get my hands on him."

"Bert, I ain't saying it again. Let the law handle it."

"You ain't telling me nothing—"

"Pa. Pa," Wanda pleaded. "He'll lock you up. He done told you so."

"Anything happens to him and I'll know who did it, Bert." Herschel felt his heart pounding under his rib cage. What was he going to do with this madman? "Which one of you is Farrel?"

The dark-eyed boy with his chin covered in fine peach fuzz gave him a snotty look. "I am."

"Who hung Billy Hanks?" Herschel demanded.

Blinking his weak eyes, Farrel drew his head back as if insulted. "How the hell should I know?"

"You boys were there."

Bert tried to intercede and moved to block Herschel's view of the boys. "They never—"

Herschel cut off Bert's protest. "Did you three boys hang him?"

Farrel began to shake his head and his eyes widened. "No, we never—"

"Don't tell him a gawdamn thing!" Bert shouted, and waved his hands at the boys to shut them up.

"Pa! Pa! We got to get out of here," the girl screamed, and pulled on the old man's arm.

"I want to know everything you boys know about the hanging," Herschel said, and came around the desk.

"We never done it," Jimmy, the youngest, shouted in defense of his brother. "I swear we never."

"Gawdamnit, Baker—"

"Hold it right there," Phil ordered from the doorway, armed with a shotgun.

Wanda began screaming. "He's gonna kill us! No! No!"

"Everyone sit down. You boys get chairs from over there and pull them up here," Herschel ordered.

Tears ran down Wanda's full face and streaked the road

dust on her red cheeks. Bert glared, but he sat down, his arms folded and a defiant look pressed on his face. The boys pulled up chairs warily, eyeing both Herschel and his gun-bearing deputy in the process.

"Now one by one, I want your stories on that night of the hanging. Wanda, go first."

She looked at Bert for what to do. In surrender, Bert nodded and she snuffed her nose.

"We went to the dance. And when it was over, we slept on the ground. Pa got us up before sunup and we drove home. Nothing more." She shook her head and her green eyes darted from side to side like a trapped animal.

"Why so early?"

She shrugged, not looking at him. "I don't know."

"Come up here and print your name on this paper." He set the pencil and paper on the desktop.

She looked for an answer, and finally Bert said, "Go ahead, we ain't got nothing to hide."

Wary-eyed, she scooted off the chair, pulled the dress down over her soggy figure, and took the pencil. Her writing wasn't smooth, but she wrote her name.

"That what you wanted?" She looked pained behind her sparse, wet lashes.

"Print 'horse rustler,'" Herschel said, keeping an eye on the others.

She shook her head and then had to get the stringy hair back from her face. "I can't spell that."

"Print what you think it looks like."

At last, in surrender, she shrugged, scratched her belly through the dress, then bent over to write something on the page.

"What the hell is this for?" Bert asked, moving to the front of his chair to try and see her writing.

"Best I can do," she said, raising up and looking hard at it.

Herschel ignored the old man, thanked her, and could barely read the words—HOASE RUSTER. "You're next," he said to Bert.

Bert rose, picked up the pencil, and scrawled his name on the paper. Then he looked up at Herschel. "I can't do no better than she did."

"Fine. Print it."

"I don't know where this is going—" He had one hand on the table supporting him. "All us writing our names and then 'hoss rustler' on this page. We ain't signing no damn confession, are we?"

"Bert, when I accuse someone, I'll do it loud and clear."

"Can't never tell," he mumbled, and copied her bad spelling of the two words. Then he slapped the pencil down on the desk. "There." And he dropped back in the chair.

"Farrel, you're next."

The boy of perhaps seventeen stepped up and blinked at the page. "Hell, that ain't how you spell it."

"Spell it yourself, then, smart-ass," Bert said, and folded his arms over his chest.

"I sure can." Farrel signed his name and then wrote—HOIRSE RUSTELER.

When Herschel nodded for Jimmy to come up, he stood and looked all around like a cat in a room full of rockers, expecting any moment to have his tail stomped on. He walked to the desk and scrawled his name under the others. Beside his signature, he carefully printed—HORSE RUSTLER.

"I'm sorry about Tucker being shot," Herschel said. "But more killing only breeds more killing. I won't put up with that. Let the law work. Do any of you know who hung Hanks?"

Subdued-acting, they shook their heads. Then Bert looked him hard in the eye. "Us Ralstons never done it."

Herschel acknowledged his reply with a nod. "Do any of you know anything to help me?"

"You need to talk to them Mannons," Farrel said as they got up to leave.

"Shut up, Farrel," Bert hissed. "You don't know a gaw-damn thing."

"Wait," Herschel said. "Why see them?"

"He don't know nothing," the old man growled.

"I ain't so sure of that, Bert. What is it about the Mannons makes you think I need to talk to them?"

"It was their hoss he stole."

"What else?"

"Old Man Mannon wouldn't let his wife, Nora, come to none of them dances 'cause he didn't want her dancing with Billy Hanks. You know she's lots younger than that old man." Farrel's thumbs were hooked in the gun belt around his waist as he smugly rocked from his heel to his toe on his run-down boots.

Herschel nodded, slowly digesting the notion. "Thank you."

Bert pursed his lips and rose. "All right, you handle the law part, but I don't like it."

"I understand. Lots in this world we don't like. I'm sorry this happened, but more killings don't make it right."

After they left, Herschel went to the open window to re-flect. Nora Mannon. An attractive woman in her twenties, light brown hair cut in shoulder-length curls, nice figure, and a handsome face with high cheekbones and blue eyes that sparkled. He'd even danced with her himself before she became Rath's wife. How long had that been? Four years—the first summer he came to Montana. She married Rath, who was a widower, the next spring. Herschel hadn't seen her in ages, and it sounded like the reason for that was Rath's jealousy. In the street below, he saw the Ralstons mount up and heard the old man's voice giving orders. Wanda sat on the spring seat and drove the buckboard team with the fresh-wood coffin in back.

"What next?" Phil asked, coming back unarmed.

"Art's gone today to tell the Crowley girl about her father. Thanks for the backup, it was getting heated in here."

"I could see that. When you going to set up the coroner's inquest?"

"I'll decide that when I can get word to Berry Kirk to get in here."

"Want me to send him a letter?"

"Will he get it?" Herschel looked back at him and smiled.

"Yes, I'll have one of his friends deliver it."

Herschel went back to sit at his desk and motioned for Phil to join him. "What do you know about Berry Kirk?"

"His folks have a ranch over east. I always thought he was rich. But they're a small outfit. In fact, last year, his pa got in a big fight with some reps from the big outfits at roundup over ownership of some brindle cow. The Kirks and that Cross bunch are all cousins. When the argument started, they jumped in to back Stone Kirk against the big outfits. It was tense up there even after that whole roundup."

"Berry prides himself on being a fist fighter, too?"

"Yeah, that, too." Phil sat straddle-legged in the chair and looked at his hands in his lap.

Herschel ran his tongue along his molars thinking back to the store incident. "The other day he beat up Wayne Farr in a fight over Kirk talking to Wayne's sister."

"Don't surprise me none. He's short-tempered all right."

"You better send Kirk that letter to come in here. I'm going to the house for lunch today. Marsha has some fresh strawberries from the garden and shortcake for dessert today."

"I'm jealous."

"Find you a good wife." Herschel put on his hat and strapped on his gun belt.

"I'm working on that. Maybe after Kate teaches me how to dance, I'll be able to find one."

"You may do that. After lunch, I may ride up and check with Barley. See if he knows anything else." Herschel paused. "That roundup business with Kirk—Hanks wasn't involved in that, was he?"

In deep concentration, Phil scratched in front of his ear. "I can't recall him being there."

"Fine. I should be back to town by dark."

"You be careful. That back-shooter about got you last time."

Herschel left the office, nodding to himself. Missed by a few inches was all. Enough to sober him to the fact someone wanted him dead. Who'd wanted Billy Hanks dead? They might be the same person or persons.

The thought of ripe strawberries made him walk faster. He felt like a lucky man to have such a hardworking wife and family. And a young'un on the way.

FOURTEEN

HE spent most of the ride over to Barley's using his tongue to pick strawberry pits out of his teeth. On the rise, he drew up in time to listen to the clack of a mowing machine. Barley was laying down some early hay. A fine team of spanking grays proudly put their shoulders to the collars pulling it. Barley waved at Herschel from the far side. Herschel rode down to the open gate and crossed the mowed grass with some small white wildflowers entwined in the mat of fresh-cut material.

"Starting early," he said when his deputy reined the team up before him and put the mower out of gear.

"Oh, I wanted to be sure the mower worked. What's up?" the lanky man asked, stepping off the iron seat.

"Well, Berry Kirk and Tucker Ralston got into a fight yesterday in the Yellowstone and that broke into a brawl. Tucker's dead. Old Man Ralston is on a tear, but I may have him settled for a day or so. Looked like a case of self-defense to me."

"What over?"

"I think over Billy Hanks's death. That was the word I got. No one is saying much." Dismounted, Herschel swept up a stem of grass and began to chew on the sweet stalk.

Busy killdeer ran about chasing insects upset by the mowing. Their cries carried as the team caught their breath. The rich aroma of fresh-cut hay hung in his nostrils. He'd miss putting feed up this year. Maybe he wasn't cut out to be a lawman. He kept hitting his head against a brick wall on the lynching.

"Nora Mannon," he said, letting his thoughts spill out.

Barley took off his sweat-stained felt hat and scratched his thin hair. "Don't see her much since she married Rath."

"I haven't seen her three times, I guess, since then."

"Why?" Barley reset the hat on his head. "What's she got to do with Hanks being hung?"

"Farrel Ralston said Rath never brought her to the dances so she couldn't dance with Billy." Herschel studied the rolling hills beyond. Was there a connection?

"A man of fifty marries a good-looking woman in her early twenties. I might lock her up, too." Barley chuckled. "Heavens, I worry about Heart leaving me."

"Nora had a baby boy?"

"I think so. He must be up walking by now."

Herschel discarded the stem. "Strange, I haven't thought about her in years."

"Lots of talk. How that wasn't Rath's son."

"What do you think?"

"If something gnaws on a man long enough, he's liable to do some crazy things. Don't get me wrong, I ain't saying her and Billy did a thing wrong, or that the boy fathered her son, but we better look closer at them."

"Hard to do. Rath plays a close hand."

"We need to separate those boys from him." Barley took

off his hat, blinked in the bright sun, and scratched behind his left ear. "That old man's tougher than rocks. He's probably part Injun, and you ain't getting nothing out of him about the deal. Those younger boys—they might talk." He set the hat back in place.

Herschel nodded. "I think you're right."

"Any word on those stage robbers?"

"Ford and that old man? No, they ran off south somewhere, may be in Texas by now."

"We've got another problem. Couple of horses have been stolen up here lately. I don't have any leads, but I suspect they're taking them up into Canada. They may be hiding them up in the Missouri Breaks until they get a buyer up there."

"You get word, let me know and we'll run up there. I need a little good news."

"They tell me that *Herald* has been nailing your hide to the wall." Barley chuckled and shook his head in surrender. "Can't please folks. Last year, the big outfits were running over this country; they never wrote nothing bad about them doing that."

"This year, those big outfits can't even afford cowboys with the winter kill-off."

"Ah, I bet they've sent buyers to South America looking for more steers to eat this grass."

Herschel nodded. "Yeah, they probably have."

"And you know what? Monkeys, parrots, and palm trees ain't surviving a Montana winter. Those cattle they get out of deep in Mexico have never seen a frost." Barley acted dismayed over the notion. Then he looked up and his blue eyes sparkled. "Where were we? Oh, horse rustlers and the Mannons."

"What about us making a scout up there toward the

Missouri middle of next week. You'll have this hay up and maybe we can locate them."

"Sure, and I'll keep listening."

"Barley, I guess I'm on the outside being sheriff now. Is there lots of talk about the lynching and what am I doing about it?"

His hand clapped Herschel on the shoulder. "You can't worry about wagging tongues. I hear a little here and there, but we're doing this by the law. It don't always work swift, but it grinds good."

"I hope so." Herschel raised his gaze to the green-brown hills. "Don't get too sweaty putting this up."

"I'll hold back the sweat."

Herschel put his foot in the stirrup, swung his leg over the cantle, and in the saddle, checked Cob. "See you next Wednesday."

"Wednesday," Barley repeated, and climbed on the iron seat. Reins undone, he drove the clacking mower away, sending the plovers scurrying away from the gray mares' feathered hooves.

Mannon's ranch was on Red Wing Creek. Herschel swung his roan horse northward, his mind set on talking to Nora Mannon. Maybe she had the answers that he needed. Strange, he hadn't even thought about her before—maybe her isolation since becoming Rath's wife for the past few years had wiped her memory from his mind.

Two hours later, he crossed the last ridge and followed the wagon track road. A grove of pines sheltered the place. Sprawling pens and sheds made a quarter moon around the main house, and the fenced hay fields beyond bordered the clear-flowing creek on both sides.

A few collies barked at his approach, and a woman shading her eyes looked in his direction from the porch. He'd been there before when he was campaigning, but that day he'd met Rath feeding hay with his boys in the bottom. In a hurry then, he'd declined an invite to the house.

"Hello," he said from the yard gate, and removed his hat. She stood on the porch in a wash-wrinkled dress; her light brown hair looked like it needed brushing. Not the Nora he recalled, all prim and proper, from a few years gone by.

"Oh, yes, hello," she said guardedly. "My husband isn't here." With her hand, she herded a small boy toward the open doorway.

"Nora? Herschel Baker here."

"My, the sheriff. Rath won't be back until—"

"I'd like a word with you."

She looked pained at him. "No, my hus—"

"Nora, I need to talk to you." Determined, he started to dismount before she went inside and closed him out.

She shook her head and looked ready to cry. "Herschel—I don't dare."

He was off his horse and through the gate, scattering collies in his wake. "Wait a minute. Don't go in that house."

"Oh, you don't know—" Her face was pale and, clutching her hands together, she swallowed hard.

"I know lots of things. I am sheriff of this county and have every right to be here."

"But what will Rath say?"

"Or do to you?"

Her violet-blue eyes blinked at him like he wasn't even standing there at the foot of her porch. Nora Mannon was not in Herschel's world—hers was one of obvious fear and possible oppression. Worse yet, he wasn't certain he could do a damn thing about it.

"Nora?"

"Yes?"

"Do you know about Billy Hanks?"

"I ain't seen Billy Hanks in years." She looked over the top of his head with gauzy vision. "My, my, that boy could dance. You tell him I said hi."

"He's dead, Nora."

"Oh, was it a horse wreck? He could sure ride them bad ones."

Herschel stood at the base of the stairs and closed his eyes. Nora Mannon's mind wasn't in this world. That was the reason Rath didn't take her to town and dances. He was hiding a dark secret, not a wife.

"I have to go," he said.

"I'll tell him you were by, Herschel."

"Nothing important," he said, and replaced his hat. "Good to see you again."

"Oh, yes. Maybe we can dance again sometime."

"I hope so."

He short-loped Cob for home. Despite the warm sunshine, he felt gooseflesh on his back and arms. It would not be easy to shed from his mind his vision of the distressed Nora.

Hours later, he sat on the porch swing with Marsha listening to the night insects. With the girls in bed and things quiet at the office, he felt halfway relaxed with his arm over her shoulder.

"You said Nora's face was blank?" His wife nestled against his chest as the heat of the day evaporated.

"She wasn't right. Talked to the wind, not me. I don't think she even understood about Billy being dead when I told her."

"You think Rath's been hiding her because of this condition?"

Herschel nodded, and felt nauseated at the thought of

the once-beautiful woman turned into a vegetable. "What caused that?"

"Bad treatment."

"I know that, but somehow I think it's more than that."

"Well, some women after having a child go crazy and never recover."

"You don't plan to go crazy on me?"

She elbowed him in the ribs. "I don't plan to."

He chuckled and hugged her. But he still didn't know everything about the situation. It wasn't likely that Billy Hanks had a thing to do with Nora Mannon's problems. That little boy wasn't his either—Hanks, by Herschel's calculations, hadn't gotten to Montana before the boy was conceived. The time did not add up, but he'd sort that out later.

"So—" She clapped him on the leg to bring him back to their world. "You have to find a jury for the cowboys that robbed the grocery, for the stage robber, and who else?"

"Mrs. Johnson will draw the names from the voter list. Then my office has to notify them they are to be in court when the judge gets here."

"Catching outlaws isn't your only job."

"No, it ain't. Art rode up and told the Crowley girl today. He's going back up there with one of his wagons and haul her down here."

"What else does a sheriff have to do?"

"Go next week and look for horse thieves. A ring of them are operating over in the far corner of the county. Barley and I plan to take a few days and find them."

"Did Jim Matson get what he needed today?" she asked, spreading out her dress over her legs.

"Yes, all the parts for the mower, and Ed over at the shop fixed his harness. He should be mowing hay late this week down at your place."

She squeezed his leg. "Our place."

"Yes, ma'am. Our place."

The swing creaked when he shoved off with the toe of his boot, and the night insect orchestra fiddled away in the starlight. Content to sit there and hold her for hours, he felt some of the job's tension drain away. Billy Hanks's killers were out there somewhere. He'd get them.

FIFTEEN

His skeleton force worked in the office the next morning. Art, Phil, and himself. Herschel was standing in the light pouring in the window to better read the name on the next slip drawn from the box.

"Tom Harkins." He looked at his deputies.

They both nodded. Harkins would do for a juror.

"Since he's of sound mind and body, then make out a summons for Tom Harkins to be here for the jury pool." He reached back in the box for another.

"Paul McGraw."

"He votes?" Art asked with a frown.

"Must have voted last time. Why?" Herschel asked.

Art shook his head to indicate that McGraw wouldn't work. "He ain't real bright. Works down at the mill."

"Too dumb to be on a jury?"

Both men nodded. Herschel put the slip down and went for the next one.

"Earl Mannon."

"Why not?" Art asked.

"No reason?" Herschel half-turned to check with Phil, who turned his palm up. "Put him down for a summons."

So the morning passed until a hundred jury members were pooled.

It looked like a monumental task to serve all of them. Taken aback for a moment, Herschel realized he'd had no idea about all the *other things* that occupied a sheriff's time. "Since this isn't a criminal process, we can use the Fellars boy to serve some of them. I can take those over in the northeast for Barley to work. Phil or the boy can deliver the ones in town, and Art, you take the west valley."

"Jury duty sure ain't going to be very popular this time of year," Art said, stretching his arms over his shoulder as he stood. "Haying and roundup all coming up at once."

"They can tell that to Superior Court Judge Mathew Conners when he gets here."

"I'm going in the morning to get Ida Crowley," Art said. "She can stay in that small house on Burns Street. Take me two days to go up there and get back."

Herschel agreed with a nod. "You get back. We'll all need to ride hard to get these summonses out. Phil, who else can we get to serve them?"

"I'll find someone."

"Good. Guess I'll have to put my campaign against horse rustlers off until this session of court is over." He shook his head, feeling a twinge of dismay over being tied down by all the obligations of his job. There were more things to keep him occupied than he'd ever figured.

Phil got up to see who'd come into the office. In a minute, he stuck his head in the doorway. "Berry Kirk is here to see you."

"Send him in." Herschel shared a concerned look with

Art. No time for them to talk it over. Kirk appeared in the doorway.

"You wanted to see me?" Kirk looked at them and the office with a haughty, suspicious glare.

"Yes, Berry. Have a seat." Herschel indicated the chair in front of his desk.

"I'll stand." He folded his arms over his chest and his spur rowels jingled when he set his boots apart.

"You know why I needed to see you?"

"I reckon it's over that ruckus in the Yellowstone."

"Yes, and you shooting Tucker Ralston."

"That was self-defense."

"That a court will decide."

"You're saying I'm under arrest?"

Herschel nested his back in the swivel chair and looked at the sullen youth standing before him. "I could arrest you, but I don't think you're stupid enough to run. Go home, get a suit of clothes to wear, and then hire you a lawyer. Ten Friday morning be in Judge Watson's office. Better bring all the witnesses you can find, too."

Kirk's dark eyes flew open in his first show of emotion. "That a trial?"

"No, it's a hearing. The judge will listen to the case and he will decide if you are to be bound over to superior court and charged with murder or not."

"It was self-defense."

Herschel shook his head. "The judge decides that, not me."

"I ain't being railroaded—"

A tinge of anger rose inside Herschel's chest—his eyes narrowed at Kirk and he cut him off. "I've heard enough from you. My good advice is over. You can do what you want, but if you don't show up in court Friday, I'll have a

murder warrant sworn for you by ten fifteen. Do you understand me?"

"Yeah. I'll be there."

"See that you're there. Now get out of here, I've got important business to tend to."

Art walked to the office door and turned back when
Kirk was out of hearing. "We going to have trouble with
him?"

"He's a troublemaker. I'm not certain how Tucker was
shot. Let Judge Watson decide that. But he better heed my
advice or he will be locked up in jail."

"Randal Squires is out here," Art said at the door.

Herschel nodded. A man in his forties, Squires lived up
in the Sharky school district. "He here to see me?"

Art nodded, and spoke to the man in the outer office.

"Send him in," Herschel said.

He stuck out his hand to the shorter man with the reced-
ing hair, his hat in his left hand. Squires wore a full white
mustache twisted on the ends until they resembled long-
horns, and was as bowlegged as anyone who'd lived his
life on a cow pony.

"Morning, Hersch. Some damn outfit stole my good
bald-faced horse yesterday. Left me some old wind-broke
nag with a T bar on his right shoulder."

"Bad trade, huh?" Herschel smiled at the man and
shook his head. No doubt a drifter already halfway to
Idaho by this time had stolen his horse.

"Bad trade!" Squires's cheeks turned red and he looked
ready to blow up.

Herschel shook his head in dismay at the man's reaction. "I was only joking."

"There ain't a damn thing funny about it." Squires's
eyes narrowed to slits. "I heard that you weren't taking this

job serious. You've never found out who hung that Hanks boy, either."

"Mr. Squires, I have a handful of deputies to protect a large area of land. We are investigating the lynching and we will look for your horse."

"Look for him, huh?" With anger in his eyes, Squires beat his leg with his hat. "Well, that ain't enough for my money."

"I'll try to do better. Now if you will fill out the paperwork with Phil, we will be on the lookout for your horse."

"I came in here expecting service. A man loses a damn good horse to some worthless drifter, and all you got to say is, you'll look for him. Hell, a five-year-old kid can do that."

"Mr. Squires, fill out the report with Phil. I don't have time to argue."

"By damn, we'll get us a sheriff that does."

"Suit yourself. You can go upstairs and get a petition right now in Mrs. Johnson's office."

Squires's glare was meant to melt iron. "What are you, Republican or Democrat?"

"Independent."

"A man don't choose sides ain't worth a pinch of salt."

"I have a job to do. I am not here to argue politics. So get the hell out of my office."

"Can I help you?" Phil asked from the doorway.

Squires used his hat for a pointer looking back while Phil had him by the arm to lead him out of the office. "I'll see what the *Herald* has to say about this. They've got your number. A do-nothing sheriff, that's what you are."

They'll have plenty to say. Herschel shook his head, still hearing the man ranting in the outer office. In the old days, he'd have gone to fists with that belligerent old goat. He pushed out of the chair and went to the window to let out some of the steam inside his chest. Sheriffs can't fight over such things. Maybe Marsha would be proud of him. New baby inside and all. There were some good things in his life, like her and the girls. That reminded him, he needed another pony. Those girls were going to ride Chico to death.

"Sorry about that," Phil said, sticking his head in the doorway a few minutes later.

Herschel turned back from the street scene of traffic and freight wagons and nodded. "Came close to throwing him down the stairs." He looked at the tin-square ceiling.

"Wonder what he'd'a done if you'd told him you were a Democrat," Phil said.

"Why?"

"He's a big Republican. He'd'a knowed what was the problem, then."

Both men laughed.

Herschel walked home for lunch. It was a cool day with clouds gathering. Phil had hired three men for a dollar a day to serve jury duty summonses. So that went easier in his mind. He still had the Berry Kirk hearing to deal with.

"We're having chicken," Kate told him, opening the front door for him.

He swept off his hat and smiled at her. "Sounds special."

"Oh, it is. We dressed the biggest of those spring chickens. Mom's frying it right now."

He sniffed the air in the living room for the aroma and gave her his hat. "Good smell."

"I thought so, too." She winked and hung up the hat on the wall peg.

"Hi, anything happen today?" Marsha asked, turning from her cooking on the wood range.

"Selected a jury pool for Judge Conners. That will be

real popular with haying and roundup on hand." He hugged her and kissed her on top of the head. "Chicken looks wonderful."

"I thought it would. Had a big hankering for some today. Kate, tell the riders to come in and wash up."

He looked after the eldest girl's retreat. "They sure enjoy that pony."

Marsha nodded, and used a fork to turn a browned piece over in the hot grease of the iron skillet. "Can't hardly get any work out of those two. I have to bribe them to even get help in the garden."

"Girls need some time to be girls."

She leaned over and put her head against his chest. "Or be cowboys."

"That ain't bad, either." They both laughed.

"What are you doing this afternoon?" she asked.

"May have to take the jury summonses up to Barley and cancel our horse-rustling trip."

"You'll be home late for supper?"

"More than likely."

She put down the fork, turned, and hugged him around the waist. "Be careful."

"I try to be all the time."

After lunch, he saddled Cob and went by the office to check with Phil. Things sounded quiet around the office, so he bundled up the summonses for Barley and headed east by northeast. There were lots of signs of haying along the way. Many mowers and teams were out in the meadows laying it down. Yellow meadowlarks darted in and out of the road and whistled their sharp calls.

Heart waved from working in her garden at his approach. With a bright smile on her copper face, she came to the fence with her hoe. "You just missed him. He went to see about some kinda trouble at Mike's store."

He frowned at her. "Any idea?"

"I'm not sure. Some boy rode up and said for him to come on the double, there was trouble down there."

"Who was the boy?"

"I think Charles Mathews's son. They bought Old Man Griscom out."

"I better go help. You feeling fine?"

Her warm smile always touched him. "How is your family?"

"Marsha and the girls are fine. Had our first spring chicken for lunch. I better go see."

Heart waved good-bye and he set Cob for the store in a hard lope. His mind was full of questions about what might have happened. If he'd gone by the road, he'd have passed through there over an hour before. He generally went cross-country to cut time off the trip and see some things of interest, like a spooked-up buck mule deer or two in the willows and a few wild turkeys. Now, as he pushed the big roan horse, his stomach churned over what might be wrong at the store.

He short-loped off the ridge and the store was in sight. Several rigs were parked about, but that was usual. At the hitch rack, he reined up and dismounted looking around for the horse that Barley must have ridden in. No sign of him.

He hitched Cob to the rack, looking up to see someone familiar come out the door. It was Cove Tipton. His face was pale. "What's happened here?" Herschel asked.

"Mike was robbed and they shot him. I'm afraid he won't make it."

Filled with disbelief that such a thing could happen, Herschel bounded up the stairs, two at a time, to the porch. "What about Sara?"

Cove looked ready to cry. "Murdered her, too."

"Aw, damn." Herschel closed his eyes. "Who did this, do you know?"

With a hard swallow, Cove nodded. "Three men. One of them was Casey Ford, according to Mike. He recognized him, he said."

"Mike dead?"

Cove shook his head in defeat. "He's in there. But he won't live till Doc gets here."

"Where's Barley?" he asked over his shoulder, going inside.

"Gone after 'em about an hour ago."

Herschel tried to think of the necessary things he had to do before he could go and back up his man. "I'll need to get word to my office and Marsha. And I have a sack of jury summonses to send back to them."

"I'll take 'em."

"Thanks. I better see if I can talk to Mike." Herschel parted the quiet throng of distraught-looking men and women at the door to the living quarters off the store. "Excuse me."

Cove's lady friend, Lucille Wynne, met him with a sad face when he entered the room. He acknowledged her and looked at Mike, who was propped up on some pillows at the head of the bed. Blood seeped through the bandages. His weak eyes blinked with recognition at Herschel.

"Glad you made it—" Mike's voice was low and strained.

"So am I. Cove said you knew the robbers?" Herschel took the straight-back chair Lucille had moved in place beside the bed for him.

"One was—" Mike went through some pain and winced at it. "Casey Ford, that tough gunhand the Powder River Cattle Company hired last year. He—I'd recognize him—anywhere. . . ."

Seated beside the bed, Herschel held his cold hand and nodded. "Go easy, pard. I'm not in any rush."

"I better be—" Mike forced a grin, then dropped his chin. "I give them all the money I had. Why'd they have to kill her?"

"Didn't want any witnesses, I guess."

"Probably so. I was mad and called him by his name. Like the devil's going to call it out when he gets to hell. My mistake—" Then tears began to run down his cheek. "Aw, damnit, promise me, Herschel, you'll find that worthless beggar and send him there for me and Sara."

"I'll find him. Won't quit till I do."

Mike choked and coughed hard. He'd either fainted or gone on.

Lucille moved in and felt for Mike's pulse on his neck, and then she nodded. "He's still alive, but I don't know for how long."

"Do what you can to make him comfortable. I'm going to ride after Barley and find those three killers. Did he mention knowing any of the others?"

She shook her head and arranged the blankets to keep Mike warm despite the day's heat. "I'll be sure the store is locked up and all if they take him to town."

"Thanks. What about Sara?"

"Some of the women and I will clean her up. Dress her, and the men can dig the grave."

"Thanks. Was she shot?"

She shook her head and looked at the pine flooring. "They cut her throat wide open."

Bloody no-account bastards. He shook his head. Hell was too good of a place for them.

SIXTEEN

Herschel tied on behind the saddle the bedroll he'd made up from store stock. One of the other women there, Mrs. Jennings, was gathering some dry cheeses, crackers, jerky, and raisins for him to take along to eat.

He handed Cove the large envelope of summonses to take back to his office. "Be sure they don't get lost, and tell Art and Phil they will have to handle the Kirk hearing, get these summonses delivered, and maybe even take care of Judge Conners's court sessions. I'll be back when I can."

Cove nodded. "I've got that letter and the one you wrote to Marsha."

"Good. Thanks," he said to Mrs. Jennings, who brought him out the poke of food to tie on his horn.

He finished hanging it on his saddle horn, then turned and saw Lucille hurrying out the front door. "Mike's dead, Herschel."

Several of the men had offered to join him, but he'd told them how important it was that they stay there and handle the double funeral and close things at the store. He and Barley could surely capture three outlaws. His deputy could probably handle them by himself. But he'd had a bellyful of this Casey Ford and his gang. Maybe if he'd pursued him harder, Mike and Sara would still be alive— this Ford must be some talker to convince these out-of-work cowboys to help him.

"Figure they got much money?" he asked Cove as he drew up the girth.

"Several hundred dollars Mike said that they got from the safe, and all the supplies they needed, too. In fact, they stole one of Mike's horses and a packsaddle, so they must have taken a lot of things."

"I guess I never expected them to come back after the stage robbery. I figured they were long gone to Texas."

"I've got a notion that Ford is wanted there, too," Cove said.

Herschel stared at the distant hills waving in grass and considered the man's words. "You're probably right about him." He undid the reins and slapped them in his calloused palm. Lots of miles to cover. He wondered how far ahead Barley was.

"You be careful. We need you as our sheriff," Cove said.

With a nod, Herschel put his boot toe in the stirrup and swung in the saddle. "I'll be back. Thanks for your help, and all of you." He looked at the sad faces standing on the porch. "You've been getting all the tough jobs lately, Cove."

"I can handle them. God be with you."

He turned Cob and headed south waving to the cheers of his friends. Some send-off. Folks counted on him. Mike had counted on him. The murder of the storekeeper and his wife stabbed Herschel's heart. He kept seeing Ford getting away, not once, but twice. If he'd only pursued him further.

Run him down into the ground. Obviously, it hadn't been long until Ford had come back again. Not this time. There would be no more next time for Casey and his gang.

He crossed the Yellowstone on the hand-cranked ferry while standing on the deck. The operator said he'd taken three men across about ten in the morning. Barley had ridden over at noontime.

Herschel checked his pocket watch. His man had a good two hours start on him. The killers four hours.

"You know any of the three?" he asked as the choppy water slapped the barge's sides.

The old man shook his head. "Your deputy asked me that, too." He strained at the winch that drew them across, his thin arms struggling to turn it. "One fella was about thirty. Tough-acting short fella, seen him before. Gunman. Then the old man with him, he was friendly and acted half-embarrassed to be with them. Third was a big bruiser. Never caught their names."

"Thanks."

"Barley said they shot up Mike and killed Sara?"

"Yes. Mike died an hour ago or so."

"Sons-a-bitches. I should have drowned them."

Herschel shook his head. "No, that's our job. We'll handle them."

"Hope you get them."

"We will." The ferry bumped into the shore. He paid the man and thanked him, then unloaded Cob and rode off.

Barley's tracks were easy to follow, as if his man was leaving him a trail to ride. No way Barley could know that he was this close to him, but intuition sometimes played a role in a Western man's decisions. Wouldn't be the first time, nor the last.

He short-loped Cob up on to the next rise, hoping in the vastness below to catch sight of his man. There was nothing in the way of a horse and rider for him to see, only more rolling grass and sagebrush country. His face to the wind, he sent the roan horse into the steep descent for the coulee far below him. One more mountain to climb was all that he could think about.

That evening, he chewed on jerky as he rode, his first meal since breakfast. He spotted a small outfit in the last rays of sundown and turned Cob off the tracks. Obviously, the outlaws and Barley had missed stopping at this place. Hoping to buy some coffee, he short-loped Cob toward the pens and low-walled shack.

A bearded man in a worn buckskin shirt stepped out of the doorway and looked hard at him. "You lost?"

Herschel reined Cob up and smiled at the man. "No, I'm after some killers that rode by here a couple of hours ago."

"Never seed them." The man spat a black squirt of tobacco to the side and wiped his mouth on the back of his hand. A cross look in his dark eyes telegraphed his wariness of Herschel.

Half-twisted in the saddle, Herschel indicated the hill behind him. "They stayed over the crest of the ridge, I'd say."

"Could have. What'cha need?"

"I was wanting to buy some food and coffee."

"You want to feed him?" the man asked, looking over his shoulder.

A woman less than four feet tall ducked under his arm and came into view. She held her hand up to shade her eyes from the red glare of sundown. "Hi. I'm Minnie and he's Jarrow. Get down. I've got some antelope stew and I'll make us some real coffee. We don't get many guests up here."

"Thanks." Herschel dismounted heavily. He figured

Jarrow to be in his forties. The short, stocky-built girl with her brown hair in a Dutch bob, he put her in the twenties. Strange pair, but the West drew all kinds. Many varied people were drawn into relationships to survive. Jarrow and Minnie looked like such a couple. No problem of Herschel's—all he wanted was a meal and his teeth were about to float out for a cup of coffee.

Forced to duck under the low lintel, Herschel soon learned the cabin had a dirt floor. Minnie indicated the rough table and benches made from planks. A couple of stiff deer hides hung on the wall and her cupboards were old gray crates.

"Nothing fancy," she said, sounding cheery and going to the fireplace. With a rag for a holder in one hand, she brought the pot and three tin cups back. "Jarrow's going to build us a real house one day."

Her husband took a seat across from Herschel, and he never answered or commented on her chattering. He acted as if having Herschel there to listen to her saved him the trouble.

"You folks run cattle up here?" Herschel asked to make conversation when he lifted the steaming cup to blow on it.

"That gawdamn outfit send you up here to spy on us?"

Herschel frowned hard at him. "What outfit? I'm passing through here after three killers murdered a man, Mike Melloncamp, that ran a store on Deer Creek. They shot him and cut his wife Sara's throat. Cold-blooded killers. Now, if you think I came to spy on you, think again."

"That damn Thorndyke Cattle Company. You know them?"

"No, but I've heard of them. What have they done?"

"Sent some rannies over here and told us to get the hell out."

"Lately?" Herschel dared sip the coffee at the cup rim, though he knew it was still too hot.

"Hell, yes, they want the spring this place sits on. Sent some fella in a suit and buggy over here, offered me two hundred dollars." Jarrow's eyes narrowed and he shook his head. "I ran him off and told him not to come back."

"You have a claim in on this place?"

"She does. We been here three years and I got a brand registered. I ain't stealing their cattle either. 'Cause we're poor, they act like we're second-rate citizens with no rights."

She stood at his shoulder and nodded.

"Why didn't you report them to me?" Herschel asked.

"My word against them." Jarrow laughed in disbelief and then dropped his chin. "The rich get richer and the poor poorer."

"You have a legal claim, they have no right to harass you."

"Get that paper," he said, turning toward her.

She nodded and lifted her skirts to leave. "Take me a few minutes. We hid it in case they tried to burn us out."

"They say they were going to burn you out?" Herschel asked.

Jarrow nodded quickly, then checked to be sure she was gone out the door. In a hushed voice, he said, "You're after Casey Ford, ain't yah?"

"You know him?"

"I might. Him and me had a falling-out six months ago."

"Mind telling me what that was over?"

"Horse deal and her. He brought four horses by here. Said he bought them in Nebraska and didn't want to sell them till planting time. Offered to cut me in if I fed them and had them in shape." He sneaked a peek at the open door and then looked back at Herschel.

"I'm listening," said Herschel.

"I went up to Miles City to get some things we needed. Her and her old man had credit up there. Ford come by and got the horses. I think he slapped her around when she asked him for pay. She wouldn't talk about it. So if Ford went over that ridge out there, I understand 'cause he knows I'd kill him if he showed up here."

Herschel nodded. "What happened to her husband?"

"She figured he had a ruptured appendix and died. She buried him by herself. We ain't got any close neighbors. I've been here over a year with her."

Both men looked up when she returned looking a little red-faced from exertion. "Whew, I really had it hid."

She put the paper on the table in front of Herschel, then went for more coffee.

Herschel read the claim. Issack and Minerva Bowen were the names on the paper. Recorded in Miles City, which was the county seat before they formed Yellowstone County. "Looks good enough to me. They have no right to threaten you."

"It's a long ways to Billings when they do," Jarrow said.

"Not as far as you think. I'll get word to them to stop harassing you two."

Jarrow held his cup up ready to sip it. "What the hell kind of sheriff are you, anyway?"

"One elected by the people. All the people in Yellowstone County."

"Guess you won't be in office very long."

"As long as folks vote for me, I'll be there."

Her brown eyes twinkled and she squeezed Jarrow's shoulder standing behind him. "We have any more trouble, we'll sure call on you."

"Good. You know where in Nebraska Ford hides out?"

"He mentioned some fella named Knowles one time." Jarrow shook his head as if lost for an answer. "I never heard him say the town or place."

"One of them horses," she said, "that he claimed he'd bought down there had a Clover brand on it. I never saw one like that before."

Jarrow nodded. "I thought at first he was a traveling horse trader. She did, too."

"He ever say where he came from?"

"Someplace in Texas. He sure hated the snow and cold up here. Bitched about it all the time. Wonder why he kilt them folks."

"Robbing them. He shot an unarmed stagecoach guard in a holdup a few weeks ago. You all were lucky he didn't turn on you."

"He ever comes back he's a dead man," Jarrow said with the frost of a winter night in his voice.

Herschel saw Minnie nod solemnly out of the corner of his eye.

"Hey, I promised you antelope stew," she said. "We all forgot you were hungry." Her skirts in her hand, she rushed over to ladle him a bowl of it out of her large iron kettle.

After he ate and they refused his offer to pay for his food, he excused himself. "I want to leave at first light. I need some hay and grain for my horse. Be glad to pay for it."

"No," Jarrow said as he stood up and stretched. "You're the first lawman I ever met wasn't in love with himself. No, sir, we've got horse feed and it's our treat."

Herschel chuckled. "I been told lots of things, but never that."

Later, under the stars, he wondered about Jarrow and Minnie. The man must have drifted in and then stayed. No telling where he came from. He probably had a checkered past, too, before coming there. No telling. Plenty of men like him in the West, and they weren't talking about their lives before. Kind of like this big-sky country cleansed those that would let themselves be cleansed and separated them from their dark pasts.

Ford was one of those who went the other way. From bad to worse. Herschel lay on his back in his bedroll under the spray of tiny lights in the vast canopy over him, a hundred yards from the dark cabin, and wondered about Marsha and the girls. But the last vision before he slipped off into sleep was the dark image Cove Tipton had described of Billy Hanks hanging from the tree and illuminated by the lightning.

SEVENTEEN

I<small>N</small> the predawn darkness, Minnie came from the house while he saddled his horse, and spoke quietly to him. "Sheriff, I have breakfast fixed when you are ready. Don't ride out with an empty belly."

"Thanks, I'll be there," he said, and led Cob for the gate.

"Good," she said, and in the gray light with her skirts in hand, went back to the cabin.

With Cob outside the corral, he stopped to tie the bedroll behind his cantle and his poke of food on the horn. Then he led the roan to the rack and hitched him. Better make the meal short, he thought. Barley might need him down the trail. Though he considered Barley the toughest of his deputies, Ford had to be the worst man either he or Barley had ever tangled with. Time would tell.

He studied the graying eastern sky. The sun wasn't far behind it. He ducked his head, entered the cabin, and found himself grateful for the warmth from the fireplace replacing the overnight chill outside.

"Morning," Jarrow said, seated on the bed that occupied the far half of the room, busy pulling on his boots.

"Morning. I'd like you to refresh my memory about what Ford looks like," he said to Jarrow as he took the cup of hot coffee from Minnie. The metal warmed his hands as he held it.

"He's about five-six. Black hair. Sharp nose and gray eyes like a bad wolf. I seen one once had gray eyes. Mean sumbitch. He could pull down full-grown cows."

"I think someone mentioned a scar."

"Yeah. Right side of his face. He said it was from an ax. Dented in his cheek on the side."

"Shame," Minnie said, using both hands to set biscuits on the table, "that they didn't chop his damn head off while they were at it." Stepping back, she wiped her wet forehead with her sleeve. "Gravy, butter, and chokecherry syrup coming next."

"This Christmas?" Jarrow asked with a wink at Herschel.

"Same as. I'm rewarding the sheriff for getting that no-account Ford."

"Hell, woman, he ain't got him yet."

After she put the butter and a mason jar of bloodred syrup on the table, she placed both palms on the surface, leaned forward, and looked close into Jarrow's eyes. "He is going to get him."

"You heard that?" Jarrow asked, laughing aloud, busy lathering a golden-brown biscuit with butter. "That woman makes up her mind, you better believe her."

She nodded and went for the gravy. "I have him convinced."

"Me, too." Herschel took his first bite of her bread. Not bad. He sure hoped she knew about Ford's arrest for a fact.

Close to noontime, he rode off a ridge several miles

southeast of their outfit and spotted a rider and dun horse.
The sight of the familiar hat made him smile. He settled
easier in the saddle, convinced he had caught up with his
deputy. In a short while, he rode up to Barley, who was
stopped on the flats.

"We still on the right tracks?" he asked, sticking his
hand out to Barley's. After they shook hands, they rode on
stirrup to stirrup.

"Near as I can tell."

"A rancher I spent last night with thinks he's headed for
Nebraska. Wasn't sure of the town where he was headed,
but Ford had mentioned a man named Knowles, and this
fella told how Ford showed up at his place with a Clover-
brand horse."

"Clover Cattle Company," Barley said, and made a
small whistle as if impressed. "Big outfit down there north
of Ogallala. It's a wonder they hadn't sent a man after him
to nail his hide to the shit-house wall. Tough bunch when I
knew them, and they sure don't mess with thieves."

"Ford brought some horses up there, including this
Clover horse. Left them for this man to winter, then come
and got them when he was gone. Ford beat up his wife, I
guess, when she complained about him not paying for
them."

"He's a hard case. Powder River Cattle hired him up
home for that purpose. To run off the small outfits. Ford
sent some of them packing; then the company pulled in
their horns after your election and laid off all their hired
gun toughs."

"Good. My lands." Herschel laughed, amused, and
shook his head in disbelief. "I really must have struck fear
in their hearts."

"You did. That wagonload of cronies you sent to Deer

Lodge Prison made them all realize their running roughshod over the little outfits was over."

"Shame the *Herald* don't know that."

"They're living in the past, too. One more winter like the last one and these cattle barons with those *corrientas* they're importing from the tropics, and they'll all be gone."

"I bet so. How far ahead are they?" Herschel motioned toward the southeast.

"Half a day'd be my guess. I figure they've rode most of the night. If they have any horses stashed ahead, or more than likely ones to steal, they'll press on."

"Ogallala?" Herschel asked as two blue grouse thundered out of the sage and spooked Cob into bolting sideways. When the horse was under control and back on the well-worn game trail they were following, he looked to Barley for an answer.

"Down in that country somewheres, I'd guess, unless he burned his bridges by stealing the Clover horse."

"We better lope these ponies. We're a long ways from there."

"A far piece." Barley put spurs to his dun and they galloped off.

That evening, they crossed sagebrush-bunchgrass flats and found a farm beside a small stream lined with cottonwoods and a new patch of alfalfa. When they rode up, an attractive young woman in a blue-checkered calico dress came to the door and looked them over. Two small children close by her side peered past her at them.

Herschel removed his hat. "Ma'am, I'm the sheriff of Yellowstone County. This is my deputy. We're tracking three men robbed a store and would like to buy a meal. We're no threat to your young'uns or you. We'd simply like to buy a meal."

"Dorothy Quin." Her eyes narrowed as if she was looking them over. "I have food. Get down. You can wash up here at the stoop." She patted the heads of the two small children who swung on her skirts.

"Herschel Baker and he's Barley Benton. We'd be grateful." Herschel replaced his hat, stepped off Cob, and went to loosening the girths when she disappeared inside the doorway.

"Polygamist," Barley whispered to him.

Herschel nodded. The back hills were full of the "other wives" of Mormon men since the U.S. marshals were so busy rounding their husbands up. Set off on small ranches and farms in remote areas to escape detection, women like Dorothy lived alone and worked the places between infrequent visits by their "man."

"You can put your horses in the corral," she said as she came outside and poured steaming water in the wash pan on the stand outside the cabin door. "There's hay in the manger for them."

"Thanks." Herschel finished loosening both girths and dropped the stirrup and fender.

"I'll put them up," Barley said, gathering reins. "You go ask her if Ford's been by here."

Herschel put his hat on a wall peg and rolled up his sleeves. "I don't guess you get many visitors?"

"No." She stood in the doorway as if overseeing his washing.

"Three men ride by here earlier?" With the bar of lye soap in his hand, he looked her in the eye.

"Those were the men you are after?" she asked, squeezing her narrow chin, her blue eyes drilling a hole in him.

"Yes, ma'am. One is a man calls himself Casey Ford, an older cowboy named Chub Travis, and the third man I don't know."

She nodded. "His name is Brigham Smith."

"You know him?" Despite the too-hot water, he began to wash his hands.

"He's some relation to my husband."

Herschel nodded. "They mention anything?"

"Like what?" She frowned at his ginger use of the hot water. "I can get some cold to put in that if you need it."

Herschel dismissed her concern with a headshake and continued to lather his hands. "Where were they going?"

"I think Nebraska. They said they were going to buy horses."

"Or steal them." He rinsed his hands off and took the feed-sack towel she handed him.

"That's why you're after them?"

"No, ma'am." After drying his hands, he mopped his face on the towel and met her gaze. "They murdered a man and woman in a store robbery."

"Oh, my. Why, I've known Brigham since he was a little boy. I can't believe they did that."

"He's tied himself in with Ford, I'm afraid, and Ford's a hardened criminal."

"Oh, that is terrible." She looked ready to cry. "And that nice old man—Chub?"

"They were with him when the crime took place."

She hugged her arms and trembled. "And those three were here in my house last night with my children. Why, I can't hardly believe it—"

"I hated to be the bearer of such bad news. But anything you can tell me would help. Describe Brigham Smith, too."

"He's tall like you are. Broad shoulders, never tans, has a red face all the time. His hair is close to red."

"Anything else?" He turned to Barley, who was coming from putting the horses up. "They slept here last night."

"But I had no idea that they had—murdered anyone," she said to Barley.

."Bad news," Barley said, and put his hat on the cabin wall beside Herschel's.

"Very bad news. I know that Hubert will be shocked to hear his cousin was involved in such a crime. Hubert's my husband. He'll be back in a day, went to take care of some business."

Herschel nodded to make it easy on her, full well knowing she was lying. Why, she'd be lucky to see him once a month when he made a circuit of his scattered *wives*.

With the bloody sun dying in the west, he followed her inside. Scurrying around, she began to dip them out bowls of stew from a kettle on her range. Then she sliced a fresh-looking loaf of whole wheat bread with a long knife, telling them about her two children and her husband's plans for the place. He wanted twenty more acres cleared of the sagebrush, leveled to irrigate, and planted in alfalfa.

She put butter in a bowl on the table and then a jar of honey. "Comes from our bees."

"I need to get a few hives for my wife," Herschel said, taking the chair she showed him.

The children sat on a nearby bench and swung their legs. Obviously trained in the old verse, *better seen than heard.*

"Has Ford ever been here before?" Herschel asked between bites of the stew.

"No, I'd never seen him or the older man before last night. I think Brigham brought them by here since he knew I was up here. Actually, he helped Hubert fence, clear, and plant that field last year."

"So he's familiar with this area?" Barley asked, looking over at Herschel with his spoon held ready for another refill.

"Yes, he knows the area."

"You think he might quit Ford then and stay around here?" Barley asked.

"Well, there are several sisters and brothers around here."

Barley looked up from his stew. "You mean Mormons?"

"Yes. We call each other that."

"I know. This Smith, he have any lady friend he might want to visit?"

By this time, Herschel understood what his deputy was getting at. If Smith wanted to separate himself from Ford and Chub, he might drop off and stay in this area. Secondly, these were his people and the kinship of Mormons for one another was well known—*clannish* was the word most people used. He listened closely as he savored the honey-sweet butter and bread. He only regretted the absence of a cup of hot coffee. Latter-Day Saints didn't drink coffee.

"Mable Green. He worked for her. She has a young daughter, Abby." She frowned as if in deep thought. "I think they're engaged."

"Where does Mrs. Green live?" Herschel asked.

"Oh, a couple miles south on this stream."

"Could I ask a question?" Herschel said to Barley. "Why do you figure he would stop overnight here and stay with Dorothy if he had any interest down there?"

"Would you take two killers to your mother-in-law-to-be's house?" Barley looked mildly across the table at him.

"I see your point. Food was good. What do we owe you?" Herschel asked, turning to her.

"Outside of your bad news, I have enjoyed both of your company so much I am not charging you."

"Thanks, we'll be on our way in the morning."

"Breakfast at sunup?" she asked looking from one to the other for an answer.

"We don't aim to be any trouble."

She raised her palms to silence his concern. "I'll ring my triangle when I get the food started cooking if you aren't up."

Later, in his bedroll in the grass beyond the corrals, Herschel raised up and asked his deputy, "How did you figure out he might stay close here?"

"If he'd stay anywhere, it'd be around other Mormons, so I went on a hunch."

"Good idea. Not to change the subject, but what's your hunch on who killed Billy Hanks?"

"Ralstons and Mannons are your two best suspects."

"Yes, but proving it, we need someone to talk."

"You know that gets harder and harder by the day. Somehow, things get buried deeper with the passage of time."

"You're right. Good night." He shook his head in grim resolve and rolled over on his side. Buried deeper meant harder for him to find out who did it.

EIGHTEEN

Hatless, the two lawmen were bellied down in the waving bunchgrass. Barley held a brass scope up to his eye as he scanned the headquarters of Mrs. Green's place. Some lodgepole pens held a milk cow that a girl had come out earlier and milked. A couple of Shanghai roosters landed on the top rail and crowed at the sunup. They tried to outdo each other.

"No sign of him?" Herschel chewed on a long grass stem and studied the place.

"Nothing yet. But he may be sleeping in."

"Can you see any of the horses in the pens?"

Barley shook his head. "They're around in front of the shed. We don't know his pony anyway."

"We saw one all tuckered out, we'd know."

"Right. You reckon we better slip down there and look closer?"

"We better. I hate to sneak up on two women that could be alone, but we won't know that until it's too late."

Barley agreed. "A man that's been in on one murder can be a desperate sort, too."

"You mean he ain't got much to lose?"

Barley collapsed the scope and nodded, chewing on his thin sun-scarred lower lip. "Which way do you want to go? Right or left?"

"I'll go left of the shed. You come around the pens."

"Herschel?"

"Yes?"

"Be damn careful, anything can happen, and might under the circumstances."

"I will. Did I tell you we're expecting a young'un next year?"

Barley's look brightened and he grinned. "That's great. What do the girls think?"

"Hell, they can't wait."

Herschel eased back out of sight from below, got on his feet, and went for the rifle and his hat. The sun's glare was blinding him without the Stetson on his head. He eased a shell in the chamber of the .44/40 and then set the hammer on safety. Barley was already headed down the sagebrush-studded hillside.

Herschel went off the steep slope. Nothing moved or looked out of place, and he soon reached the base. Moving through some head-high box elders, he heard voices and stopped to listen.

"He up yet?" a woman asked in a coarse voice.

"I told you no."

"He going to sleep all day?"

"He might. Told us hadn't sleep in two weeks."

"Go out there and wake him up. He can eat this oatmeal."

Herschel stopped. If they were talking about Smith, he must be sleeping in one of the sheds—not the main low-roofed structure Herschel considered the cabin, which was twenty feet from him. Which shed was he in? One was a chicken house with open doors and glass-bottle windows facing the south. Not likely. The big shed had an open front and was for hay and horses. Likely. The last one looked like a toolshed, and from the back he couldn't see the door.

He wondered about Barley coming from his right and the far side of the pens. Had he heard the voices? No, it was doubtful. Through the box elder leaves, Herschel could see a woman with her skirts in her hands coming around from the house to wake the man in the shed. With a swipe to dry his right hand on his pants, he moved to be close to the side of the shed.

"Brigham, wake up," she said.

Herschel held up his hand to stay Barley, who was coming bent-down close to the corral. With his thumb, he indicated the shed.

"What's wrong?" a sleep-soaked voice asked.

"Oh, she's worried about feeding some oatmeal she has left to the pigs."

"Oh, baby—I'm so glad to be with you—"

"Not now. Besides, she's on a tear."

"About me being here?"

"She don't need a reason. I'll be so glad when we can leave here."

"Soon, baby. Real soon."

The red-faced man was seated on the cot putting on his boots when he blinked in disbelief at the sight of Herschel and his rifle blocking the door's opening. For an instant, he looked ready to spring up, but that passed and he settled down with a look of surrender on his face.

The girl screamed. Hands to her mouth, she about fell backward getting out of the way.

"Don't go for the gun," Herschel said, reading Smith's glance at the gun belt hooked on the wall above the cot.

"What's going on out there?" the woman at the house shouted.

"Law business," Barley said. "Stay there."

"What kind of law business?" she demanded, and Herschel could hear her coming.

"I'm arresting you, Brigham Smith, for the murder and robbery of Mike and Sara Melloncamp. Now get on those boots."

"Tell him you didn't murder anyone!" the girl screamed.

"Where you the law from?" Smith asked, getting ready to pull on another boot.

"Yellowstone County."

"Montana?" He strained to pull the boot on and then sat with his hands in his lap.

"Yes. Put these on." Herschel handed him the handcuffs.

"You ain't got no authority here." Smith looked at him, grinning and shaking his head. "This is Wyoming."

Herschel used the rifle muzzle to punctuate his words. "I don't give a damn if it's Fort Worth. Get those cuffs on. I'm taking you back for murder."

"Wait, you can't—" The girl started to move in.

"Ma'am, you don't get back, I'll take you in for harboring a criminal."

"But you have no authority—"

"This rifle is all I need."

"Abby, get out here this instant," the older woman shouted. "This lawman out here says Brigham killed a man and a woman up there."

About to cry, she looked in disbelief at Smith. "You do that?"

"Of course not."

"See?" she said. "You have the wrong man."

"No, he was there all right when they cut that woman's throat. If he didn't cut her throat, then he held her so Casey Ford could."

"Tell 'em it wasn't you!"

Smith shrugged in defeat. "I guess they've got their minds made up."

Herschel reached in and tightened the cuffs another notch so Smith couldn't slip them. Then he jerked the big man up by his shirt collar. "Get moving."

"Abby, Abby." The older woman rushed over and drew her away. "They say he's a killer." The gray-headed woman tried to shield the sobbing girl from all of them.

"Mrs. Green, they ain't got no authority here to arrest me. Have them stopped."

"Ma'am," Herschel said to her, shoving his prisoner toward Barley. "We ain't asking no one for their authority. He's going back and stand trial in Billings, Montana, for those murders."

"Which one's his horse?" Barley asked.

"The lineback dun," Mrs. Green said, hugging and petting the hysterical Abby. "If he did that, you're better off without him," she told her daughter.

"But Momma—" Sobbing cut off her words, and she buried her face in the woman's dress.

"I'll go saddle him," Barley said.

"Fine," Herschel said. "How much of the money do you have left from the robbery?"

"I never—"

Herschel saw red and grabbed Smith by the shirtfront and shook him. "I asked you how much."

"Don't know. It's in my saddlebags."

Barley led the dun horse out of the corral and had heard the admission. "I'll check on it."

Mrs. Green set her daughter aside. Raw anger clouded the older woman's face. Only Herschel stepping in and blocking her stopped her from getting at Smith.

"He did kill that woman and man—" She looked angry enough to fight a bear. Inches away from Herschel, she stood straight-backed, opening and closing her fists. She seethed to get by him.

"He's going to be tried by the court. They'll decide his fate. That ain't our job."

"Well, it won't matter if it's a boy or girl, that child will never carry your name," she said to Smith, indicating Abby.

"Oh, Mother!" Abby cried out.

"The money was for us and the baby," Smith shouted over his shoulder as Herschel guided him toward the saddled dun.

"Blood money!" Mrs. Green shouted behind him. "Filthy blood money!"

It was a long climb on foot up the steep hillside. Herschel led his prisoner on his dun. At the top, Herschel looked back and saw no sign of Mrs. Green or her obviously pregnant daughter.

Smith's hands, in irons, grasped the horn as he looked back and shook his head. "Now she can marry that damn bishop like her mother wanted her to in the first place."

Herschel's entourage made Jarrow and Minnie's place after dark.

"One of the three killers?" Jarrow asked as they dismounted in the light coming from the open doorway.

"One of the three," Herschel said. "Could we buy some food?"

"Land sakes, it ain't often we get celebrities around

here. Famous lawmen and outlaws. I never seen him before." Minnie peered out the doorway.

"Brigham Smith." Herschel told him to sit on the
ground while he loosened the girth on Cob.

"Guess the other two got away?" Jarrow asked, standing, arms folded by the lighted doorway.

Herschel looked at the man. That was obvious.

"There'll be another day," Barley said, and took the
reins of the horses. "I'll put them up."

"Thanks," Herschel said, then turned back to Jarrow.
"Casey Ford's using his nine lives up fast."

"I imagine so. Come in. What part did Smith here play
in the deal?"

"Ask him. He says he's innocent." Herschel took the
prisoner by the arm and stood him up. "The man wants to
know."

"Ah, go to hell."

"We may all go there, but you'll be working the gate for
us to get in." Herschel guided him to the doorway. "Duck."
Then he seated him on a chair.

"Eggs, fried potatoes, and ham enough?" Minnie asked.

"Sounds wonderful," Herschel said.

"I wasn't expecting you back so soon."

"We found him down the way."

"Yeah, in Wyoming, where he didn't have any authority," Smith said loud enough that the world could hear it.

"Shut up," Herschel said sharply. "I've got the authority
all right."

"Do you reckon he can get off on that?" Jarrow asked,
looking Smith over.

"No, but a man in his position needs every small hope
he can muster."

Jarrow nodded slowly as if deep in thought. "Get much
of the loot back?"

"Couple hundred dollars." He fished the small notebook out of his vest and read from it. "Two hundred twenty-seven and some change."

"Wonder what them other two got out of it."

"Damned if I know, and Smith here ain't saying."

Seated at the table, Jarrow nodded. "I figure them Mormons will hire a big lawyer and get him off."

"Anything can happen. He'll be in jail until then."

"Them Mormons do that."

Herschel agreed for the sake of not having an argument with the man. Barley's entrance was a welcome intrusion. Maybe they could get off the subject. He had grown tired of talking about it. All the past day he had wondered if he should have sent Smith back with Barley and gone after the other two.

He'd no doubt hear about it from the *Herald*.

"Food's about ready," Minnie said. "You taking his handcuffs off for him to eat?"

"If it would make you happy—" Herschel glanced over at her.

She shrugged. "No matter."

"He can eat with them on, then."

The clink of the chain between the cuffs accompanied the meal. Smith ate with the bracelets on like he'd done it all his life. No one in the room said much. Not even Jarrow, who sat and watched them.

"Good food," Herschel said when finished. "The county will reimburse me for this food, so I'll pay you."

She wrinkled her nose. "In the morning you can pay me. I'll have breakfast cooked before sunup. I know how you like to get to traveling."

"Thanks," Herschel said, and took his sullen prisoner out of the room. He headed him for the corral, where the bedrolls were stacked in the starlight.

"You try anything during the night and one of us will kill you. Savvy?"

Smith yawned. "Yeah, I understand."

"Just don't get to thinking we love you. We don't."

Barley took the first watch, and stirred Herschel in the night for his turn. He awoke heavy-eyed, sat up on his bedroll, and waved his deputy off to get some sleep. It reminded him of his trail-drive days. Only, he didn't need to sit in the saddle and sing to cattle so that if the horse bumped into one, it didn't use that as an excuse to stampede.

His back to the corral rails, seated cross-legged with the rifle over his lap, he looked at the snoring Smith in his bedroll at the side. No worry about the prisoner escaping. He yawned. Poor Marsha. She no doubt was beside herself with worry by this time. Don't worry, won't be long and we'll be home.

NINETEEN

AT mid-afternoon on the second day after leaving the Bowen place, Herschel arrived at the courthouse. He dropped heavily from the saddle and his legs held him up, though he grasped the saddle horn with both hands for a moment to be certain. An itch in his whisker stubble caused him to smile—must look a mess. Be plenty of time to clean up later.

"Get down," he said to his prisoner, and undid Cob's girth. Absently, he went around Cob's butt and ran right into the raging Smith's face, his handcuffed hands reaching for him. They grasped Herschel's vest and Smith began to shake him. Herschel's right hand closed on the Colt's wooden grip. Staggering backward, he tipped the six-gun out of the holster, raised the muzzle upward, and jammed it against Smith's gut.

"You ready to die?"

Smith wilted—shook his head.

"Don't try me," Herschel said through his teeth, and

drove the prisoner back against his dun horse. "I'd shoot you down in the wink of an eye. You killed a friend of mine."

His face bleached white, Smith nodded and swallowed hard.

"Now get in that door and don't be slow."

"That one of Mike's killers?" someone asked from the boardwalk.

He holstered the Colt. "Don't get any ideas about a lynching. He's standing trial for it."

"Oh, I didn't mean that—"

"Good," Herschel said, and propelled his man by the collar for the door.

Someone opened the door for them and when Herschel looked up, Phil was on the top of the stairs.

"You back, sir?"

"I hope so." He smiled at the sight of his concerned-looking deputy, who came down the stairs two at a time.

"He the killer?" Phil looked Smith over and shook his head.

"He's one of them. Two got away. Lock him up—oh, here's the keys to the cuffs. How's things going here?"

Phil took them and nodded. "Judge Conners is holding court. Art's handling that."

"I'll ride home and check on Marsha and the kids."

"Things are pretty quiet. Judge Watson ruled Tucker Ralston's death as self-defense. Berry Kirk's free."

"Nothing else?"

"No, sir. Oh, yes, I asked Ida Crowley out for the schoolhouse dance Saturday night."

"Nice young lady. She find work?"

"Nanny for the Thompsons."

"Lock Smith up and don't trust him." Herschel gave the sullen-looking outlaw a hard glare.

"I won't, sir."

"See you don't," he said, and turned on his heel to leave.

"Sheriff, Sheriff Baker," Ennis Stokes shouted, coming pell-mell down the stairs. "This the killer of that store-keeper and his wife?"

"That's for a jury to decide. I'm tired and have no time for questions. See me tomorrow."

"He can't hold me," Smith interrupted. "He arrested me in Wyoming. I'll be loose in no time. He ain't got any authority in Wyoming."

"What do you say to that?" Ennis asked Herschel, taking down notes with his pencil.

"I say he's in my jail and Judge Conners can decide the rest."

"What about the others? The other gang members?"

"Stokes, it can wait." He went outside to Cob. Weary beyond words, he drew up the cinch, took the roan's rein to lead him, and headed for his house. A few hours sleep and he'd be better—he hoped, anyway. Barley should be home, too, by this time—sleeping.

Marsha came on the run at the sight of him. Trailed by the three girls, she raced from the garden with her skirt in hand. "You're home at last. Kate, go stoke the stove. I'd bet he hasn't eaten since—when?"

He dropped out of the saddle, gathered her in his arms, hugged her to his chest, and rocked her back and forth. "Days and days and days." Then he laughed, and they all did, too.

He about fell asleep at the table eating her hastily prepared food.

"You need some sleep," Marsha said, looking across the table at him.

"I'm filthy."

"Sheets can be washed. Get up. We're hauling you up-stairs and tucking you in."

"I feel so bad—" His mind was too numb to even argue. Minutes later, he closed his eyes and slept.

Thunder woke him from a bad dream. From his sleep-blurred vision, he looked at the flash of lightning on the windowpane. Must be close to sundown. A strong rain had obviously swept into the country. The drum of the big drops with some hail on the roof told him that. Then, more thunder and flashes.

He threw his legs over the side of the bed. Better try to get cleaned up. A million things to do. No word on Billy Hanks's killers, either. What did Barley tell him? The far-ther away in time you got from a crime, the harder it was to solve it.

"You awake?" Marsha asked, sticking her head in the doorway.

"I think so."

"I've got hot water if you're ready."

"Lands, girl, I'm coming."

The sound of the thunder shook the house and wind lashed it with waves of rain. "If we don't blow away," she said.

He shook his head. "I'm glad to be home."

"So am I. Good to have you." She led him downstairs and sent the girls to their bedroom so he could bathe. The kitchen soon was steamed from the hot water she poured in the copper tub.

"Phil brought me all the signatures and the printed words. None of them look like the printing on the note to me," she said, scrubbing on his back with a brush.

"It was just a hunch. Who have I missed, I wonder?" Busy lathering himself in the hot water, he tried to think.

Someone out there wrote that note. Damn, he wished he had more leads on the lynching.

"How are you feeling?" he asked. "You're the one I was worried about."

"Fine." She swept the lock of hair back from her face. "I've done this birthing before."

"Maybe you'll have to coach me, then."

"Some babies never seem to get here and when they do, you can always wish they'd taken longer." She pursed her lips, then laughed. "Stop looking at me so serious. Serious is for the sheriff's job."

"Yes, ma'am." He pulled her around and kissed her. "How is the garden coming?"

"We'll be shelling green peas in a week for supper. Will you be here to eat them fresh?"

He stopped and considered the question. "I may need to go to Nebraska."

"So soon?"

"So soon. Casey Ford and Chub Travis were headed that way."

"Can't Art or one of the others go after them?"

He shook his head and started at the next roll of thunder. "Dang, the rain isn't over yet."

"No, it's not." With a pail of water she climbed on a chair, ready to douse him. "Rinse time."

At the supper table, the girls had a thousand questions about his chase of Brigham Smith. He did his best to tell them all they needed to know—aside from Abby Green's condition.

After supper, he and Marsha were alone on the porch. The rain had moved south and lightning still danced down there. The swing creaked and with Marsha under his arm, they simply enjoyed the reunion.

"How soon must you leave?"

"In a few days. Casey Ford may not stay long in that country. I can't seem to learn where his roots are at."

"This other outlaw?"

"Some old drover. No family I can learn about. Folks that like him say he never hurt no one."

"How did he ever get hooked up with a killer like Ford?"

"No telling. Ford finds help like Newton Crowley. No one believed he'd ever rob a stage."

"It's the hard times, isn't it?" She snuggled against him.

"Hard times don't give you any rights to take to the owl-hoot trail."

"Oh, I worry so much about you when you are gone."

"Don't."

"I can't help it."

He bent over, lifted her chin, and kissed her. Kissed away all the worry he could and enjoyed the intimate moment. Casey Ford still had to be apprehended.

At seven the next morning, Herschel was behind his desk reading the *Billings Herald*.

Yesterday, Yellowstone County Sheriff Herschel Baker returned with one of the reported criminals in irons that perpetrated the bloody Deer Creek Store massacre that claimed the lives of Mike and Sara Melloncamp. The outlaw, whose name is Brigham Smith, is twenty-seven and a resident of Clay Bank, Wyoming. Mr. Smith claims that the sheriff illegally removed him from Wyoming Territory without the expressed consent of Wyoming officials, and hence has made an illegal arrest. He plans for his legal team to sue the sheriff and Yellowstone County for wrongdoing, violation of the U.S. Constitution and of his civil rights.

An ex–ranch foreman, Mr. Smith alleges that he was

*helping some families out with spring chores and hay
cutting when arrested. He claims that he has not been
in Montana in six months and has no idea why Sheriff
Baker singled him out as a suspect in the cruel murder.*

*Sheriff Baker was not available for comment. The
question stands. How does one gang of criminals keep
attacking our citizens? The sheriff goes off on his own
and leaves the entire county vulnerable to attack for
days at a time. When he does return, he brings in some
underling, like he did the last time. The Yellowstone
County Republican and Democratic Parties plan to
have large conventions this August, and each have reported they will field strong candidates to end Baker's
short term this coming November.*

"There you are," Mayor McKay said, storming into his
office.

Herschel lowered the paper. "I see you didn't do much
good with this newspaper."

"Oh, the Good Lord could not dissuade them. But you
have one of the killers?"

"He's back there if you want to talk to him."

"Heavens, no. Now what about the others?"

"Down in the Nebraska panhandle, best I can tell."

"Why are we getting all this bad publicity?"

"The *Herald* is egging it on."

"What are you going to do about this outlaw leader?"

"I'd need two hundred and fifty dollars in expenses and
I'll go get him." Herschel folded the paper and sat back.
He'd see how strong McKay's convictions were about end-
ing Ford's career.

"My God, man, that much money?" McKay paused,
pulled on his beard, and frowned. "You say you can get
Ford if you have the money?"

Herschel nodded.

"How will you arrest him down there?"

"I'll have a deputy U.S. marshal badge."

"That would solve the problem. Who would go with you?"

"You have more money to spend on expenses?"

"No." McKay looked affronted by the mention of more money.

"Then I'll go and hire any help I need down there."

"I think the railroad would pay some of that." McKay cupped his right elbow in his hand and squeezed his chin with the other, looking hard at the painting of George Washington on the wall.

"What I don't use, I'd bring back." Herschel clasped his hands together on top of the paper. "But I can't say how much."

"I'll be back this afternoon." McKay rushed off.

"What was his problem?" Phil asked from the doorway.

"Money, like usual."

"Oh, here's how things went in Conners's court. The judge gave that stage robber Felton four years in Deer Lodge Prison. Them two cowboys that robbed the store got off with agreeing to get out of Montana. They ever come back, they'll serve two years in prison."

"Sounds all right. Now we can keep Smith in jail until his fall session."

"He told Art that he'd hold a special session here if you got that whole gang since it was such a terrible crime."

"Let's hope that we do."

"You reckon we will?"

"I have my way, we will."

"Man, it would be nice to have them tried before they hold the county election conventions." Phil smiled. "Sure be nice."

"What would be nice?" Art asked, strolling into the office.

"Getting Ford and Travis," Herschel said. "Thanks for all your work in court. Must have gone well. We have one of the gang in jail."

"I already read that damn Stokes in the *Herald*." Art shook his head in disgust. "Didn't I see McKay also leaving the building? What's he after?"

"My expenses to go after Ford in Nebraska."

"Aw, hell, Phil, we'll have to run this place again."

They all laughed, and Herschel told them to take seats. "What else is happening?"

"I told Phil already," Art began. "That Earl Mannon acted awfully nervous the whole time he was in town for jury duty. I never saw a fella that nervous wasn't guilty of something."

"I told Art that word's out. One of those two outfits, either the Ralstons or the Mannons, lynched Billy Hanks."

"What else?"

"There's also rumors that Billy Hanks got one of them Ralston girls with child."

Herschel sat back until the springs creaked. "What else?"

"Hanks was after Earl's betrothed."

Herschel scratched the back of his neck. He needed a haircut. "All hearsay and not admissible in court. But we need to know some answers."

"Is one of the Ralston girls going to have a baby?" Art shook his head and gave him a frown. "I ain't asking her."

"We can have Marsha do that at the dance Saturday night."

"We sure can." Phil smiled, looking relieved that he didn't have to do that job.

"I guess I need to talk to Barbara Ann Kelly," Herschel

said, and gazed out the window at the bright blue sky, tenting and untenting his fingertips.

Art made a face like he was about to blow up, then said, "Judge Watson's decision that the shooting was in self-defense ain't helped things."

"Some of them think Berry Kirk is the avenger for the cowboys' side?" Herschel asked.

Both of his deputies nodded.

"Bad enough that there's horse rustling, not related to Hanks, going on up in the northwest part of the county. Barley and I intended to make a raid on them. All this has put it off for the moment."

"Know who the rustlers are?" Art asked.

Herschel shrugged. "More out-of-work cowboys would be my guess."

"Plenty of them on their way here now," Phil said with a shake of his head. "And word is they're bringing fifty thousand more cattle up from Texas for these ranges."

"Yeah," Art said. "Even shipping some by rail and then driving them over from the end of the tracks."

"Ain't they learned their lesson yet?" Herschel asked.

Art scowled at them and shook his head. "Another winter like the last one and they can all go broke."

"That's for sure. I'm giving Mayor McKay some time to get me the expense money to go after Ford. Meanwhile, I'll take the stage over and see Art's friend Otter Washington at Miles City. He's the U.S. marshal now and can get me a deputy marshal's badge."

"He'll fix you up," Art said.

"Figured so. Guess we all have work to do."

"I've got a lead on that bald-faced horse," Art said. "I thought I'd go down on the Crow Reservation today and see if I can locate it."

"Good idea. I'd like to have him back for that crotchety old man Squires."

Phil agreed and their meeting broke up. "Oh, yes, I have the jail expenses and the circuit court costs for you to go over before I turn them in," Phil added.

Herschel closed his eyes and dropped his chin. "I better look them over next then." What else did a sheriff have to do? Was there a woman involved in the Hanks lynching? Maybe there was an answer out there. The weekend would tell something about it.

Phil brought in the report. Herschel took the papers and looked at the columns of costs. At times, he wished he had been a bookkeeper instead of a cowboy. He'd be better equipped to handle the job if he'd had that kind of experience. He'd just gotten to the third item on the list when he heard a commotion in the outer office. Phil was arguing with someone.

He rose and went to the doorway.

"I demand to see the sheriff!" Stokes shouted as Phil physically blocked him from going past his desk.

"What do you want?" Herschel knew the scowl on his own face must have been black. It felt red—red-hot. "Get in here."

Stokes shrugged, raised his chin, jerked down his green-checkered suit's coattail, and slipped past the angry-looking Phil. "So there."

"I ain't through with you, either," Phil said.

Herschel wanted to smile. Phil's actions reminded him of the first time a guard dog pup raised his hackles at an adversary. That boy might make a real lawman yet.

With his right hand, Herschel scratched the side of his head and looked at the flushed face of the *Herald*'s star reporter. "What is all this about?"

"I'm here to ask you about progress on the Hanks

lynching. Any leads—" He fumbled in his coat pocket for a stub of pencil and his pad. With a lick of the lead point, he was ready to write.

"Under investigation by this office."

"No new leads? Nothing? Word on the street is that you deliberately were out of town so this Berry Kirk wouldn't be vigorously prosecuted in the shooting."

"That's the prosecutor's job, not the sheriff's."

"Yes, but the word is if you had been there and given your full support to the case, the results would have been different."

Herschel walked to the window. He'd never offered Stokes a seat. This was to be a lesson in endurance for him. Traffic in the street looked busy. An eighteen-hitch oxen team's freight outfit with two wagons threaded the ruts.

"I doubt Judge Watson based his decision on my not being there."

"Ralston had a knife?"

"I'm satisfied that he did."

"The word on the street—"

"What street?" Herschel half-turned and frowned at him.

"All over Billings."

"Well, what are they saying, since I don't hear them?"

"That Berry was hired to kill him for his involvement in the lynching."

"How much was he paid?"

"How would I know?"

"You're hearing things I'm not. They must be telling you the price on Ralston's head. Why didn't these people come forward and testify at the hearing? Hearsay is not evidence. The prosecutor needed hard evidence and testimony."

"Casey Ford?" Stokes sounded ready to move on.

"He's riding south."

"Never to return to Montana?"

"If he knows what's good for him, he won't ever come closer than Cheyenne."

"Do you have a vendetta with this man?"

"Are you asking me if I have a personal grudge against Ford?"

Stokes nodded, looking as if he was ready to write something important down.

"Casey Ford is a two-bit outlaw who killed a man and woman in cold blood and has been in on several robberies. I want him to face a judge and get his deserves. That's my job."

"But each time you go after him, you only get an accomplice, and then Ford strikes again. How can society believe he won't strike again?"

"They can't. I guess they better keep their doors bolted and a gun handy until he is behind bars, since you have compared him to Jesse James in your articles."

"Mayor McKay says that this rash of crime could make the railroad go around Billings and avoid the town."

"I think he said that exaggerated news stories about our local crime going out to the rest of the country would do that."

"How do you intend to bring Ford to justice?" Stokes had ignored what Herschel said.

"We have plans."

"We? Who's that?" Stokes looked around the room.

"I have some hardworking deputies and they cover lots of miles and territory. The apprehension of Casey Ford is number one on their list."

"But if he's in Wyoming, as you say . . ."

"Wyoming?" He frowned at the reporter.

"You said for him not to come north of Cheyenne. How will you know when he does?"

"A little bluebird is going to fly up here and land on my windowsill and tell me so. That's all I have time for." He about laughed aloud; he could see the next headline. "Sheriff Uses Blue Birds for Passenger Pigeons." With his hand he waved Stokes to the door, knowing full well he'd never get rid of him that easily. "Go on. I have work to do."

"But—"

"I have work to do."

Stokes made it to the door. "If Berry was hired to kill Tucker Ralston, do you think he'll kill any of the other Ralston men?"

"Why don't you go interview him?"

Stokes's blue eyes opened wide. "Why—why, he might kill me."

Seated at his desk with his nose in the figures, Herschel nodded and never looked up. *What would Berry charge for doing that?*

TWENTY

A SMALL deputy U.S. marshal badge pinned under his suit coat, Herschel returned to Billings by the afternoon stage. His twenty-four-hour trip to Miles City had been a busy one. The federal deputy position would give him some authority when he went after Ford. Not a matter of *if,* but *when.* Ford would surface somewhere, he'd hear about it and go arrest him. That outlaw better sleep in his boots so he was ready to run in them.

Herschel intended to make his nights short. Besides, after U.S. Marshal Washington filled out the papers, Ford was wanted for obstructing and robbing the mail, a federal offense.

Phil was still in the office when Herschel returned. Phil looked up and nodded. "Barley sent a note today. I figured you'd need to know about it."

He took it and opened the folded paper.

Herschel,

   Hoss thieves have taken over a dozen good horses

*from the area. The tracks go north. I am following them
while they are fresh.*

Barley Benton

It was in a woman's handwriting. No doubt Heart,
who'd been educated, had written it for him. Herschel
hated the fact Barley was going alone. He'd better cancel
all his plans, get up early, and track him down.

"I'll go up there and help him in the morning. You and
Art handle things. Art back yet?"

Phil nodded.

"Did he find the bald-faced horse?"

His deputy shook his head.

"You need to get out of here?" Herschel asked.

"Yes, Ida is cooking me supper tonight."

"I wouldn't miss her cooking, either. Tell her I said hi.
She like the nanny job?" He scanned his own desk for anything he might need to check on.

"Yes, well enough, I guess."

"Get out of here. Art get any leads on the stolen horse?"

"No," Phil said. "The horse was gone out of the country
from what he learned."

He picked up the newspaper. YELLOWSTONE COUNTY
SHERIFF MUM, the headline said. "Sheriff Herschel Baker
could only allude to bluebirds bringing him messages
when questioned about the large number of unsolved
crimes in his territory," the article said. He'd not missed
it far.

"That sumbitch," Phil swore.

"Haven't you left?" He looked up and frowned at his man,
then smiled. "I must be beginning to have some fortune-
telling talents. I saw that coming when I ran him off."

"I'm like Art. Stokes is getting under my skin."

"Go on. Have a nice evening. We can't stop him."

"I had my way, I'd poke him in that big nose."

"No. We can't do that."

"See you," Phil said and left.

Nothing on his desk looked urgent, and soon he strode the blocks for home. Looking forward to an evening with the girls and Marsha.

"Father's home," Marsha called out, and his stepdaughters came from three directions to tackle him. He distributed the small nickel presents to them, then went in the kitchen and hugged his wife. There were times like these when he wondered if the whole situation was real. He felt ten feet tall. The smell of supper cooking filled the kitchen and she laughed. "Your favorite, of course, beef pie. Did anyone ever make it on the trail drives for you?"

He shook his head and kissed her on the top of the head. "Trail cooks fried steaks in tallow and boiled lots of beans. I was with an outfit once with a boy and that fella got more sand in his beans every day than I did swimming a flooding river."

"Oh," Kate said, hugging her arms. "Was that gritty on your teeth?"

"Yes."

"Father, Mr. Tipton came by yesterday and left us a small bay horse. He said if it was all right with you, we could ride it until he needs it again."

Three sets of blue eyes waited for his answer.

"Did he buck any of you off?"

Kate dropped her chin. "No. How did you know we rode him?"

"Who would take candy out of the jar?"

"We would," came the chorus, and all three hugged him and began babbling all at once about how nice Brownie was.

"Time to eat," Marsha said, opening the oven, and everyone hurried to get everything ready.

"When do you leave again?" she asked.

"In the morning. Barley has some horse thieves he's gone after. I need to go help him."

She nodded and gave him a look.

"Something wrong?"

"Oh, no. We're fine, aren't we, girls?"

"Yes," they all said, looking up from chores.

After supper, he played the harmonica and the girls danced. Marsha leaned against him on the porch swing, and by the time the crickets started their night song, he'd worn the girls out dancing. They sprawled on the porch floor and laughed at his comment that they would one day waltz with princes.

"It's always good when you come back," Nina said.

"You mean we appreciate him," Marsha said, correcting her.

"Sure, but it's good when he comes home, too."

In surrender she sent them to wash up and go to bed. After a barrage of kisses and thanks, they fled inside and in the growing shadows of twilight, Herschel and Marsha were alone.

"Something wrong?" he asked with her tucked under his arm.

"Yes. I couldn't talk around the girls, but I am afraid our baby may not go to term."

"You need to stay in bed?" He looked hard at her.

"No. It happened once before to me. My granny told me everyone conceived wasn't intended for this world."

He rubbed his palms on the tops of his pants. "What can I do?"

"Nothing. I just wanted to warn you."

He turned and squeezed her. "Hey, I want you and the girls and that's fine with me."

"I know. Just hold me," she said, and began to sob. With a knot in his throat that he couldn't swallow, he held her tight and they rocked until the full moon began to rise.

It was a horse-thief moon that reminded him that under such light, horse takers moved on with their ill-gotten animals. When he was a boy growing up in Palo Pinto County, Texas, during the fall full moons, settlers lived in fear expecting Comanche raiding parties to sweep down from the north, raid their ranches, steal horses, kidnap women and young boys.

He'd seen the painted faces and hard murderous eyes from the security of a mesquite thicket. The file rode past not twenty feet from a trembling youth of eleven sprawled tight on the sticker-covered ground, hoping and praying hard that they didn't discover him. He never forgot how their ear-cropped ponies danced on their bare hooves under the decorated saddles. And the bells, he would never forget the musical jingle the small Mexican bells made that adorned their gear on that cool afternoon.

Under a layer of red dust, their short, bare, red legs showed in the sunlight when he chanced to peek through the leaves. Such sights made his stomach cramp harder. But they also awed him, these people were real horsemen. Each rider was so much a part of their steed, he considered them molded on those horses since they'd been born. But the wind carried a strong musk of horse manure, death, and carrion from the riders. A bathless society from a waterless land.

Later that night, when the full moon set, a half-starved, weak-kneed Herschel reached his neighbor's place. His family was there and safe in Horton's two-story rock dwelling where they had held off several charges from the war party. Hugging Herschel, his mother shed tears that felt like ice through his thin shirt.

His brother Tom told him the red devils had killed their collie Buster. At the news of Buster's murder, Herschel had wanted to cry. He knew all about full moons and the harm they held for ranch folks. Horse rustlers, red or white, used them often.

He finally took Marsha upstairs and they slept in each other's arms.

Before dawn she had him up, letting the girls sleep in. He wondered if she wanted him to herself without having to share his attention. Concerned, he asked her if she thought she should see the doctor.

"I will while you're gone. Now—" She straightened his vest as if it needed it, and forced a smile when he bent over to kiss her. "You don't worry about me. You take care of yourself." Her finger poked his chest. "The girls and I need you."

"Yes, ma'am."

Cob had one of those mornings. He buried his head between his knees and bucked for a full block alongside the garden and pasture on their property. He even sunfished twice, and the sun wasn't even up that early to shine on his belly. Herschel was about to get angry when Cob's head finally popped up and they were off.

At noontime, Heart fed Herschel a meal. She seemed worried about her husband's decision to go on alone. She'd wrapped herself in a blue and orange blanket despite the midday heat, and could not sit still over a minute at the table with him.

"It'll be all right," Herschel kept saying as she hovered around him. "He'll be fine. This ain't his first time."

"I know—" She raised her smooth copper face and then

tossed the thick braids behind her back. "I still worry this time."

"I'll be with him by nightfall."

"Good," she said, and reached out to squeeze his hands. "You know, an Indian woman who's lived with a white man can never go home."

"Don't worry. Barley will be fine."

He left for where Barley told her he'd take up the rustlers' trail. According to Heart, the Crawford Cattle Company had sent a rider to tell Barley that someone had stolen twelve head of using ponies from their line shack on Cherry Creek, leaving the hands there afoot. Herschel could imagine the cowboys mad as hornets when they awoke and learned that they would have to hoof it back to headquarters for something to ride.

Herschel carried some crackers, dry cheese, and jerky to eat. With that, plus the noontime meal he'd just eaten, he felt equipped to get by till the next kitchen or chuck outfit came along.

No one was at the Crawford line shack, but he discovered that Barley's horse tracks went north, so he fell in at a short lope and by sundown was miles north. No sign of Barley, but he hobbled Cob and threw down his bedding. A coyote came over the ridge, yipped a little at the rising moon, then was gone in the sagebrush and bunchgrass. Seated cross-legged on his bedroll in the twilight, he gnawed on some peppery jerky and washed it down with canteen water.

About midnight, he awoke in the silver brilliance of the huge moon and decided he could see enough of the tracks to ride on. His mind was like a butter churn in the hands of an aggressive kitchen helper. Hanks's lynching, Casey Ford's whereabouts, Marsha's health, and even Barley's safety had all begun niggling at him. Even trying to find some way to stop Stokes's black journalism.

Somewhere, a wolf howled on a distant ridge, and another answered closer by. The cold long-winded cry made him kind of hunch his shoulders against the night's coldness, and be grateful for the .44/40 under his right leg deep in the scabbard. Damn stock killers anyway.

TWENTY-ONE

A T mid-morning, he cut the tracks of two shod horses that looked fresh. He swung Cob westward, and soon overtook the rider, who reined up when he hailed him.

Herschel didn't know the man, whose eyes were shaded under the wide brim of a felt hat. The cowboy in the saddle hadn't shaved in a week, and his clothes looked like it was longer than that since they'd been washed.

"Howdy," Herschel said and set Cob down. Hands on his saddle horn, he stretched his tight back muscles. His senses were alert, but the rider made no threatening move for the gun strapped on his waist, so Herschel settled into what he hoped would be helpful palavering.

"Howdy yourself," the man said. "Got the makings? I'm out."

"Sorry, I don't smoke."

"Must be a preacher," the man said as his saddle horse went hip-shot under him.

"No, I'm looking for some horse rustlers."

"Don't know any."

"I figured you been riding the grub line. You might have slept a night with some boys in this country that borrowed other horses."

He shook his head.

Injun'd up, Herschel called it. No need to waste any more time on this one unless Herschel wanted to beat the soup out of him, and then the answers might only be what he wanted to hear.

"See you down the trail. Sorry I didn't have a smoke," he said, and started to leave.

"Hold up." The man kept looking at his hands in the thin goatskin gloves that held the reins and rested on the pommel. The expression on his hard face said he intended to tell Herschel something but didn't know how to word it. "There's a place in the Breaks north of here. I've never been there. But they say Hootie Brown is holed up there."

"Who's Hootie Brown?"

"A sorry sumbitch. One time, Hootie and two kids held up a Wells Fargo stage. When they got away and were stopped for the night, Hootie shot the lock off the strong-box and told them boys to get all they wanted out of it, then he'd get his part. Pretty generous of ole Hootie, huh? Both them poor Texas boys dove in that strongbox like starving hawgs at a trough full of milk and sour corn. They were so busy sifting them silver and dollar coins through their fingers that they didn't hear him cock his pistol and shoot both of them in the back."

"You survived?"

"I ain't saying. He just shot them two in the back, took the money, and vamoosed."

"I reckon you're telling me this Hootie Brown ain't worth much?"

The man nodded. "Mister, don't ever turn your back on the sumbitch."

"I appreciate it." He reined Cob around and set out in a short lope. There was no way to warn Barley that they might have a real badger in on this rustling business instead of some itinerant cowboys. It could make a world of difference from the sound of things.

At midday, he found a cow camp and the horse wrangler was there. The waddy took off his sweat-stained gray hat and scratched his head when Herschel asked him about Barley passing through.

"Yeah, Benton was here last night. Told us about them rustlers passing right by here. But after grub this morning, your man lit a shuck about daylight. Headed for the Breaks after them." He indicated northward.

Herschel nodded and thanked him. He left the camp still on what he thought were the tracks of Barley's dun. A long narrow shoe that stood out in the soft spots kept reminding him that his deputy was ahead of him and close to the rustlers. By late afternoon, he knew he was near the Musselshell River. It was long past the Yellowstone County line. He wondered how far the thieves had ridden before resting. Perhaps as far north as the Missouri Breaks.

In the late afternoon, he spotted smoke coming from a large cottonwood grove. Had he found their camp? Plenty of horse tracks led there from a bunch on the move. The horse droppings were scattered, which meant the horses were being pushed. It was an old Texas Ranger trick to tell unshod horses from Comanche horses. Since the Injuns were on the move, their barefoot horses left scattered horse apples. The mustangs' were in a pile.

He leaned back and jerked the rifle out of the scabbard. He levered a shell in the chamber and sent Cob off the high hill for the camp. No need to take any chances. Even the roan felt the tension. He began to prance despite the hard day's ride he'd been through. Sidling off the hillside, Herschel kept a wary eye on the trees and the smoke. The rush of the river and the dancing dollar-size leaves overhead were the only sounds he heard. No whinny of horses. He began to realize they probably were gone.

At a hundred yards from the grove, he saw some scattered bedrolls, then a body lying facedown and not moving. Alert to everything around him, he stepped off the roan and dropped the reins. Cob would ground-tie. The skin on the back of Herschel's neck itched. He dried his right palm on his pants, and then took up the rifle in both hands and advanced toward the camp.

The dead man wasn't Barley, he was certain of that. Herschel saw nothing else, but the coffeepot still hung over the dying fire. He knelt and turned the corpse over. To judge by the man's unshaven pale face, he looked to be in his early twenties. Two bullets in his back had stopped his life. The blood from the wounds had mostly dried, telling Herschel it had happened a few hours before. He found a letter in the man's pocket addressed to L.T. Rademacher, and a return address on the worn envelope in Gonzales, Texas. Enough to notify his next of kin, anyway.

Despite his conscience growling at him about not burying the dead rustler, he felt he needed to ride on and catch up with Barley. Obviously, his deputy had the rest of the rustlers on the run. Before he left, he downed some of the thick coffee and stuck the tin cup back in his saddlebags. Where were the horses?

Cob crossed the Musselshell easily, and the tracks of the herd went north. Still, Herschel felt confused. One rustler shot, their bedrolls and some packs abandoned. There must have been a gunfight in that camp. There was lots to find out. Barley would tell him the details when he caught up with him.

In a new land of rolling grassy hills, he short-loped Cob, at times squinting hard against the sun's glare for a sight of anything that fit the tracks he followed. Recent rains kept down the telltale cloud of dust that a herd of horses would usually stir on the move.

At mid-afternoon, he caught sight of them. Maybe a mile ahead and moving hard—the streak of mixed colors had to be the rustlers. Where was Barley? Herschel wet his cracked lips and stood in the stirrups. Still too far away. He dropped in the saddle and pushed the roan. Cob responded, and in a short time he drew close enough to see the three men driving the horses. No Barley. When the riders saw him, they left the horse herd and started to ride away. He could hear them swearing at him above the wind and the drum of Cob's hooves. Their foul words meant nothing to him. He wanted to know what had happened to his deputy, if he had to beat the information out of them.

The rustlers went in different directions, and he went after the one going left. Later, he planned to track down the other two. In a short while, he was gaining on the outlaw and closing the gap. The wide-eyed outlaw looked back twice at him as if that would stop Herschel's pursuit. Then, the desperate outlaw went to beating his horse on the butt with his pistol and lost it.

Herschel sent Cob in for a burst of speed, and undid the lariat from the pommel as he drew closer. At a full run, he built a loop, then stood up in the stirrups and made three swings above his head. The rope flew out and settled over the rider. Herschel slung the slack to the side to cinch the rope around his quarry. In a swift move, he dallied the hemp around the horn and sat back. When he braced himself, on cue, the roan horse planted his feet in the sod and plowed up some dust.

The rider came out of the saddle off the tail of the still-running horse, and landed hard on the ground. Herschel tossed the rope and stepped down, six-gun in hand. He checked to see if the other two had come back to rescue the moaning outlaw on the ground. Herschel saw no one. He strode over and jerked the rustler up by the collar. He was hardly more than a boy. Tears ran down his peach-fuzz cheeks as he rubbed his backside from the fall.

"Where's my deputy?"

"Don't—don't shoot me." He held his hands out and his voice sounded whiny, like some girl. "I never kilt him. I swear—Hootie shot him—I couldn't stop him."

"Where in the hell is he at?"

The boy blinked his wet eyes. "He must be back in camp on the ground."

Herschel frowned. "All I found was some dead puncher."

"No—no—that's Dicky. I mean where the horses were up the bottom."

Damn, had he missed him? "You go catch that horse of yours and ride up there and meet me. Try one trick and I'll shoot you when I find you." He hauled him up close to his face. "You savvy that?"

The boy pulled away from him. "Oh, yeah, I'll be right back. I promise."

Herschel turned him loose and went for Cob. In the saddle, he watched the boy, with his hand on his hip, no doubt sore, limping after his mount. If he did run away, Herschel could catch that half-pint easy. At the moment, he wanted to try and find Barley. He spun Cob around and sent him hard for the camp.

He crossed the Musselshell in a big splash, avoided the

copse of cottonwoods, and circled left of them. Cob cleared patches of sagebrush in leaps and then hit a game trail that led up the bottom. They passed through a head-high thicket of box elders. The branches whipped Herschel's legs, and on the other side he spotted the familiar saddled dun horse, who threw its head up at the sight of them. A knot began to form in his throat—if anything had happened to Barley, what would he tell Heart?

The sight of the fringed buckskin coat and Barley lying facedown made him sick to his stomach. The wounds in his back were obvious as Cob slid to a halt and Herschel bailed off him. In his rush to Barley, a sage bush caught his boot toe and about tripped him. He caught himself before he sprawled facedown, and moved up to the body on his knees to turn Barley over.

The sight of the lifeless blue eyes kicked him hard in the gut. How long ago had it been? A few hours? He hugged the stiffening body in his arms. What had he done wrong for this to happen? He closed his eyes as hard as he could. Despite the lump constricting his throat, no tears came, and the muscles in his arms tightened on the dead man. At last, he released him in dismay and filled with guilt.

He'd had no last words with his best friend, the man who he considered his mentor as a lawman. The one who'd aided his campaign from the start, and told him all he knew about people and how they might behave. Herschel had lost his brother on the last cattle drive coming up there a few years before. Their father had ridden off one day when they were young boys, and never returned. Barley Benton was both father and brother to him. Damn, oh, damn.

He looked up and saw the boy coming. Herschel hefted Barley's body in his arms, staggered some getting to his feet. "There a shovel in camp?"

The boy, still at a good distance, reined up and shouted, "Huh?"

"There a shovel in camp?"

"A small one."

"Good. Catch them horses." He indicated the dun and Cob. "Bring them along."

"Yeah, I will. He's dead, ain't he?"

Herschel nodded and walked on toward camp with the heavy burden in his arms. There was no way to get his body back to Heart. He'd have to bury him there. His arms and shoulder ached like penance for letting this happen, but he strode on under the load. The cottonwoods looked a mile away, but they weren't that far. Each boot heel struck the ground, step by weary step.

He never looked around when he heard the boy and horses catching up with him. The boy went past him looking shaken. "I'll go find the shovel."

Herschel nodded like a wooden Indian. Step by step, he bore his best friend—like a pallbearer—he closed his eyes to the reality. Maybe he wasn't cut out to be a sheriff. He'd screwed up by not catching Casey Ford twice, had not found the lynchers of Billy Hanks, and now had gotten Barley killed.

The boy met him at the edge of the trees holding up a small shovel. "I got it."

Herschel stopped like a man in a trance. He dropped to one knee and gently laid Barley's corpse on the ground. Before he rose, he shut his eyes. Then, looking around, he decided he wanted his friend buried above the flood line.

"We're going to dig his grave on that rise."

The boy nodded and with a limp started in that direction.

"What's your name?" he asked, realizing that he didn't even know it.

"Toby, Toby Grayson."

"I want a grave, not a hole, Toby. You know the difference?"

"Yes, sir."

"I'll fix the bodies."

"East to west?"

"I always heard the morning sun should shine on his face."

"I'll dig it that way."

"What's the story on L.T. Rademacher?"

"Who?" Grayson asked.

"The dead man over there." Herschel gave a toss of his head toward the other body.

"I thought his name was Dick Smith. I called him Dicky. He was all right—my friend."

Herschel shook his head. "His name was L.T. Rademacher."

The kid stuck the short shovel in the ground, took off his weather-beaten hat, and scratched the unbrushed thatch of wild black hair. "Guess no one uses their right name in this business."

"I guess you're right. Get started."

"Yes, sir." And he moved off toward the rise.

Herschel removed the few things from Barley that he knew Heart would want and tied them up in a bundle. A skinning knife, some money, a few Indian tokens, and the charm that hung around his neck—Herschel spent little time examining anything. The job was tough enough, he didn't want to linger on it any more than he had to. Then, as much as it hurt him, he went and took a canvas ground cloth from a bedroll abandoned by the rustlers. He popped it free of the blankets and then wrapped the body in it. He used a lariat he found to make the bindings around the canvas shroud.

With Barley's body prepared, he went and checked the rustler's pockets again, removed a small sum of money and change, pulled off the man's boots and found ten dollars more. He stood. Rademacher's mother would like him buried without his boots on. Then he wrapped the corpse in another groundsheet. Seemed like such a waste to Herschel, two men dead over a handful of horses. Especially Barley. . . .

The boy had made good progress when Herschel went up to check on him. Herschel knew digging under the tough sagebrush must have been hard, but the dirt the boy was tossing out of the knee-deep hole was alluvial and had only a few small rocks in it.

"Look all right?" Toby asked, raising his sweaty face to look at him.

"Looks respectable. I'm going to search for a board to carve a marker. There may be some in the river."

"Yes, sir," Toby said, and went back to work.

Herschel walked the banks until he found a small log-jam and spotted some boards in the tangles. They were too far out to reach from the shore, so he removed his boots, rolled up his britches, and waded into the river to extract a couple of short boards, which he tossed on the bank, then came out.

Out of the river, he looked at the two pieces. One carried dim traces of green paint, and he suspected it had been a gate board on the back of a wagon, probably lost crossing the Musselshell somewhere upstream. He dried his feet, then replaced his socks and boots. Above the sounds of the rustling cottonwoods and the river's murmur, he could hear the boy chunking out dirt and rocks. Satisfied, he picked up the green board and began to carve BARLEY BENTON—DEPUTY KILLED ON DUTY.

The letters cut into the wood board looked deep enough

to last awhile. He didn't notice the time his painstaking efforts took, until a pair of run-down boots came into his vision and he looked up into the sweaty face of the boy.

"Can't dig any deeper and get out of the hole."

Herschel nodded. "We'll put Dick in there first."

"Oh, thank God," the boy said, and wiped his face on
his wet sleeve, looking relieved.

"Why?"

"I figured you needed two graves."

Herschel rose stiffly and shook his head. "One's fine.
Let's get Dick up there."

They carried the rustler's corpse up there and, gently as
they could, placed him in the fresh-smelling hole. Then
they went back and brought Barley to the site. Somehow,
wrapped in the dull weathered canvas, he now seemed to
Herschel just another body to bury.

When they straightened and stood on the brink of the
hole, Herschel removed his hat and the boy did the same.
A strong gusty wind like the hand of God swept Herschel's
face and he raised his chin.

"Dear Lord, deliver these men to heaven. Barley was a
family man and leaves a wonderful woman alone and
she'll need your help and strength. Lord, he was a good
man"—a large knot in his throat cut off his words for a few
seconds—"and my best friend. Lord, L.T. was another
wayfaring cowboy, lost in the hard times. He'd rather've
been working cattle than stealing horses, I'd bet a good hat.
Take these men to heaven. In Jesus' name, amen."

The kid's green eyes were wet. He nodded. "You had
Dicky right. He told me time and again, we didn't belong
with Hootie Brown and should go on. But we had little
money and no jobs or prospects of getting any."

"Tell me who is with Brown."

"Frenchy, Bateau is his name. He's a Canuck. Mean bastard. He's maybe as mean as Hootie."

Herschel rubbed his palms on his pants. "I'll go make us some food. You cover them up."

"Yes, sir."

He stopped and looked at the boy. "You pick up your pistol back there?"

The boy shook his head.

"Get them covered up, then go back up there and find it."

"Any reason, sir?"

Herschel gave him a short bob of his head. "Before this is over, you may need it."

"I'll find it."

Satisfied, Herschel went to camp. He restarted the fire, then found some dry brown beans and some bacon. He put some river water on to boil for the beans and coffee. Then he set in to sort the beans. Gave him plenty of time to think about the boy and his trustworthiness—armed, he might— no—he shook his head. He'd give Toby a chance, but the boy had better not disappoint him. At last, the beans were on to cook. He sliced off some bacon to toss in. Toby came back and told him the job at the grave was done—did he want to check it?

The sun was dropping low in the west. He considered the boy's question and answered him. "Go find that pistol. I'll have food here in a while. I trust you did a good job."

"Yes, sir."

When the youth rode off, Herschel went to the rise and looked in approval at the marker and the pile of fresh soil and rocks. Hard to believe it contained his friend. Tougher even to think about the task of telling Barley's wife. Heart would be torn up by her loss.

He looked at the thunderheads piling up in the south.

Sunset bled on the taller towering ones. Better try to make them a shelter. He hurried back to camp and stretched some of the ropes he found from tree to tree. With the wagon sheet from the rustlers' things, he soon had a tent up. He looked up from driving some quickly hacked-out stakes to hold it down when the boy arrived on the run.

"I see you got some shelter," Toby said, jumping off his horse.

"Better get our saddles in under it." Herschel used the small shovel for a hammer to finish the job.

"Looks like a mean storm," Toby said, unlacing his latigos.

"It'll be bad enough," Herschel agreed, and threw his own saddle inside. They were better off there than on the trail, anyway. Thunder growled like a mad silver-tip grizzly and the storm opened its huge mouth to eat them.

When the first winds, filled with the sourness of rain, struck, Herschel knew the beans would never be done before the storm came. The few airtight tins of tomatoes and peaches he'd found would have to be their supper, along with the fried bacon.

"I'll get the coffee. We can have it, anyway," he said as Toby finished hobbling the horses and came on the run.

Fierce gusts threatened him as he used his kerchief for a holder to carry the granite pot and ran for the "tent" Toby held open for him. The canvas sides danced in the wind and pulled at the tie-downs as their world turned into darkness. Big drops began to batter the material; soon pea-sized hail struck and made the tent's sides drum, as bolts of blinding lightning flashed and deafening thunder boomed. Seated on the ground, cradling a cup of hot coffee in his hand, Herschel listened to the storm.

A limb cracked overhead, broke off, struck the tent's top, then toppled off, but the structure held.

"Heckuva storm," Toby said.

"Yeah," said Herschel. "It's like he wants to tear us from this earth."

"I never thought of it like that. But I've been in some bad ones that sure tried to get me."

Thunder rolled across the land. Tall cloud tops, still in sunlight, were laced with brilliant streaks of lightning. It would be a tough night. They'd be lucky if his makeshift shelter lasted till the storm was over.

Rain began again, then big drops, and the world grew darker. Soon pea-sized hail began to rap the sides of the tent again. Waves of thunder boomed again. Lightning illuminated the boy's solemn face as they sat out the fierce weather.

In a while, the rain let up, but the storm stayed around them. Herschel looked out, and could see more dark clouds churning like a stampede coming in their direction.

"Don't count your chickens yet," he said. "The next round is coming."

Toby stood up and stretched all he could under the canvas. "I'm plumb grateful for this tent."

Herschel turned back from the gathering weather and nodded. "I'd gave my soul a couple of times driving cattle to have had one like it. 'Cept there weren't any trees down there to tie it on."

They both laughed.

"Oh, yeah. I found my gun." Toby started to take it out.

Herschel shook his head. "In the morning, you better take it apart and clean it. I don't figure you plan on killing me."

Toby's face turned red in the dim light. "No, sir."

"Clean it up. A gritty gun won't work when you need it."

"Yes, sir. This deputy that Hootie shot, he was your friend?"

"Yeah, we knew each other for years. Helped me get elected. Had lots of good advice."

"I had a good pal once. We borrowed some horses and ran off together twice. Our pas must have got tired of running us down the second time and gave up on us. Johnny was good-looking and all the girls liked him. Dark eyes and real curly hair. I was surprised he wanted to go with me.

"We was in west Texas and he got the bends. You know bending over, hugging his guts, and about crying from the pain. Weren't no doctor out there—nothing. He died two days later under a mesquite tree, and all I could do for him was hold his hand and cry."

"Bad deal for you to go through."

Toby nodded quickly in agreement. "I packed him over his horse and rode another day to borrow a shovel off a Messikin to bury him. And you know, Sheriff? Things ain't gone good for me since then."

"How did you ever get hooked up with Brown?" Herschel turned his ear to listen to more thunder roll. It was coming back.

"I did some horse wrangling on roundups. You know, that's the worst job in camp. Frenchy told Brown I was good with wrangling horses. So he said for me to come along."

"Who's this Frenchy?"

"A cowboy, I thought. Dicky and I met him after roundup and we were out of work. Frenchy's older and he knew Brown, so I figure they had worked together before."

"Frenchy wanted anywhere?"

"I can't say. You know, you meet lots of cowboys looking over their shoulders a lot and don't ask no questions."

Herschel nodded. He never believed his best friend Buck Jones had murdered his wife and her lover. But they hung him for it after some Texas deputy sheriff finally ran him down in Dodge and took him back for trial.

The boys in the cow camp considered jumping that banty-legged badge toter and giving Jones a head start, but in the end, Jones waved them off. "Hell, they ain't going to do nothing to me back there."

Herschel never took that answer for the truth from the hard look on the deputy's face. Buck might not have told them all of it. Men like that always tell their side as they see it.

"Tell me what happened here," Herschel said.

"Your man, the deputy—he rode up where I was gathering the horses."

Herschel nodded for him to continue and took a seat. It would be raining again in a few minutes.

"He told me who he was and asked me to give him my gun. I did. Figured we were caught."

"Where was Brown?"

Toby shook his head. "I ain't sure. Maybe out scouting. I told your man he wasn't in camp. Your man—"

"Barley."

"Yeah, Barley and I rode into camp. Frenchy acted kind of prodded, but he dropped his gun. Dicky was beside himself. I mean upset. He never liked Brown or the deal from the start."

"He go for a gun?"

"No, sir. About then, Brown snuck up and got the drop on Barley. Dicky, he got all nervous and started to run off. Brown shot him. I never saw—"

Herschel turned an ear to the increasing rain as darkness settled in their world. "He ain't the first of his own men that Brown shot in the back."

"I don't doubt that. Anyway, we got on our horses and Brown said to get the horses moving, there'd be more law behind this one."

"When did he shoot Barley?"

"I guess when Frenchy and I were starting the horses in the Musselshell ford. I heard the shots, and pretty soon Brown caught up.

"Frenchy asked about our stuff in camp. I wouldn't of asked Brown nothing 'cause he was mad as a rabid dog. Figured my life wasn't worth ten cents. 'We're getting out of here!' was all he said, and we headed north."

"Thanks," Herschel said, knowing the boy had had a hard time telling him the story.

The storm had returned in fury. Herschel sat in the darkness, listened to it batter their fragile shelter. Marsha and the girls were in the solid house at home. Barley Benton was resting on the rise above this copse of trees. Herschel would sure have to screw up lots of courage to tell Heart about him, and Billy Hanks's killers still walked the stormy night.

TWENTY-TWO

THEY hit their saddles in the predawn. Herschel checked the ford and figured they could cross, but they needed to be across before the water rose any higher. They'd picked the things they needed the most, loaded four panniers, and caught Barley's dun and another loose horse left behind to use as pack animals. The loose one was an older cow pony with white scars on his back who had taken up with their mounts. Herschel decided the rest of the stolen horses would be too scattered after the storm and take too much time to recover—so his decision was push on after the outlaws.

Herschel and Toby gnawed on some jerky for breakfast on top of the far bank of the river, then turned their wet-bellied ponies and headed north. In the weak cloud-shrouded light, Herschel looked back, grateful they were across the stream—the river would surely rise all day. He knew the outlaws' tracks were gone, but he led the way north. The outlaws couldn't hide their horse tracks for long.

At mid-morning, he discovered signs and they nodded to each other. They were on the right course. By noon, Herschel found an old cow camp where the outlaws had corralled their horses. The roof had fallen in on the shack, but a nearby shed must have been their shelter during the storm the night before. Squatted on his haunches, he found some recent cigarette butts on the floor.

"They both smoke?"

Toby nodded.

Stiff, Herschel rose and flexed his tight shoulder. "They were here last night."

"Then we ain't far behind?"

"Half a day. They're probably hungry, ain't no sign of a cooking fire here."

"They ain't got nothing to cook or cook it in."

"Right, we have it. So they'll strike for a place that has food."

"I never been in this country before—and I ain't coming back." Toby looked around in disgust at the abandoned camp.

"This was probably built by some of the first cow outfits came up here," said Herschel. He swung on Cob ready to go.

The tracks became easy to follow from there. Herschel set Cob in a long trot and they ate up lots of ground. They found a used road with wagon tracks cut through the short grass that was waving in the afternoon wind. The horse sign went east on it.

In the late afternoon, Herschel spotted a soddy. The small house looked freshly built and sat on a rise with wash flapping on a line. Not a tree for miles, not a soul in sight. A half-acre of hilled corn churned out of the prairie. The plants in the hills looked pale; their sheaths rattled in the wind when Herschel and Toby rode by them.

The front door stood open, and that made Herschel frown. Perhaps someone was home. He dismounted heavily, straightened the crotch of his pants, removed his hat, then called out. "Hello."

No answer.

"Look over there," Toby said.

"What's that—" Herschel blinked. Then he saw the small multicolored dog in the grass beside the house, shot several times.

A knot rose in his throat. He unholstered his gun and barged in the door. In the dim light coming in the bottle window, he saw the woman's pale flesh and the crimson blood. The long hair obscured her face and he turned to block the door.

"Bad?" Toby asked, stopped short by Herschel in the doorway.

"Real bad." His gun arm hung like a pendulum at his side.

"What're we going to do?"

Herschel drove the Colt back in his holster, feeling useless. "Bury her and leave a note. No telling when her man will be back."

"Bad, huh?"

Herschel stepped aside and let him in. He went out and squatted on his heels. What kind of a killer was this Brown? Shot his own man, raped and murdered an innocent woman. He needed to be removed from society.

Seconds later, Toby came out and made it a few feet before he vomited. Bent over, he choked and then puked some more. "Jesus, that's bad. I never—"

"Best we get that shovel. You start the hole and I'll wrap her body up in some quilts. Then I'll come help you."

"Where?" Toby blinked his watery eyes and wiped his mouth on the kerchief.

"On the high point, I guess," said Herschel.

"Yes, sir."

Two hours later, they ate some pancakes Herschel cooked and spread on them some lick, a sorghum and molasses mixture the woman kept in a crock. It was a quiet meal and they ate outside off tin plates. Neither man had said much since the brief funeral and Herschel's terse words over her body wrapped in the blood-soaked blankets.

"I need to write her man a letter."

Toby took off his hat, scratched his thatch of hair, and nodded. "You better. I ain't no good at words."

Herschel took a pencil and some paper from his saddlebags and they went inside. Toby lighted a couple of candles.

To her family,

> *We found her murdered, no doubt at the hands of an outlaw called Hootie Brown who we are chasing. Not knowing your time of returning, we buried her on the rise and spoke the word of the Lord over her as best we could. Regretful we cannot look you up but we did the best we could.*

> *God bless you*

Herschel Baker, Sheriff Yellowstone County

Billings, Montana Territory

"I sure don't aim to sleep in here tonight," Toby said, hugging his arms and looking around in the dimly lit interior.

"Me, either," Herschel said, and put a saltcellar on the paper to weigh it down if the door blew open before the man came back. He put out the candles and went through the doorway into the twilight after Toby.

"You reckon we can catch him—Brown, I mean?"

Herschel considered the last rosy light of day on the western horizon. "We ain't stopping till we do."

"I better clean my gun, then, just in case."

"Good idea."

At dawn, they pulled out with their packhorses, and at mid-morning, they met a wagon coming on the road. Herschel spotted it a mile away and shared a grim nod with Toby. The meeting he faced wouldn't be nice—no way. He hoped the man was strong.

At last, the homesteader reined up two large draft horses. Young and fresh-faced, he set the brake and nodded to both of them, using the stop for a chance to roll himself a smoke.

"How's it going today?" he asked.

Herschel stepped down and gave Toby the reins. "You mind getting down?"

The man looked at both of them. "No, what's wrong?" He blinked and looked hard as if disturbed by the request. "I ain't done nothing wrong."

"It ain't you."

"Oh." And he bailed off and stuck the roll-your-own cigarette in his lips. "What is it—" He was trying to strike a light when Herschel reached out and stayed his hand.

"We have some bad news. Is that new soddy back there yours?"

"Something wrong with my Dorie—" His eyes opened wide.

With the man's hand still in his grasp, Herschel nodded. "Yes, she was murdered yesterday."

"Oh. My God, no!" The man fell to his knees and began bawling like a baby.

Pale-faced, Toby stood by holding the horses, and shared a pained look with Herschel, then joined him in the search for some words of comfort for the distraught husband.

"We gave her a Christian burial."

"Oh, no," the man cried out. "Why my Dorie—"

"Mister, I'm sorry, but did you pass two men on this road?"

"Yes, after I left Edwards."

"That a town?"

"Got a bar, store, and wagon yard."

"Good. They'll stop there," Herschel said.

"Went after some handles for my cultivator." The man snuffed his nose and wiped the free tears off his cheeks onto his sleeve. "I was only gone a day." Then his eyes turned to coal. "Them two kill her?"

Herschel nodded. "Why do you ask?"

"I gave them the makings not two hours ago. Said they was out and said that they'd waved at Dorie riding by yesterday—sonsabitches."

"You can leave Brown and Frenchy to us. We'll get them. Go home and cultivate your corn. It'll help take your mind off the loss of her."

"He your deputy?"

Herschel looked over at Toby and considered him. "Yes, he's my deputy." He'd give Toby a chance.

The man staggered to his feet. "Guess I owe you two."

"No, but we need to get after Brown."

"I hope he hangs forever on that hangman's rope strangling to death," the man said through his teeth.

Herschel nodded and mounted Cob. They had work to do. "I never caught your name."

"Argus McCord."

"God be with you, Argus McCord," he said, and nodded to his new deputy to ride.

An hour later, they spotted the buildings that marked Edwards. Two false-front stores and a low rambling soddy with pens alongside that had to be the wagon yard. One store was actually a saloon. Herschel could read TEXAS SALOON in big black letters on the graying boards. EDWARDS MERCANTILE was on the second store. If those two killers were still there, they must have put their saddle horses in the yard pens. No horses were hitched at the racks. No one was in sight. Only an azure sky, a bright midday sun—not a tree for shade or even a cur dog to bark at Herschel and Toby.

"You ride around the back of the saloon," Herschel said under his breath. "One of them two busts out—shoot them. If they don't stop and surrender, you shoot them. You're a deputy sheriff."

"I-I never shot no one."

Leaning back, Herschel jerked out the rifle, levered a cartridge in the chamber, and put it back on safety. Straightening in the saddle, he said, "I know that. But you remember they're killers and they won't hesitate to kill you."

Toby swallowed hard and nodded with a grim set of his mouth. He reined his bay to ride around the saloon and set out in a trot.

Herschel kept riding Cob straight toward the saloon. He noted Toby's disappearance behind the building. When Herschel was two hundred feet from the batwing doors, they parted and a rough-dressed, white-bearded black man stepped into the sunlight. In his right hand, he held a pistol aimed at Herschel.

"If you're the law, mister, you be dead."

"Brown?" Herschel asked and, using Cob as a shield,

dismounted. In one swift move, he jerked the Winchester out of the scabbard. He knew he had to chance Brown shooting the horse because the outlaw would know that Herschel would come up firing. Herschel counted on him being a dedicated killer and not wanting to waste a shot at Cob. A shout at the roan and it bolted forward. He dropped to his knees, rifle to his shoulder, and saw the black smoke from Brown's pistol barrel through his sights. In a fluid motion, Herschel squeezed the trigger and acrid smoke blew in his eyes. Through the tears, he watched the big man stagger backward to the door frame from the force of the bullet, and despite his wound, begin to raise the six-gun again.

The second round from Herschel's .44/40 struck Brown in the chest and smoke began to come from the bullet hole in his vest. He slumped down to his butt and dropped his chin.

Several shots from behind the saloon forced Herschel to rise and run for the saloon's batwing doors. He wondered if Brown was playing possum and might make one last try to kill him. Only a few feet from the boardwalk, he decided the man was unconscious or dead, and he hit the doors holding the rifle in front of him and shouting, "U.S. marshal!"

The bartender raised his hands behind the bar.

"Which way did Frenchy go?" He surveyed the empty place.

The shocked man indicated the open back door, and Herschel headed for the well-lit frame with sunlight streaming in.

"Toby? Toby!" he shouted as he ran.

"I'm all right, Sheriff. I'm all right."

In the doorway, Herschel stopped and glanced down at the foot of the stairs and the buckskin-clad figure sprawled facedown among the brown bottles. The bulldog pistol in his right hand still smoked.

"You sure you're okay?" He looked hard at the boy, who was collapsed cross-legged on the ground.

Toby nodded. "It ain't easy killing someone, is it?"

"No."

"I knew when he came through that door and looked at me I was dead. How he missed me I don't know, and I shut my damn eyes and went to shooting at him with both hands. I must have opened my eyes sometime. . . ." He stood up and holstered his gun. "You get Brown?"

"Yes. I don't know how you feel about drinking whiskey, but we need something." He reached down and turned Bateau over. His brown eyes stared into eternity. Three wounds in his chest wept lots of blood.

"Come on in, I'm buying."

A smile of relief crossed Toby's face, and he removed his hat to wipe his forehead on his dusty sleeve. "I didn't know if I had it in me."

Herschel nodded and started inside. He almost bumped into the curious bartender.

"He dead, too?" the man asked, letting both of them by.

"Yes, can we get a grave dug for them?"

"One or two?"

"One's fine with me. They can share it going to hell." Herschel headed for the bar with Toby in tow.

"Cost you ten bucks. Coffins are more."

"Toss them in the hole and cover them up."

"You don't want a coffin?" The man blinked and wiped the bar with his rag.

"No. Good whiskey, a bottle and two glasses. Can you get us some food?"

"Ah, yes. Steak and bread okay?"

Herschel looked at Toby for his answer.

The youth pulled out a chair at a table. "Fine, I could eat a bear."

Herschel turned back to the man. "That's what we want, and a ten-dollar funeral."

"That's just for digging the hole."

"He can cover them up, too, for that."

"No services?"

Herschel set the bottle and glasses on the table. A thread of anger was in his voice. "You go see about our food and the undertaker. They're both too far gone to pray over. Now go."

He poured some whiskey in Toby's glass, and watched him lift the glass with both hands and sip deep.

"Easy, this stuff is like a mule, it'll have a big kick."

Toby stopped drinking. "I need a kick."

"It'll be all right after a while," Herschel promised him, and let the first shot slide down his throat and cut the dust. There hadn't been many times in his life when he figured he needed a drink—this was one of those days.

A man in his forties stuck his head inside. "This Hootie Brown out here?"

"He used that name," Herschel said.

"Where's his partner?" the man asked.

"Out back."

"You know there's a two-fifty reward on Brown and Bateau," the man said.

Herschel frowned at Toby. "You know what that means?"

The youth put his whiskey glass down. "No, what's that?"

"We need to get an ax and take their heads with us."

Toby slid his glass over for a refill and his shoulders quaked in a big shudder. "I'll sure need to drink me some more whiskey for that job."

Herschel refilled his glass halfway and they both laughed.

TWENTY-THREE

Horses gathered, saddled, and packs loaded, both Herschel and Toby still hung over, the two started south at daybreak. Herschel had picked out Barley's dun for Toby to ride. It was the only horse that he could give the kid a bill of sale for, and somehow he felt Barley would have given him the horse if he'd been alive. They drove the other horses.

"I'm sure glad you got them fellas to sign the paper that they saw Hootie and Frenchy dead and we didn't need to pack their heads back for proof," Toby said as they rode stirrup to stirrup.

Herschel agreed with a nod. At the moment, his mind was on how tough it would be for him to tell Heart about her husband's death. The next day or so would be hard. Dread stabbed his chest as he rode in a long trot.

At midday, they rested and grained the saddle horses to keep them moving. There was no sign of the homesteader when they rode by his place, but his grazing horses raised their heads and nickered. Herschel and Toby rode on. Herschel wondered what he'd do if someone had killed Marsha—probably spend the rest of his life crying.

"What are you going to do next?" Toby asked after bringing back one of the horses that had strayed.

"Go home. After I see Barley's widow and then get on a stage for Nebraska. There's a killer down there I'm going to bring in."

Toby shook his head and looked over at Herschel. "I thought you had deputies."

"I do, but I can't ask one of my men to do my job."

Toby squinted over at him. "I don't think you're like other sheriffs."

"I can't tell," he said, and motioned him to boot their horses to go faster.

The long day passed with many miles covered. At sundown, they crossed the Musselshell, turned the hobbled horses loose to graze, and made camp in the twilight.

"What are you going to do next?" Herschel asked Toby as they sat on the ground and listened to some coyotes yap.

Toby tossed some sticks on the fire. "Guess look for work."

"You know, there's other things to do besides cowboy."

"I'd been thinking on that for a while now."

"When we get to Barley's place tomorrow, we're splitting. I'm giving you the dun horse and a bill of sale. Some cash I have on me, so that'll be your share. But I want you to line out, find a real job, and make something out of yourself."

"You're serious, ain't yah?"

"Serious as I ever get."

"Whew—I never—I never figured it would end like this." He wiped his forehead on the back of his hand in the flickering light.

"How did you figure it would end?"

"Figured I'd do hard time, be lucky not to be lynched."

Herschel nodded. "Well, you have a chance many don't ever get, don't waste it."

"I promise I won't."

"Good enough. Let's get some sleep."

"If I can even sleep." Toby shook his head in dismay.

Late afternoon the next day, they split. Toby rode south and Herschel took the trail-broke herd and headed southwest for Heart's place.

He let the loose horses stop and graze while he rode up to the yard gate, and she ran out of the house to greet him. Halfway to him, she stopped. "He's dead, isn't he?"

He put his arm on her shoulder and managed a raspy, "Yes."

She buried her face in his vest. His hands felt strange—like they were trespassing, holding her as she wept.

"I'm sorry I was too late," he said.

She raised her wet brown eyes in the flare of the sundown's last fire. "Oh, he knew his way. He would not have waited even for you."

Herschel nodded. "That was his way."

"I am sorry his best friend had to bring me such news."

All he could do was nod. There was no way to swallow the knot behind his tongue.

He left the extra horses there, planning to send for them later.

Close to dawn, he reached home and dismounted. He glanced up when the back door slammed open. Skirt in hand, Marsha crossed the yard. "You're back. You're back."

He wrapped his arms around her and rested his cheek on her head. "I'm back."

"You sound sad." She raised her face to look at him in the first light.

"Some rustlers killed Barley."

"Oh, no." Her eyes filled with tears. "I'm so sorry."

"Any trouble here?"

She shook her head and fingered his vest. "I lost the baby."

"Oh." He looked pained at her.

"I'm fine now. But I told you all of them weren't made to come into this world."

He hugged her. "Sorry I wasn't here."

"I'm so glad you're back—safe."

"Let me get Cob put up."

"Fine. I'll go make some breakfast." She smiled through her sparkling tears. "I prayed a lot for you."

"Must have worked." He laughed and led Cob off to be unsaddled.

The next day at mid-morning, the mayor burst into Herschel's office waving the newspaper. "More of these headlines and Billings will never be the railroad center of the Yellowstone River Valley."

"What did they say today?"

"Sheriff Saves Trial Costs." The mayor thumped on the page with his fingers to show the story. "This sort of thing—"

"McKay, we can't stop them from printing that stuff. It sells papers."

"But if the Northern Pacific—"

"How did you do raising money for my trip to Nebraska?" He had little time for the man's ranting.

"Oh, my, I have close to two hundred dollars."

Herschel leaned back in his swivel chair and tented his fingers. "Good, gather it up. I'm heading for Ogallala."

"Now? I mean right now?"

"Yes, the sooner I have Casey Ford in jail, the sooner I'll be able to enjoy my family."

"But they say that's a vast area and not controlled by any law."

"That's why he is down there."

McKay leaned forward with his fingertips on the desk. "But you have no authority—"

"I have a deputy U.S. marshal's commission."

"Good." The mayor straightened. "I will collect what money I can get and be back in the morning."

"Fine."

He saw the mayor to the doorway and nodded to Phil. "What else is news?"

"Well, Ida Crowley has agreed to marry me." The deputy swallowed hard.

"Wonderful news."

"I thought so."

"Send someone after Art. I need to speak to him."

"He's probably sleeping. He's been doing the night watchman shifts since Dave broke his leg."

"We better go to billing McKay for our services."

"You think he'll pay us?"

"No, but he will get a bill. I'll speak to Art later."

"I overheard you say that you were going after Ford—"

Herschel nodded, deep in his own thoughts about all he must do first. "Yes, I plan to leave as soon as possible. No new information about the lynching, is there?"

"Nothing. Been pretty quiet. Except for some rowdy cowboys in town."

"I'll need to hire another deputy, too. Barley gone and all." The thought of his loss stabbed him. "I need to send someone out to his place and bring in those horses I recovered."

"Oh, yes, the telegram is back from Wells Fargo. They will pay the reward on those two."

"Fine. But they'll be months sending the money, I'd bet."

Phil shook his head. "Supposed to be here in a few days."

"Good, I'm going down and arrange for my stage tickets to Cheyenne. I can catch an eastbound train from there and be in Ogallala in a few days."

"Big country and they say there ain't much law up in the panhandle, either."

"Ford's there, I'll find him."

"I don't doubt it. There was a fella by here looking for work the other day. Said he'd worked law in Kansas. I never figured we'd need someone."

"See if you can find him if he ain't left town. I'd sure talk to him. Anyone with experience would be valuable."

"His name was Ty something. I see him, I'll tell him."

"Good. I'll go down and see Lem Pascal at the stables and get him to send one of his work hands up there after those horses."

"Word's out, you know, by October there will be quarter of a million new cattle up here. They left Texas last spring."

Herschel looked hard at his deputy. "I guess they haven't learned yet. No hay, no cattle, come the Chinooks."

"Another bad winter and even the rich ones will know."

"You're right. Think of the name of that lawman from Kansas. Tell him to drop by." Herschel went back into his office for his hat and gun. Lem should be able to send someone after the horses.

"I'll find him if he hasn't gone on."

Herschel agreed, left the courthouse, and walked the block to Lem's stable.

"Morning," Lem said, and swung his boots off the desk when Herschel came to the office door. "You're about a stranger around here."

"Been busy."

"Come in. I was sorry to hear about Benton."

"Damn shame." Herschel took a kitchen chair and sat down. "I need you to send a hand up there and bring some horses back from his place. We can pay them out of the claims fees."

"No problem. But I've been surprised that you haven't kicked that reporter's butt."

Herschel smiled. "Trying to be respectable."

Lem scowled. "I'm sure tired of him."

"Maybe they can get up a good candidate for sheriff against me."

"Hogwash." Lem cut him a disapproving look. "They can't field anyone that is electable."

"We'll see. I'm heading for Nebraska to find Casey Ford, probably leave in a few days. I want you and some more men to carry deputy badges while I'm gone."

Lem rubbed the top of his legs with his palms. "I've never been one, but I'd sure try to back your men up."

"Good, think of a few more."

"I'll do that. What else?"

"Gather those horses in and I should be back in a week or ten days." He stood.

"I can handle that."

"You ever hear any word about the Billy Hanks lynching?"

Lem shook his head and made a grim face. "Lots of talk, but nothing real solid about it. Folks speculate a lot."

"Listen close."

"I'm glad you ain't forgot him. Someone did that for a reason, and I ain't buying horse rustling."

Herschel stopped in the doorway, his back to Lem, and considered the matter again. "I'm not either. See you."

"Any time."

He left the stables and headed across the street for the stage office. Jim Brooks was working under a celluloid visor, and looked up from his work when Herschel entered the office of the Yellowstone Overland.

"What can I do for you?"

"In the morning I want a seat on the southbound coach."

"No problem. Put your money away. Ticket's on us."

Herschel looked hard at him. "I can afford one."

"Nope." Brooks rose and came over to the counter. "Where are you headed?"

"Ogallala."

"When you get to Cheyenne, show that deputy U.S. marshal badge to the train master. He'll give you some passes."

"How did you know about that?"

"My business to know, and I know about the Fargo reward. Brown was really wanted for his activities against Wells Fargo."

"He won't do anything again."

"I wish we could tone down the damn paper's rhetoric."

"Guess that's their right."

Brooks gave him a hard glare. "Enough is enough."

"What time does she pull out?"

"Seven sharp."

"I'll be here."

He hiked home from there. The girls were all under sunbonnets and hoeing in the garden. They looked up in relief at the sight of him.

"Daddy's back," Nina said, and they came marching out of the neat garden with their hoes on their shoulders. Sarah came at the end eating raw green pea pods.

"Everything at the office all right?" Marsha asked, looking relieved he had come back.

"Fine. I need to pack a few things. I'm going to Nebraska in the morning and find Ford."

She nodded. "I figured that. We'll miss you."

"I'll miss you, too. But I won't be satisfied until he and his henchman are behind bars."

She put the crook of her arm out for him. "No rock unturned—" Then she laughed and tossed her head back. "I sure hope these folks appreciate all you are doing."

"Me, too."

They made ice cream with the crank machine and he played music. It was a free day and the girls danced. Herschel forgot about his problems and enjoyed the company. Kate told him Phil was marrying Ida Crowley and he told her that he had heard.

She wrinkled her nose. "I guess that's the way things go. Teach them to dance and they leave you."

He hugged her. "Oh, he was a little old. A handsome prince will come by and sweep you off your feet."

She frowned. "A nice cowboy would be fine."

Herschel laughed and ate some more of the rich vanilla strawberry ice cream. With a shared look across at Kate, Marsha nodded in approval over his answer to her eldest.

"You have plenty of time," Kate's mother said, and then looked at heaven for help.

In late afternoon, he went back by the sheriff's office and found Art looking sleepy-eyed sitting on the edge of Phil's desk.

"Hear you're going after Ford."

"Right. Sorry about the night watchman job. You still look sleepy."

"I'm feeling worse about Barley. I know you are. Damn shame."

Herschel agreed. He'd tried to sweep the whole thing under the rug, but it wasn't staying under it well. Every time someone mentioned Barley, there was a lump in Herschel's throat, and he tried not to see the fresh grave above the Musselshell. That image might follow him forever.

"I got there too late," he said.

Art shook his head. "Some things can't be helped. Like they were going to happen anyway and there was nothing anyone could have done."

"Maybe. I'm headed for Ogallala in the morning."

"Phil said so. Can I hire that Kansas lawman?"

"You all find him?"

"I sent word. He's staying with someone south of the river."

"Keep an eye on him, this isn't one of those Kansas cow towns. What's his name?"

"Ty Martin."

"Never heard of him. Just watch him if you think he's all right and I'll be back."

"I hope you're back by the Fourth of July. Things can get rowdy that week."

Herschel left the office after going over some small details with Art. The hardest to leave again would be Marsha and the girls. After the nice afternoon of ice cream and music, he'd felt better than he had in days. Maybe when he had Ford rounded up, he could do more of the same.

The thought of Billy Hanks hanging in the lightning's flashes reminded him of another pressing matter. Ford needed to be dealt with, but so did Billy's death.

TWENTY-FOUR

Hᴇ left on the swinging stagecoach and headed for Sheridan and the long ride on to Cheyenne. With his rifle and saddle in the boot, this would be the quickest way. In three days he'd be at the railroad, and stiff as a board. He looked out the open window grateful for the morning's cool air. If there was anything left of him, he'd be in Sheridan that night. Seated in the back-facing seat, he viewed the man and woman across from him.

"Jerome Calhoun," the dapper-dressed man said. "This is Emma."

Herschel touched his hat and introduced himself. Calhoun was his age, in his thirties, with a trimmed thin mustache, a silk scarf, and a fine suit. Emma looked to be in her early twenties, maybe even younger. She wore a green silk dress and a wool shawl against the coolness. Her hazel eyes avoided him as if deliberately. Somehow, the pair did not match. He'd almost thought Emma was a courtesan rather than a wife. Calhoun looked like a promoter or fancy tinhorn. No matter, they were southbound with him.

Once over the grade, the horses made good time going downhill. The driver on top, in a loud voice, called the horses by name when they weren't doing right. How he knew them apart, Herschel could never figure, since they changed teams and animals so much, but this driver did, or pretended he did.

"We're going to Buffalo, Wyoming," Calhoun said. "I'm looking for some investments."

"Nice place. Been through there several times bringing up herds."

"Should be some there."

"They say that there's coal in the Powder River country." Calhoun said it more as a question than a statement.

"I guess there could be, but it's so far from anything. I doubt it would be worth much."

"Ah, the future."

"In a couple hundred years." Herschel chuckled at his own idea, and gazed out the window. They'd pass the site of Custer's demise sometime later in the day. Lots of settlers were taking up land along the streams. Get rid of the buffalo and Indians and the cattle came, behind them plodded the farmer.

"You aren't impressed with such resources," Calhoun said.

"I wouldn't know how to get it from the ground or how to sell it." He still could not figure out Emma, who reminded him of one of the girls' best china-faced dolls. Oh, well, she was no concern of his.

Through the day, the stage made stops and changed teams. The fly-infested outhouses offered little solace for the traveler, who just wanted to get in and get out. Any food served in the stopovers tasted rancid and old—left over from something the last passersby didn't eat. Even the coffee tasted bitter and scorched. It no doubt had pan-browned barley for its base. In Sheridan, they'd lay over two hours, the driver said, but that would be late at night. Herschel curbed his appetite and lasted until they rolled up the streets past the lighted businesses.

"We should find some fine cuisine here," Calhoun said, and smiled at the silent Emma.

"Yes," tumbled off her lips in a quiet whisper.

She could talk, Herschel realized, and he nodded in approval at her. "The Grand Café is the best place. I've eaten there."

"Show us the way."

"Certainly," Herschel said as the driver opened the door.

"Two hours and we pull out," the man said.

"We will be here," Herschel promised. He planned not to miss it.

The restaurant meal of roast beef went well, and Emma even ate some from her plate, though he suspected she never ate much. After supper, the three strode back to the stage office.

"I may step in a den of iniquity for a moment if you would show her to the stage office," Calhoun said.

"Sure." Herschel nodded at Emma and she went along without a word.

Two doors down, Calhoun went in the swinging doors.

"He a good gambler?" he asked her casually to make conversation.

"He's a gambler."

"He must win sometimes."

She raised her eyebrows and shook her head at him. "Yes, he won me."

"Won you?" The notion slapped him between the eyes.

She nodded and kept on walking.

"Excuse me. The sale of anyone is prohibited by federal law."

She looked up at him and smiled. "Blacks maybe, but not women."

"I'm a federal marshal."

"Thanks, but nothing you can do. A soiled woman has few choices."

"You mean nothing you can do but be a slave?"

"The alternatives are not very pretty."

The time slipped by as they waited in the stage office, and Calhoun still did not return. The driver looked up and down the dark boardwalk, grumbling about his absence.

"I can—" Herschel started up to go after him, but Emma's hand touching his forearm stopped him.

"He knows when the stage leaves," she said.

He settled back and nodded. "Shall we get on board?"

She took his arm and he helped her inside, then climbed up. The driver shut the door and the coach rocked when he went up on top. The lines in his hands, he shouted to the horses, and they were off for Big Horn and Buffalo in the darkness of night. Some dim-lit lanterns hung on the coach, but the driver needed to know the road for he had to go by feel in the starlight.

Herschel pulled the hat down over his face and slumped down to try to sleep.

"Thank you," she said in a smoky voice.

He raised his hat and looked in her shadowy direction. "What's that for?"

"For not going after him."

He smiled. "No problem, ma'am."

Two days later, he parted with Emma in Cheyenne. She refused his offer of money and when he last saw her, she was walking away with her carpetbag. Head high and proud as anyone, she soon disappeared. He hoisted his saddle on his shoulder and with his rifle and war bag in his other hand, headed for the train depot. The next eastbound passenger train would be there in two hours, which meant he'd be in Ogallala by the next day. Maybe he could sleep on the train. He hoped so.

During his wait, he left his gear with the ticket agent and found a café, where he ate some better beef and frijoles. In Montana, the brown beans were scarce. So it was a treat. Cooked long in smoky ham and onions with a hint of Mexican spices, it reminded him of the food on the cattle drives.

Full at last, he headed back for the brick depot. Cheyenne at night sounded quiet compared to the old days. But it had grown, and many men dressed like Calhoun—Eastern-fancy, not nearly like the drovers he recalled from past visits. Maybe the drovers just weren't up there yet. What did Phil say? Big herds were coming in the fall.

In the morning sun, he dismounted from the train in Ogallala. Plenty of wagons were choking the streets and lots of honyockers were strolling on the boardwalks. Farmers with bib overalls had obviously found that end of Nebraska. The Sioux were all on reservations up in South Dakota, which opened lots of country for homesteading. Some great grassland, in his opinion, lay north of the Platte for many miles. A shame to bust it up for crops, but they would. Somewhere up there, Casey Ford and his henchman were camped out. Herschel would find them.

"Baker! Herschel Baker!"

He turned and saw a familiar face coming through the wagons and parked rigs. Texas Jack Bailey, with his long curly blond hair and buckskin-fringed shirt, was booting his buckskin pony and soon drew up in front of Herschel. A longtime friend from the cattle drives.

He blinked his blue eyes at Herschel. "Thought you were in Montana."

"I am."

"How the hell come I'm seeing you here?"

"Long story. Get down and I'll buy you a beer."

"Man, you must have sold the herd, if you've got enough money to buy me a beer." He swung down. "What're you doing here?" He jerked off his fringed glove and shook Herschel's hand.

"Looking for some killers. I'm the sheriff of Yellowstone County."

"Damn, that's impressive. Let's go inside and have that beer. I'm dying of thirst."

They climbed the porch and entered the yellow sunlit canvas tent behind the false front. A crowd dressed in everything from suits to overalls was shouting over a faro wheel. They found a space at the bar. Herschel had left his gear and saddle at the depot until he could find a horse.

They ordered beers, took them to a vacant table, and sat.

"I heard about you losing your brother," Texas said, and slouched in the captain's chair.

"Been a while," Herschel agreed. "I have a wife and three girls now."

"Well, my lands, that ain't filtered down my way."

"Great woman and her daughters are four, seven, and ten."

"You look like you've done fine. Bet she's a looker." Texas shoved his hat back on his shoulders and laughed.

"Marsha's a handsome woman."

"I bet she is. I'll have to see her sometime. Who are you after down here?"

"Looking for a man killed some folks and his hench-man. Casey Ford and some out-of-work cowboy called Chub."

"Casey Ford—he got a scar on the right side of his face?"

"Yes, you know him?"

"He ain't worth much. He robbed a bunch of our riders of all their money when they got drunk once in Dodge. He told them they spent it—but we figured it out later."

"Lucky he didn't cut your throat. He did that to a man and woman he robbed in Montana."

His stein of beer halfway to his mouth, Texas stopped, frowned, and shook his head in disgust. "The worthless outfit."

"He's that all right. You on any payroll?"

"No, why?"

"I can pay two bucks a day. Ride with me up there and we'll find this no-account."

"You've done hired you a posse man, sonny boy."

They shook hands on the deal. Herschel ordered another round and sat back. He had a man could handle himself. They'd choused enough cattle out of the Lone Star State to cover Kansas over in cowhides if they all were laid out. No one he'd like better at his back when a fight broke out than Texas Jack Bailey.

They left the saloon and went to find Herschel a saddle horse and a pack mule. After two hours dickering, Herschel owned a big bay to strap his saddle on, plus a long-legged red mule to carry their bedding and gear. He was pleased when they had the things they needed in panniers at the livery by supper time, including food for the trip and their animals.

They left Ogallala before sunup with a few tips that Texas learned, somewhere along Pine Ridge they should find Ford. It was only a tip, but he felt certain that someone might know something or had heard about Ford. Worth heading that way anyhow for starters.

They pushed hard, covering forty miles, and found a ranch to stay at that evening. The cook was an old friend of Texas Jack called Toad. The short man had some large red growths like mushrooms on his face and the name suited his ugly looks, but he laughed a lot and fixed them steaks fried in tallow, although the crew had already eaten.

"What you doing up here?" Toad asked.

"Looking for some range for a herd," Texas said, and shared a quick look with Herschel to make sure he backed him.

"There's plenty grass," Toad said. "When is the herd coming?"

"Late, I figure. They've had trouble. Fences and hon-yockers down south."

Toad made a fist and raised it. "I would kill that one he made bob-wire, huh?"

"He'd be a good one to start on," Texas said as they stayed busy eating.

Herschel offered to pay him for the grub, but he waved it off. "I always feed the good ones I know passing through. Boss, he can afford it, he's got lots of money."

"Thanks."

"We have breakfast at four."

"We'll hear the triangle," Texas assured him.

"You fellas are really looking for grass," Toad said, "could have fooled me. I figured you were just drifting through."

They laughed, thanked him, and rolled out their bedding upwind from his fire's swirling smoke.

"No need to let out any word we're looking for Ford. He might get that message before we find him." With that said, Texas rolled over and went to sleep.

Herschel took a while longer. He wondered about Marsha and how she was making it. Heavens, she'd run a ranch by herself for two years before they married. Art and Phil surely could hold down the office and jail. If only they learned more about the lynching. Then he fell asleep.

At dawn, they were in the saddle and hauling the loaded mule over the next ridge. Herschel called him Red, and the long-legged stout horse Bay. They made good time, and reached a freighter stop by evening. Several double wagons were parked around some low-sided buildings, and lots of oxen were spread out grazing, when Herschel and Texas topped the ridge to view the place in the sunset.

"Amos Seaman's Ranch," Texas said. "We can rest our horses here a day and listen. There may be some hard cases here. So stay on guard. Several wanted men drift in and out of here all the time."

"Good idea. Make camp on the creek." Herschel followed the line of cottonwoods upstream as they rode off the rise.

"Yeah, after we eat and drink some of the old man's firewater. Want him to think we're only looking for a place to set a herd."

"Good notion," Herschel agreed. Texas would earn his money before this was over.

The hard-eyed freighting bunch in camp looked them over with suspicion when they rode up. They were an unshaven lot that hadn't bathed, and their clothes were soaked in road dust. They were snorting whiskey from crocks, and someone played a banjo. A half-drunk kid was hopping around like a clumsy black minstrel he'd seen somewhere on a stage.

A man stuck his head out the door of the hewn cottonwood log cabin. He had a long nose, a ring of black whiskers, and a shiny bald scalp. He spat tobacco to the side before he spoke. "That you, Texas?"

"Yeah, me and a pal, Amos."

"What brings you this far from a whorehouse?"

"Looking for some range where we ain't crowding in."

"Hell, don't lie to me. You want some sweet-grass country."

Texas looked at Herschel. They'd been caught. They dismounted heavily. It had been a long day. They'd trekked across forty miles. Herschel looked over at the revelers in the twilight, and the man with the banjo was still picking away. The dancer was on the ground lying on his back, as if he couldn't go another step.

"Come on in," said Amos. "The whiskey's hot and the girls ugly."

Texas nodded as they undid their saddle girths. "He ain't lying about that. Ugly women."

Herschel smiled and shook his head. Been a long time since he'd been on the move. He'd forgotten the road camps and the freighters. Most of the cargo they carried were supplies for the Indian reservations. Tough bunch of men, and it wasn't unusual for someone to be killed over cards or anything at every stopover.

The smoky yellow light in the interior came from candles. A hefty woman moved about serving the few customers and gathering dirty dishes. She used her large butt to intentionally bump men in the back when she went by, to get a reaction from them.

"Suppose you two ain't ate?" she said, more as a demand than a question, as she inspected them.

"No, we ain't ate," Texas said, and laughed.

"It ain't funny either." She went off in a huff cussing all late arrivals.

They took a bench behind a table with their backs to the wall. Soon, she brought them steaming coffee in tin cups, and mumbled that she'd have them food directly. Then she went by and propositioned a freighter, and when he agreed, she put a ham of a hand on the rise of her hip and glared back at Herschel and Texas. "I'll be ready, darling, when I get them fed," she said.

"Aw, I can wait that long, Cindy," the old man said.

When she brought their food, Texas stopped her. "We got an old friend up in this country owes us a few bucks, named Casey Ford. He ain't been in here lately, has he?"

She put the heaping plate of bread, beans, and stringy meat in front of Herschel, leaned over so he could see her cleavage if he wanted to, and then straightened as if thinking about the question.

"He was over on Blue Crick. But that cheap weasel hears you want money from him, he may ride to Dakota to get out of paying you."

"Cheap, is he?"

She looked at Texas like she couldn't believe he didn't know that. "We're talking about the same Casey Ford?"

"Got an ax scar on his right cheek." Texas pointed to that side of his face.

"Yeah, yeah, that's him. It's a gawdamn shame that was only a glancing blow. Should have chopped his head off." She put a plate down before Texas. "You can tell him Cindy Evans said stick it up his you-know-where."

Texas looked startled. "Why, I'd never believed that." Then he went to laughing and waved her on. "We're talking about the same fella. Except he owes me twenty bucks."

"You won't ever get it," she said over her shoulder. Then she stuck her large flabby arm out for the white-bearded freighter. "Darling, we've got business to tend to."

The old man jumped up, did a jig, and then locked his arm in hers. They went out the back way.

Texas looked after them and sat for a long moment tapping on his plate with his fork. Then he shook his head in amused disbelief. "Young love."

Herschel nodded. He now knew a possible place where Ford might be hiding out—Blue Crick, wherever that was located. The notion of being that close restored some of his confidence about finding his man that the vast rolling empty grasslands they'd crossed had wrung out of him getting to this place. Beyond the next horizon or even the next—Casey Ford was enjoying his last days as a free man, and probably his last days on earth. Herschel planned to make them as short as possible.

TWENTY-FIVE

THEY bedded down a half mile from Amos's place on the stream. Under the stars, they unloaded Red and set the panniers aside. After they watered the animals, feed bags were hung on them and they were hobbled. Herschel was anxious to get some sleep. He undid his bedroll, wrapped in the canvas ground cloth, and strung it out.

Texas squatted on his boot heels and smoked a roll-your-own. "You ever have a gut feeling about something?"

"Sure. Why?"

"I got me a big one tonight. That drunk kid dancing. I seen him somewheres before. He ain't with them freighters, I'd bet a month's pay. Something about him got me uneasy."

"Better to be ready than sorry. Wake me up when it's my turn." Herschel decided to sleep in his boots in case there was any trouble.

"I seen him before somewhere. Damn, I wish I could re-call where that was."

"It'll come to you." Herschel lay back and looked at the

starry sky. He'd rather have been in his own bed in Montana.
A million constellations, and a fiery comet sped over the
earth. He closed his eyes—been a long day.

"Hersch, be really easy," Texas whispered, waking him
from a sound sleep. "We're getting company. One's coming
down the creek side, and I seen another sticking his head up
to the north. I think they want our horses and mule."

Half awake, Herschel nodded, and his finger closed on
the grip of his .45. He rolled over and got on his hands and
knees beside his partner. Fully awake, he tried to see the one
in the north. The bay horse, a hundred feet away, had been
awakened, and to judge from his dark silhouette, the gelding
was looking in the direction of the invader.

"You get him. I'll get the one on the creek side."

"Right." He watched Texas slip off into the night in a low
run. Then he tried to focus on his man. In a low run, he
moved twenty feet closer to the horse, staying down, and
stopped to listen. All he could hear were the creek's murmur
and some crickets chirping away. The mule must be snoring
some, too, he decided, locating it beyond the bay.

Then he saw a bare head move, and wondered if the
thieves were Indians. It was moving toward Bay. He wondered how vulnerable Texas was as he cocked the .45. Then
the crack of the rifle from the watercourse was heard, and
Texas shouted for someone to halt. More shots.

Herschel was on his feet, gun ready, and moving past the
bay. "Put your hands up."

The cherry-red fire of a pistol shot cracked the night.
Herschel returned fire with deadly accuracy as he ran toward
the shooter. It spooked the mule, and he began to bray like
he was hit.

Herschel had no time. He rushed over and found the
would-be horse thief moaning on the ground. He ripped the

pistol from his fingers and checked him in the dim light for any more weapons.

"Oh, Gawd, I'm dying," the wounded man cried out.

"Mister. I ain't got one drop of sympathy for you. You'd'a killed me or Texas in a minute and stolen our horses if we hadn't figured you out."

"We never killed—nobody."

"But you stole lots of horses and left folks stranded and maybe they died 'cause of you."

"Never killed no—one."

"You ain't fetching no tears out from me. You better talk to your maker. I think you're going to see him soon." He looked in the direction of the stream, and in the starlight saw the familiar hat coming his way. "You all right?" he called to Texas.

"Fine. But my man's on his way to hell. I told him throw it down and he never listened."

"This one's going there, too."

"What's your name?" Texas demanded of the man Herschel had shot.

"John Smith."

"Bullshit, you're dying. I'll send a letter to your people and tell them you passed on. What is it?"

"Jenny Perkins, South Fork, Texas—tell her I was trying to—get home."

"Your mother?"

"No—my—w-wife."

"I'll do it." Texas looked closely at him. "He's gone to his place, too."

"I guess we can bury them tomorrow," Herschel said. "We've got all day."

"Yes, we have. I may need it to get enough sleep."

Herschel looked around. He would, too.

At dawn, Herschel rode in and borrowed a shovel. Amos

never asked why, simply handed him one and nodded. Herschel mumbled thanks and rode back. They worked for hours, taking turns digging the grave, and at last dumped the two bodies in minus their money, boots, and guns. Thirty dollars, sixteen cents, a Cleveland for President button, three whorehouse tokens, and two jackknives. Both pistols were cap-and-ball—hardly worth anything.

"Dear Lord, receive these two. They wasn't worth much on earth. Maybe you can make them better up there— amen." Texas nodded at Herschel when he finished, and they started the tedious job of covering the bodies up.

They made breakfast next. Then they bathed in the creek, and let their clothes dry on the bushes while they shaved. Except for some sore muscles in his back, Herschel felt better. Still, he grew antsier by the hour to get after Ford, but he knew the animals deserved some rest. Besides, they had another thirty or forty more miles to cover to find his man from what they had learned about the Blue Crick's location.

Amos rode down to their camp on a flea-bitten, spavin-toed gray horse in mid-afternoon. He reined the exhausted horse up, and it snorted in relief with its head down in the grass.

"Don't pay to keep a good horse down here," Amos said, and spat sideways. "They'll for sure steal a good one."

"Two of them won't steal no more horses." Texas had an angry scowl on his face.

Amos nodded like he was considering what to say. "They was wondering."

"Who's they?" Herschel asked.

"Oh, them freighters. They wondered if their swampers had run off."

"They have," Texas said. "They went to hell last night without telling them, I guess."

Amos spat again and wiped his hand over his whiskered

mouth. "Guess they won't be going to the Rosebud Reservation."

"They ain't going anywhere." Herschel handed him back the shovel. "We won't need it no more, either."

"Boys," Amos began. "Horse stealing is so bad up here, I can't tell you how terrible it is. They even stole this gray once, but let him go and finally he came home. You understand?"

"I think we do now. We'll be sleeping with one eye open," Herschel said.

"Good." Amos turned his horse and rode off on the coughing gray with his shovel.

Texas was looking after him. "Kind of nice of old Amos to come out and check on us."

"I ain't so sure he wasn't looking like a buzzard for something for himself in the deal."

Texas snorted. "Second thought, you may be right."

The next morning, without an incident in the night, they loaded Red and rode northwest. Not many cattle to speak of in the country, but Herschel knew for certain they were on their way. He felt grateful he didn't need to be a drover again. Nights without sleep, stampede after stampede, swollen rivers to cross—no, he'd take man-hunting over that any day.

At midday, they reached a small soddy and some corrals. A woman with two small children hiding in her skirts met them at the doorway.

"Afternoon, ma'am," Texas said, looking around.

She looked stolid and was straight-backed. "You come to steal our horses, you're too late. My man is out tracking your brothers right now."

"Brothers?" Texas looked pained.

"Cousins. You horse thieves are all kin."

"How long has he been gone?" Herschel asked, wonder-

ing how prepared her man might be for fighting such outlaws.

"Since daylight. But he ever gets them in the sights of his
old Greener, they can count on going to hell on an express."

"Ma'am, I'm a deputy U.S. marshal." Herschel booted
Bay in closer. "Which way did he go?"

She pointed toward the northwest. He nodded to Texas.
Without another word, they reined around and broke into a
long trot for the high ground.

"I'd'a left ole Red at that place till we got back, but they
might steal him," Texas said with a grin.

"We better keep our stock all under lock and key."
Herschel could hardly believe the state of affairs in that
country. They needed law badly.

Texas nodded, and they rode on.

After an hour's ride, they spotted a distant figure and rode
toward him.

"Better tell him you're law," Texas said as they approached the armed figure.

"Deputy U.S. marshal," Herschel shouted.

The man stopped, set his gun butt down, and took off his
hat to wipe his face on his sleeve.

"Didn't catch your name," Herschel said.

"Thompson, Clyde Thompson."

"Your wife said you were after some horse thieves."

"They got my team last night."

"Any idea who they are?"

"No, but I aim to track them down if it takes forever."

"Get up behind me." Herschel took his foot out of the left
stirrup. "I never tried Bay double, so hang on," he said, taking the shotgun as the shorter man attempted to mount.

When Thompson was on behind, Bay went in a circle,
but Herschel got him settled and they went on.

"You on their tracks?" Texas asked, catching up and coming beside them.

"There's plenty of tracks. Mine's shod," the man said. "You know, leaving a man out here without a horse is worse than criminal."

"Damn serious," Texas agreed.

"Hell, it's murder. I can't go for supplies, make a crop, or do anything without horses."

The first sign was the smell of wood smoke. Herschel couldn't see the thieves yet when he turned to Texas. "May need to leave our honker here. If he goes to braying, they might scatter. Let's hobble him."

Texas agreed and bailed off his horse. In minutes, the mule was hobbled and left to graze. Herschel hoped he didn't get too lonesome too fast and give an alarm.

"Want me to get down?" Thompson asked.

"Not yet. They break and run, I'll want you off."

They topped the next crest, and Herschel saw two men jump up and run for their horses at the sight of them. Thompson slid off, and Herschel sent Bay after them. The thieves were busy gathering up saddles and pads to throw on their horses.

"We're the law," he shouted with his six-gun in his right hand.

Stirrup to stirrup, Texas rode beside him, and they bore down on the panicked horse thieves.

"They're going for their guns!" Texas shouted over the drum of their horses.

Herschel saw the ring of black smoke from the hatless one on the right, hanging onto the lead of a spooked horse and trying to shoot at the same time. He shot once at the man, and the rustler was forced to let go of his horse. But it was too late to turn back and shoot—a shot from Herschel's

.45 struck him in the chest and he fell on the ground, the fight gone from him.

Texas's man kept shooting. Herschel's deputy stood tall in the stirrups and began to make his shots count. The bullets' impact spun the rustler around, and Texas hit him twice more before he struck the ground.

"Any more?" Texas shouted, whirling his pony around and looking the area over.

"Looks like we got them." Herschel set Bay down and stepped off, handing his reins to Texas.

Thompson came on the run. "Those are my horses over there." He stopped to catch his breath. "Sure glad you two were here for this. I never saw two braver men than you two."

Texas smiled. "Or dumber ones, either. You know these two?"

"That's Pauley. Webb Pauley, I've seen him before." Thompson walked wide of the dead man. Pauley's eyes were open to the bright sun.

Herschel squatted by the rustler he'd shot. "You got any next of kin you want notified?"

The man half-raised up, then fell back. "Naw. They wouldn't care." He made a face. "What's a damn U.S. marshal doing—after horse thieves?"

"Part of the job."

"Yeah, yeah—" He grabbed his sides and looked pained.

"You seen Casey Ford lately?"

"You after him?"

"I asked you if you've seen him lately."

"Sure, he's on the Blue, staying at the U7."

"How much money you got on you?" Herschel asked, still on his haunches.

"You figure on spending it?"

"No, but I figure the man who's going to bury you can use it."

The man's breath caught, and he winced. "That the hon-yocker—owned them horses?"

Herschel nodded. "You got a name? We know the other fella was Webb Pauley."

"B.J. Flowers."

Herschel rose and nodded to Thompson. "You can have your horses back, their horses and saddle gear and any monies on them. Give them a proper burial."

"But he ain't dead yet," Thompson said, looking upset.

"He will be by the time you ride back to your place for a shovel and get back here."

"Wait—lawman—pull—my boots off," Flowers said.

Herschel nodded and obliged the man. He began to gather up the rustlers' firearms, and noticed Texas had rounded up the four horses and had them all picketed.

"Learn anything?" Texas asked.

"Where is the U7?"

"West a ways and north some on the Blue like I figured."

Herschel checked the sun. They still had several hours of daylight. "Let's get closer."

Texas agreed. "I'll get the mule."

"I'll tell Thompson."

In a few minutes, Texas was back with Red and they headed out. By evening, they were camped on the Blue.

"U7 is upstream about ten miles, I'd guess," Texas said, squatted on his heels and rolling a smoke.

"Big outfit?"

"Naw, another two-bit place, but sure a hornet's nest of worthless ones like Casey."

Herschel put the skillet on to heat up and he sliced some bacon. No time to make bread, but he had some crackers that weren't wormy to go with it. Maybe in another day, he'd be headed for home and his girls. As he bent over, turning bacon in the sizzling skillet, he missed all of them.

TWENTY-SIX

Texas led the way in the predawn. Red trailed him, and Herschel came last on Bay with the .44/40 across his lap. The wagon tracks they followed ran parallel to Blue Creek and wound their way down the bottoms. Pine trees grew on ridges in this land, which was more broken than the rolling prairie country behind them. In fact, some hills soon began to appear. Herschel and Texas spooked some cattle watering in the creek. They were wary critters that ran as the riders approached.

Herschel and Texas were in a land that neither knew much about. They had made no human contact since they'd left the dying horse thief. Thompson had mentioned that the U7 was north of the Deer Creek Fork, but the scratches he'd made in the dirt for a map seemed unrelated to the country they were riding through. Not seeing any human habitation in all their riding amazed him more than anything else. Of course, this land had no doubt been part of the Sioux land before the reformation of that treaty, and maybe folks had not dared come in here as they had elsewhere.

The skin on Herschel's neck crawled for no reason he could pin down. Since reaching the Blue and this dim road, he'd felt uneasy. When he twisted in the saddle to view more of the country, he expected to see some form of opposition to their presence. But nothing appeared despite his edgy feelings.

An hour later, a second stream flowed into the Blue. Letting Bay drink beside Texas's horse, the two men considered the crossing.

"This the stream Thompson called Deer?" Texas looked around, stretching his arms above his head. He covered up a yawn. "Aside from a deer or two, I sure ain't seen nothing that indicated there's a ranch up here."

"We may be close." Herschel motioned northward.

"There ain't been a horse on these wagon tracks since Hector was a pup."

"If you were stealing horses, would you use this road leading to your place?"

Texas laughed and slapped his pommel. "Hell, no. I'd keep to the ridges so I could see who was eating my dust."

"We don't find the place by dark, or someone who can tell us how to get there, we'll try something else tomorrow."

"Fair enough." Texas drew his horse up, jerked Red away from snatching grass, and bailed across the shallow watercourse.

Herschel didn't feel any better after they talked. It was still an eerie country to him. Maybe his mind was trying to warn him. He'd never felt quite like this before—trapped in an empty land of grass and ridges in pines with raw cuts of yellowish bluffs.

"Wood smoke," Texas said, sniffing the air. "Smell it."

A smile crossed Herschel's face and he nodded. "We must be close."

"Maybe we better scout this place," Texas said. "We don't need this canary braying, 'we're coming' either."

"My sentiments. Let's take him back a quarter mile or so and hobble him. Then we can ease up and see who's over that ridge."

"I'd sure feel safer about that than riding into a hornet's nest."

With Red hobbled, they rode back and chose a game trail to the top of the hill. Under the brow, they left their horses and snuck along until they could crawl out and observe from the rim.

Texas used a brass telescope to scan the setup. Herschel studied the pens and low buildings. Some horses in the corrals, but not many. The place wasn't new, and might have been built by some outfit grazing cattle to sell to the agency later. It was not an Indian camp. Besides, the Sioux didn't live in houses—they used tepees.

"Five horses in the corral. Wait—" Texas handed him the glass. "Who's he?"

Herschel peered through the eyepiece. A short, white-whiskered, stove-up cowboy went to the shed and returned with some wood in his arms.

"That could be Chub." He looked over at Texas on the ground beside him. "All I know is Ida Crowley's description of him."

"How did he ever get in with a killer like Ford?"

"Hard times is all I can say."

Texas agreed with a sharp nod. "How we taking them? I mean, if Ford is down there."

"We need to be certain he's there and not off horse stealing."

"If he's down there in that cabin, sooner or later his bladder will drive him outside."

Herschel agreed with a grin. "Sooner or later."

They had whiled away a few hours on the ridge when a rider came from the east. Texas raised a hand and then used the scope. "Your man just stepped out of the cabin."

"Recognize the third one?"

"No, but I'd say he's telling them two about something. Maybe he brought them word about us being up here."

"Could be. They get hasty about leaving, we'll know shortly."

"What then?"

"We'll try to stop them."

"Good enough. Hey, Ford just went inside and brought out his saddle."

"Time to act," Herschel said, and rose to his feet levering a cartridge in the Winchester.

"We going off the hill on foot?"

"Be as quick as on our horses."

"I guess so." Texas collapsed his telescope. "Reckon they can shoot worth a damn?"

"I doubt it." Herschel reached up, pulled down his hat, and started off the hill.

The way was steep and, over the cry of some quail, he heard a shout. They'd been discovered. The short one was pointing up the hillside at him.

"U.S. marshal!" he shouted, but doubted they could hear him in the gathering wind.

The third man on the scene drew his pistol and emptied it. His shots sent up dust far below Herschel, who drew the rifle butt to his shoulder and took aim. The rifle report echoed back and the cowboy went down. It panicked the other two. The older one ran into a shed. Ford dropped his saddle and headed for the cabin.

The wounded one on the ground had begun moaning by the time Herschel reached flat ground. Texas started for the shed, and Herschel went toward the cabin. Two shots rang out from the front door and he answered them, with his bullets splintering the wood door facing.

A shot from the shed distracted him for a second; then, a figure appeared in the cabin doorway. Hands high, the hatless Ford came out in the sunlight.

"I give up."

"Keep walking this way," he said, and called out over his shoulder, "Texas, you all right?"

"Fine. It was the old man. Shot himself. Guess the thought of prison or hanging got to him."

The wounded one wailed.

"Who in the hell are you, anyway?" Texas asked, standing over him.

"Gus—Gus Jenks."

"Well, Gus Jenks, guess you're wanted all over hell."

While Texas talked to Jenks, Herschel disarmed Ford and then shoved him in that direction. Herschel's handcuffs were in his saddlebags; this time he'd come equipped.

"Only thing they ever got me for before was pig stealing," Jenks said.

"Damn, I wouldn't have admitted that in a court of law." Texas shook his head in disgust. "What we got here is a dead man, a pig rustler, and a killer."

"I'm dying—"

"Die, then. You come to warn those two we were coming."

"How did you know that?"

"We heard you." Texas knelt down and split the man's pants leg. When he twisted the right one to see it better, the outlaw screamed. "Amputate is all I can see to do."

"No!"

"Give me your kerchief." Texas held out his hand for it.

"What you going to do?" Jenks asked.

"Bind it up. Hell, you're barely scratched."

"Oh," Jenks moaned, and fell back on the ground.

When Jenks was in irons, Herschel went to see about fixing some food. Texas took Ford and made him dig Chub's grave. The sound of the shovel ringing on the gravel carried to where Herschel stirred the beans in an iron pot over the fireplace inside the cabin. After he put the Dutch oven over the coals to heat, he went to the shed and cut some steaks off the hanging deer wrapped up in canvas.

Soon, his biscuits were cooking in the oven, steaks sizzling in hot tallow, and the coffee was made. He was sipping on a tin cup of it when Texas brought Ford in and sat him on the floor in cuffs. The candles Herschel had lit gave off a smoky yellow light inside the low-roofed cabin.

"Coffee's done. Food won't be long now," he said to Texas.

"I could eat a bear," Texas said. With his handkerchief for a holder, he reached for the coffeepot and filled his cup. "Man, it sure smells good."

"Not half as good as my wife's."

"Yeah, but I don't have one of those."

"Then you don't know what you're missing."

Both men laughed. Herschel realized that for the first time in two days, the skin on his neck wasn't crawling.

"What are we going to do with Jenks?" Texas asked, seeing that he'd gone to sleep in the cuffs seated on the floor.

"I guess turn him loose. I'd hate to pack him back to Montana."

"Good. I guess the job includes me going up there with you?"

Herschel nodded and used a big fork to turn the steaks. "Unless you've got other work?"

"Naw, just asking." He sat in the chair, his legs spread apart, and bent over with his elbows rested on them, he rolled himself a cigarette. "I ain't got nothing better to do."

"We'll head north, then."

"Guess we can swing by Lead and Deadwood going back?"

"I guess. What've you got on your mind?"

"I thought if you'd stake me to a few bucks I'd get a shave, a bath, lubricate my throat, and see how ugly the ladies are."

"Ford can rest in the jail for one night, too."

"Good idea. I'll be looking forward to that." Texas blew steam off his coffee. "You know we're a *fur* piece from Montana."

Herschel considered his words and nodded. "A *fur* piece."

Deadwood, nestled in the deep canyons, proved hotter than an oven. Miners floured in blasting dust, prospectors, fancy-dressed gamblers, and the dregs of society all milled on the boardwalks and streets with scantily dressed show-girls, wooden-shoed Chinese whores, and fancy silk-gowned prostitutes. Herschel led the way on horseback threading around double-wagon freight teams with eight teams of patient oxen in front, mule-powered freighters, buckboards, ambulances, and buggies. To judge from the horses standing hip-shot at the hitch racks and the noise and the tinny pianos, Deadwood, despite the sweltering heat, was alive and booming.

The town marshal took one look at Herschel's federal badge and agreed to board Ford for two bucks a day. Herschel and Texas took the horses and Red to the livery and stabled them there. Texas thought thirty cents a day was highway robbery, but Herschel paid the man.

"Inflated mining town prices, I figure," Herschel said.

"Inflated? Plain thievery!" Texas shook his head in disgust.

They twisted through the throngs of people making their way up the steep hill, and had almost reached a saloon that Texas wanted to visit when a horse at the hitch rack caught Herschel's attention—a bald-faced horse stood at the rack under a Texas saddle.

"Wait," he said, and stepped off the wooden walkway. A closer examination showed Squires's brand. Herschel looked at the peaks high overhead to give celestial thanks. He'd found Squires's lost horse.

"Know him?" Texas asked.

"Yes. He was stolen west of Billings a few weeks ago."

"Bet that cowboy riding him is around here." Texas searched the crowd and then shook his head. "No telling where."

"I'll wait for him." Herschel climbed back on the boardwalk.

"I—"

"You go get a bath. I can wait. I'll tell you the story later." He counted out twenty dollars for Texas. "Enough?"

"Plenty."

He watched Texas disappear in the crowd, and then settled in with his shoulder to the frame of the saloon's plate-glass window. He could hear most of the goings-on inside and see part of inside while he waited.

His wait wasn't long. Three cowboys came out of the saloon, and he could tell they were going for the hitch rack. A tall one and two shorter ones, all in their twenties.

The shortest one began tightening the cinch on Baldy when Herschel stepped off the boardwalk as if crossing the street, and once he was beside the cowboy, spoke. "Stealing horses in Montana is not gainful employment."

"What?"

"I'm a deputy U.S. marshal and this horse was stolen in Yellowstone County."

"How did you—"

"Next time steal a plainer horse. You're under arrest. You have a gun?"

"No, sir."

"Carl, we'll get you a lawyer," the tall cowboy said, looking defiant.

"Ain't no use," Carl said. "You play the fiddle, you pay the fiddler."

"Right," said Herschel. "He'll be along in three years or so. He can get mail at Deer Lodge Prison, Montana. Come on, they've got a nice cell for you here, too."

Herschel undid the reins and looked at the defeated-looking cowboy. "We'll put him in the stable. What's your name?"

"Carl Tibbs."

"All right, Carl, you're on your best behavior. I won't cuff you, but don't give me an excuse to. We're several days' ride from Billings."

"I won't give you an excuse."

Tibbs shook hands with his pals, exchanged a few words, and they parted. He marched with Herschel to the livery and the horse was put up. Then Herschel took Tibbs to the jail.

Then, Herschel walked across the street and stepped inside the telegraph office. He sent a wire to his office. HAVE FORD STOP HAVE BALD-FACED HORSE STOP BE HOME IN A WEEK STOP HERSCHEL BAKER

An hour later, after a bath and shave, he found Texas in the Gold Dust Saloon. His deputy was dancing with a bar girl. Several of the onlookers were cheering him on. Herschel ordered a beer, and when the barkeep delivered the stein, the man said, sounding impressed, "That damn cowboy can sure dance."

"Not bad at all." Herschel took the mug and went to the free-lunch bar and made a sandwich. Texas was almost as good at dancing as Billy Hanks had been. Herschel fixed a sandwich from sliced bread, piled with sliced dry sausages, mustard, pickles, and some deviled eggs. Then, seated at a table, he grinned when Texas swept by with his dance partner.

"You must have got him," Texas said, going by a second time.

Herschel smiled and nodded, then considered his food. He'd soon be headed home. *Marsha, I'm coming.*

TWENTY-SEVEN

T HEY crossed the Little Big Horn River and stopped off at the Atwood Cattle Company summer camp. Jim Hayes, the superintendent, looked them over with a critical eye as they rode up. He stood in the doorway of his head-quarters, a low-walled cabin next to the cookshack, harness and supply shop, and two bunkhouses.

"That you, Baker?"

Herschel booted Bay in close. "It's me. You remember Texas Jack?"

"Not since Wichita." With a big smile under his bushy handlebar mustache streaked with silver, Jim stepped out and shook their hands.

"Who are they?" he asked, looking at Ford and Tibbs.

"Prisoners."

"I heard you were the law up there."

"Yes, I'll be glad to be back."

"I bet you will be. I'll get Yonky to fix you some food."

"We'd appreciate it. These fellas think my cooking's bad."

"Texas, you remember Wichita?" Hayes asked him.

"I remember a helluva hangover."

They talked about the old days and cattle drives they'd shared. The prisoners did as Herschel directed them, and sat side by side on a bench outside the cookshack to wait.

The cook Yonky fixed a pile of breaded steaks fried in hot tallow, served with German potatoes and onions, fresh sourdough biscuits with cow butter, and plenty of hot coffee to wash it down.

Herschel thanked Hayes, who refused any pay, and an hour or so later they rode north for the Crow reservation. He was within a good hard day's ride and anxious to get back home.

They crossed over the high country, and he shared his ideas with Texas about the Hanks lynching.

"You think one of them two families hung him?" Texas asked.

"They're my suspects. One of them was even shot in a bar fight supposedly because of his involvement."

"And you have the word of a drunk that he saw three of them ride off, but couldn't see their faces?"

"He also saw the man that cut him down awhile later."

"I guess that says three were there for the hanging, huh?"

"Why don't you stick around when we get up there? I want to interrogate both families and see what they really know. Besides, you'll like Marsha's cooking."

"Hey, I'm footloose."

"Good, I want this lynching solved."

"Sounds like you've been working hard at it."

"Not hard enough. I haven't solved it."

"I'd say you haven't done bad."

Herschel nodded, and looked back at his downcast prisoners. It would be good to be home.

Two days later they rode up Main Street, drawing lots of attention from the onlookers. At the courthouse, Herschel told the prisoners to dismount, and removed the Winchester from the scabbard. He looked carefully around the area. No sign of any mob, but he expected one before it was all over—Mike Melloncamp had lots of friends.

Keeping his eye on everything, he backed to the open door where Texas and the prisoners had entered.

"You're pretty anxious, aren't you?" Texas asked under his breath.

Herschel nodded, and looked up to see Phil's smile on the second-floor landing.

"You're back," Phil said.

"And with guests. How are things?"

"Quiet."

"Too quiet?" Herschel asked, halfway up the staircase.

"Art says the lynching and murders are on lots of minds. People are worked up. Now we got Ford it could turn tough."

Herschel nodded and introduced Texas to Phil. They shook hands and the prisoners were taken inside and, after Herschel filled out the papers, were put in cells.

Back in Herschel's office, Phil and Texas sat around his desk.

"I am afraid we all need to sleep here," Herschel said. "A bunch of agitators'll get to drinking and work up their courage for a lynch mob. Better tell Art. He sleeping?"

"Yes, we're still in charge of the town law," Phil said.

Herschel shook his head in disgust. "McKay better hire him a chief of police. Money or no money."

"Stokes has been pestering me for a story since the telegram."

"Guess he got a copy?"

"I never gave him one."

"I imagine a couple of bucks bought him one."

"Isn't that illegal?" Phil asked.

"I think so. But it isn't a felony. Texas and I are going out to the house, and we'll be back here in a short while."

Phil wrinkled his nose and then agreed. "I can hold them off that long."

Herschel looked hard at his deputy. His man had no idea about the power of a large mob to swarm in and take over the jail and carry out their plans to lynch everyone in the cells. "Send word to Art and get him in here."

"Yes, sir."

"Come on, Texas, we can put the horses up and meet my wife and girls."

"Right."

"Something wrong?"

"No, but you're sure on edge about this lynching business."

"I have a reason to be. Montana has a reputation for it."

Texas agreed, and followed him out the door.

Nothing looked out of place when they rode out to the house. Still, Herschel could hardly stand to think he had left a young man in charge of so much back at the jail. Not that he didn't trust Phil, but he knew in his heart that someone would make a try at getting to his prisoners with rope justice.

When they rode up with the extra horses, Marsha rushed out the front door to hug him, and the girls charged out after her. Everyone talked at once, and he tried to answer them all.

"I'm fine. I'm fine. This is my good friend Texas Jack." They all nodded at Texas.

"Now, I've got to go back to work," said Herschel. "I

only came out to see you a few minutes, put these horses up, and I need to get back."

Marsha frowned.

"I'm concerned about vigilantes," Herschel said.

She nodded. "How many to feed? We'll bring you supper."

"Four or five of us."

"Nice to meet you, Texas," she said, looking very somber.

Texas smiled again and then waved his hat at the girls.

"You all right?" Herschel asked as Marsha walked beside him and they led the horses out back.

"I'm fine. We've been very worried about you. The telegram helped. Phil showed it to us."

"He's a good man." Herschel and Texas stripped the saddles off and carried them inside the tack room.

"How long will you have to do this?" she asked.

"Until they all get calmed down about it. Until I'm sure it's safe."

"We understand. Don't we, girls?"

"I think so," Nina said, and hugged his arm as he went by her.

"Good, we'll have a big picnic and go down to the ranch when this is over."

"Yeah!" came the cheer.

Herschel kissed Marsha on the forehead after the animals were in the pen.

On their way back to the jail, Texas laughed. "You did good, ole cowboy. That bunch really likes you."

Herschel nodded in agreement. He hated not being able to stay with them right now.

At the jail, Wally came in and brought Herschel his bedroll. "Figured you might need help."

Herschel nodded his approval from behind his desk. "If

we have to sit in here, I want to talk with both the Ralstons and Mannons. Phil, send Donnie up and tell Bert Ralston I want him and his boys in here in the morning. No need to waste our time just sitting here."

"What will you ask them this time?" Art asked.

"Who owns this arrowhead? Who wrote that note in the schoolhouse after the dance?"

"You reckon we'll get someone to break?" Art asked.

"I think they all know more than they're telling us."

"I'll send Donnie right away," Phil said. "What about the Mannons?"

"He can go up there, too, and tell them to come in here on Wednesday."

"What if they won't come?" Art asked. Phil and Texas both turned an ear to listen.

"I'll go out and arrest them," Herschel said.

"Want Donnie to tell them that?"

"Only if they refuse."

"I'll go find Donnie."

"Phil, they may try to pick us off one at a time. Be careful."

The deputy nodded with a grim face, put on his hat, and left.

Herschel looked around the room. Texas was half-asleep slouched in a chair. Art prowled the floor, and Wally looked out the window at the street. No one said this job would be easy. Times like this, he considered quitting on the spot and going home to be with his family. Maybe go back to breaking horses and ranching, it would be a damn sight easier. But he and Marsha had set out to make Yellowstone County a better place to live. Vigilante law was over in the territory and it was his job to enforce that.

Phil came back and reported Donnie was on his way to the Ralstons and the Mannons. They all jumped to their feet when someone called out from downstairs. Herschel picked up the double-barrel Greener off the desk. He went out through the outer office on soft feet, followed by Phil and Texas.

"Sheriff Baker, can I come up?" Ennis Stokes stood at the foot of the stairs.

"What do you need?"

"Your story. I heard you rode in with two prisoners."

Herschel nodded and handed Phil the shotgun. "We have Casey Ford in custody and the horse thief—took Squires's bald-faced horse."

"Can I come up there?"

"No."

"But I'm a reporter," he pleaded.

"Stokes, I think you've written enough bad things about this office and the job my small force of men do. I don't care what you print."

"This is the story of the century. It could make you as famous as Buffalo Bill Cody."

"I don't want to be famous. I just do my job. That's it. This building is closed to everyone." He paused. "Clear out."

"Baker, you'll regret this day."

"I've been regretting you and your yellow journalism for weeks. Clear out," he shouted, and it echoed in the empty courthouse. "This place closed at five p.m."

Stokes went off cussing to himself and when Herschel was certain he was gone, he dusted off his hands.

"He ain't giving up that easy," Art shook his head. "But no more civil than he is, we don't need to be nice."

"Amen," Phil said.

Herschel went back inside his office. "Marsha's bring-ing supper for us. I guess the prisoners have food coming?"

"Café sends food about this time," Wally said. "I'll watch for them."

"Good."

Herschel checked the schoolhouse clock on the wall, 6:10 p.m.

The prisoners' food arrived. Two boys in their teens carried it in pails covered with napkins to keep the flies out. The process was uneventful and following the boys' departure, Marsha drove the buckboard up in front, and the crew went down to help her and the girls carry up the food. She oversaw their work, skirt in hand, apologizing that she had not had time to cook all she wanted to, and saying she hoped it suited them.

"They'd eat old nails if you cooked 'em," Herschel said, and hugged her shoulder as the food went up the stairs. He took a look around, but things in the street appeared quiet—too quiet.

His office became the banquet room. The rich smell of her cooking saturated his nose. Man, how he had missed so many things about her. Plates were unwrapped by the girls with care and silverware soon appeared. Sliced hot beef straight from the oven. Browned new potatoes, new green peas fresh from her garden, sourdough biscuits, and yellow homemade butter. The talking ceased and the feast commenced. The girls kept everyone's coffee cups filled, and Herschel looked up once from eating the mouthwatering food and nodded in approval at Marsha.

He sure hoped this wasn't a last supper.

When the meal was over and the buckboard packed, his crew was still bragging on the food. Herschel had only a moment to tell Marsha thanks and promise this situation would be over soon. She nodded, put her arms around his neck, and kissed him. "I'll be waiting for you."

"I'll be back soon," he said.

With sundown bleeding on the front side of the court-house, Art slipped out to check on the town. He knew it better than anyone else, and he was confident he could find any trouble before it festered.

They waited.

Art returned after sunset and came upstairs. "They're gathered in the Buckhorn." He shook his head. "It's getting louder by the hour."

"Old man whiskey is fortifying them," Herschel said. "Art, you and Wally stay here. You can hold this jail. They've got to come up those stairs to get to the jail. Shoot if you have to." He turned to Phil and Texas. "Get shotguns."

They nodded and went to the rack. Herschel broke out a box of twelve-gauge brass cartridges on his desk. "Take some extras."

"Texas, you will go up the alley. Phil and I will go in the front. I'll fire off one round outside and then bust in. Texas, you do the same in the alley and come in gun ready through the back door. Phil's backup."

"Good plan. That should throw them off guard," Texas said.

Art agreed with a grim set on his face. "They're sounding tougher."

"That's where we need to cut them off. I may need to shut the bars down for a week, but I hate to ruin those fellas' business."

"This should work," Art said, sounding confident for the first time that evening.

Herschel gave Texas a good description of the Buckhorn's back door, so he could find it when he went up the dark alley. Then, Herschel and Phil set out on the boardwalk. The few folks still out stepped aside in awe for the two armed lawmen.

Herschel dried his right hand on the side of his pants two doors short of the Buckhorn. Then he gripped the stock and trigger again. A pattern of light from inside shone on the boardwalk in front of the saloon. A few steps short of the saloon, he cocked the right barrel's hammer and stepped to the edge of the boardwalk. He fired the Greener, and the blast woke up a half-dozen horses at the rack. They tore loose in a wild scramble and in three steps, shotgun ready, he stepped into the brightly lit barroom.

Texas's blast in the alley made all the customers whirl around to see him charge in from the back.

"Everyone sit down," Herschel ordered, standing blocking the door with his boots set apart. He aimed to intimidate them. With a loud scraping of chairs on the floor, they all wilted into seats.

"I have only one message. My deputies have orders to shoot and shoot to kill anyone breaches that jail. I mean some of you will die. I have plenty of buckshot. We're leaving the law to the law in this county, is that clear to all of you?"

"Mike was—"

"Mike was my friend. His killer will hang by a judge's order."

"What's he like? I mean his killer."

Herschel answered. "A little self-centered rat that has no feelings about it or remorse."

"But he damn sure ain't worth dying over," Texas said.

"Save you the expense of a trial," someone shouted.

Herschel's eyes narrowed. "There's lots of things depend on how we act as citizens over this matter. The railroad is looking hard at us. I don't want them to bypass Billings. The federal government is looking at us. Our statehood is at stake here. Boys, we don't need a lynching."

"Baker, we'll back off if you say he'll hang."

"Back off, then. Ain't a jury in Montana won't find him guilty and hang him."

Texas came across the room, nodded to Phil, and whispered to Herschel, "You've won. Let's go back."

Herschel agreed and turned to leave. One battle down, one more to fight. Learn who lynched Billy Hanks.

TWENTY-EIGHT

L IKE a rumpled banty rooster, the billy-goat beard shaking under his chin, Bert Ralston stood up defending his rights as a citizen. "I've got my rights—"

"Sit down," Herschel said, pacing the floor with the entire clan seated around two tables in his office. "You were asked here to answer questions, not defend yourself. Now sit down and listen."

Farrel and Jimmy looked ready to jump and run. The eldest, Wanda, hugged her father's arm and kept talking to him about how everything would be okay.

"Now you camped there all night, right?" Herschel looked hard at the youngest, Jimmy, who he felt was the most vulnerable. Herschel's hand cut off Bert, who was starting to speak for the boy.

"I want Jimmy to tell me."

The boy's head bobbed and the rooster comb in his blond hair shook when he spoke. "All night—we stayed there."

"Did you see anyone after the dance go in and out of the schoolhouse that night?"

"Hell, that's dumb, how could he? He was asleep."

"Bert, I want his answer." Herschel waited.

Jimmy looked up and shook his head. "No."

Innocence was all over his face when he shook his head. "Thanks," said Herschel.

"I saw someone," Wanda said. "I don't know who it was. It's all right, Pa. I saw someone lighting matches inside from where we camped. I was curious and went over there to see who it was and what they were up to, but they ran off before I could tell who it was."

"How many?" Herschel asked.

The pudgy girl held up one finger.

"Before the rain?"

"Yes, it liked to never rained."

Herschel looked at Art and Texas seated in chairs to his left. Then he dug out the arrowhead. "This belong to you, boys?" He started by handing it to Jimmy, who quickly shook his head and passed it to Farrel.

"You ever see that before?"

Farrel nodded. "But I can't remember where."

"Think hard."

"I never owned it, but I seen it before." Then he shook his head. "I remember, I'll tell you."

"Good. Now I have a witness seen three of you ride away from the hanging."

"He's a gawddamn liar. Our horses was all picketed that night. We've got witnesses," Bert said.

Nothing pointed to the Ralstons, Herschel realized. Wanda had no reason to lie about seeing a person in the schoolhouse writing the note. Someone had written the note in there. It was a dark night, and it would have been hard to identify anyone at any distance at all.

"Bert, hold on. He saw three riders. Did any of you see three riders after the dance?"

They all shook their heads.

"Thanks for coming. You remember who had that arrowhead, you send me word."

Bert stood up and stared hard-eyed at Herschel. "That mean you don't think we done it?"

"Bert, I don't think your family was involved."

"Good, 'cause we never done it."

Herschel nodded and they filed out.

"That leaves the Mannons," Phil said when the Ralstons were gone.

"They have to answer some questions, too," Herschel said, picking up the arrowhead and pocketing it.

"That second boy had seen it before or one like it," Texas said.

"I agree that sounded good to me," Art said as if in deep thought. "Means that it might lead us to the killers."

"I want to toss this out. Mannons do the same thing to us tomorrow and where are we?" Herschel asked them.

"Still looking," Art said.

Yes, Herschel agreed, still looking.

Things appeared to be settling down in town, but his force remained in the courthouse. Mayor McKay came by acting all upset, and wondered if they should ship the prisoners to Helena.

"No, we have to show everyone we can do things civilized here."

"It's a big risk. A big risk."

"There's been less organized mob activity each night since we busted up the Buckhorn mob."

"But what if?"

Herschel dismissed him and showed him the door. "We can handle it. You need to hire a police force."

"It's the money. Money I don't have." He went off mumbling to himself.

Herschel began to feel better about his efforts to prevent a lynching. Various leaders in the community paraded by offering him support. Several offered to stand guard. Politely, he thanked them and said things would be fine. More than anything he wanted his force to be sufficient to handle things, if for nothing else than to show his potential opponents he could handle the job.

His time with Marsha was short, but she agreed his plan was working. All he had left was the interview with the Mannons. He'd have no other suspects in the lynching of Billy Hanks—unless he could incriminate the Mannons.

Rath was in no better a mood than Bert had been the day before. He sat in the chair assigned him and slouched, all humped up like a mad bulldog ready to snarl or bite. His eldest, Earl, sat up beside him, clasping and reclasping his hands on the table. Derrick, Sloan, and Harry the kid whispered to each other until Herschel cleared his throat.

"I want to go over that night at the Sharky Schoolhouse."

"This a hearing?" Rath demanded.

Herschel shook his head. "Phil's taking notes for my files. I wanted to thank you for coming. But I need some answers."

"You heard ours."

"Except one. Three of you rode by the body hanging there." He searched their faces, and knew from the shocked expressions he'd hit a chord.

"Who says?" Rath asked quietly.

"The man who saw you ride away."

"All right, we saw him hanging there in the lightning. I didn't want the blame. I swear we never hung him."

"But all of you saw him hanging there?"

"We rode past him when we spotted him."

"Why didn't you tell me the truth to start?"

"'Cause you never know about them things. We thought we might be next on their list. I figured at the time them big outfits was out to get all of us small ranchers and out-spoken cowboys."

Herschel nodded.

"Then Sam came home with his saddle and I figured they done that to tell us to get the hell out," said Rath. "We talked about it for a day before we brought him in." The others all nodded.

"I want you boys to look at this arrowhead and tell me if you've ever seen it before." He put the piece on the table before them and watched them. "You ever seen it before?"

Harry nodded and raised his blue eyes to look at him. "Sidney had one like that once that he wanted to trade me out of a jackknife for it."

"Sidney who?" Herschel asked.

"Sidney Cross."

"They live on Deer Creek," Rath said.

Herschel recalled the name, but it meant nothing. "He have any others?"

"No, he just had one like that."

"It's obsidian," Earl said, picking it up.

Herschel agreed. "Can any of you add anything to this investigation?"

They all shook their heads.

"Where did you find it?" Earl asked, handing it back.

"In the frog of Billy Hanks's horse."

"How the hell—"

"I've asked myself the same thing for weeks. You get the answer, tell me."

Rath stood up. "You see where we were at?"

"I see you had problems, but honesty with me might have helped."

The rancher slapped on his hat, then stopped and turned back. "I ain't looking for no forgiveness, but you've been as fair a lawman as I ever dealt with."

"Thanks," Herschel said, and turned back to his deputies.

"Wonder if Farrel Ralston saw the same arrowhead at school?" Art asked when they were gone.

"We can't lead him into the question," Herschel said. "I want the truth."

"But if one remembered that stone, I'd bet there's more kids at that school do, too," Texas added, and the heads nodded around the room.

Herschel looked up at Clare Scopes standing in the doorway.

"Clare? What can we do for you?"

"I need to talk to you." She swallowed hard and looked ready to cry.

"Fine. Everyone out."

Texas shut the door as the last one out. Herschel showed her to a chair and sat on the edge of his desk. "What can I do for you?"

"Oh, Sheriff, I know who killed Billy Hanks." She began to sob in her kerchief.

"Who?" He waited.

"Berry Kirk—"

"How do you know?"

"He—he asked me to marry him last night." She buried her face in the wet cloth.

"And?" He waited.

"He tried to give me Billy Hanks's grandmother's ring."

"You're sure?"

"Yes, oh, yes, it's her ring. I mean, the same one Billy made me try on."

Herschel looked out the open window at the building across the street. The Cross boys—two of them fled at the sight of him on Mike's store porch. "Are the Cross boys any kin to him?"

"His cousins."

"They pal around together with him?"

She made a disgusted face. "They do his beck and call. Why?"

"Clare, what did you tell him?"

"Oh, I said I had to think about it." She raised her face up. Her eyes glazed with tears. "I knew I had to tell you and I didn't want him warned that I knew about the ring."

"Good girl. That ring he might say he bought or traded for, but I have a second piece of evidence we discovered today that is the key."

"What's that?" she asked as he stepped to the door to call his deputies back in.

"An arrowhead." He recalled the day Barley dug it out of the cow pony's hoof and handed it over. The thought of his friend's death knifed him in the gut, but he felt secure they at last had the killers to arrest. He went to the door and called for the others to come in the room.

"I'll have a warrant sworn out for Berry Kirk and the Cross boys," Herschel said. "Kirk tried to give her Hanks's grandmother's ring last night."

The men around the room looked at Clare in appreciation.

"What's the Crosses' names?" Herschel asked.

"Roman and Sidney," she said to Phil, who was writing it all down.

"Can I go arrest them?" Art asked.

"Take Texas along for a backup. I don't need to lose another deputy."

Art nodded and patted her on the shoulder. "Thanks for helping us." She smiled bravely and thanked him, too.

"What next?" Phil asked.

"Send for Stokes," Herschel said. "I have a story for him about the last illegal hanging in Yellowstone County, which was a disguised murder."

Two nights later in his own bed, he snuggled with his wife.

"It's good to at last have you home with me," she said.

He raised up on his elbows and looked through the open window at the distant lightning flashing on the horizon. "I hope that isn't an omen out there."

She sat up and hugged him. "We won't answer the door."

"Good idea." He settled on his back. Maybe he'd make the grade as a lawman. The *Herald,* in their latest edition, had even written a good story about him. Maybe he was settled in—something didn't seem right. He closed his eyes and listened to the distant thunder—*let it rain.*